# LETHBRIDGE STEWART

## SPHERES OF INFLUENCE

Violet Addison &
David N Smith

CANDY JAR BOOKS · CARDIFF
2024

*Spheres of Influence* © Violet Addison & David N Smith 2024

*Characters from The Web of Fear*
© Hannah Haisman & Lincoln Estate 1968, 2024
*Lethbridge-Stewart: The Series*
© Andy Frankham-Allen & Shaun Russell 2014, 2024
*Major Bugayev created by Simon A Forward*


*Doctor Who is* © *British Broadcasting Corporation, 1963, 2024*

ISBN: 978-1-915439-51-2

Range Editor: Andy Frankham-Allen
Editor: Shaun Russell
Editorial: Keren Williams
Licensed by Hannah Haisman
Cover by Martin Baines & Will Brooks


Printed and bound in the UK by
4edge, 22 Eldon Way, Hockley, Essex, SS5 4AD

Published by
Candy Jar Books
Mackintosh House
136 Newport Road, Cardiff, CF24 1DJ
www.candyjarbooks.co.uk

# PROLOGUE

**ANNE TRAVERS** strolled slowly through the park.

She was taking her time. Enjoying the scenery. It was a very ordinary January morning, a little grey and overcast, but she still felt snug and warm inside her big winter coat.

There were no monsters or mysteries clamouring for her attention.

It made a refreshing change of pace.

She and Bill had taken advantage of the break in their otherwise chaotic lives, to spend some time with his sister and her six-year-old son, so they could all enjoy a few precious hours of normal family life.

At that moment, Bill was enjoying a kick-about with his young nephew, often allowing Dean to steal the ball and clumsily fire shots at their makeshift goal. The boy was loving every minute of it. Bill was too. He would feign disappointment each time he conceded a goal, but she could see the delight in his eyes, as he revelled in the joy of the game.

She supposed it was a lot more fun than following Lethbridge-Stewart's orders, getting shot at, or generally being wrapped up in top secret missions vital to the future of the country – or possibly the world.

It was so different to the rest of their lives.

'Your life could be like this too,' said Bill's sister, who was walking alongside her, watching the boys' antics on the pitch. 'You and Bill must have discussed having kids?'

Anne almost laughed.

How could they possibly hope to look after a child given the nature of their lives? The thought made her a little sad. She'd always assumed she'd have children one day, but when…?

'We've talked about it.' She shrugged, toying absently with the engagement ring on her finger. 'And I know Bill will make a great dad.'

'Oh, I know,' Samantha said, smiling as she watched her brother pretend to lose the ball again. 'There's no doubt about that. And you'll make a great mum too.'

Anne nodded, saying nothing, feeling less certain.

What did she know about parenting? Her father had rarely been around, he'd been too busy with his madcap expeditions to remote corners of the world, and her mother... She'd been taken from them far too soon. Anne had spent most of her life lost in academia, pursuing her career. It all left her feeling too ill-prepared to even consider looking after another human life.

Samantha glanced at her. 'You'll be amazing,' she stated encouragingly, clearly able to understand exactly what Anne's silence meant. 'It's normal to have doubts. But you can't let that stop you. Gotta live life while you can.'

Anne nodded. 'I know.'

Watching Bill and Dean enjoy their game, it was difficult to deny that there was something special in such ordinary everyday pleasures, which was too often missing from their lives. Didn't they deserve to have a little slice of normal happiness too? Heck, even Lethbridge-Stewart had got married.

'I just want to wait a while.' Anne sighed. 'We're always so busy. And there's so much more I want to do.'

Samantha nodded. 'You don't have forever, you know.'

'I know.'

As she spoke, a wailing noise sang out across the city. It rose and fell, repeating over and over, a dull droning noise which sent a shiver of fear down Anne's spine. She recognised it instantly. It was the air-attack warning siren.

Dean continued playing football, too young to understand the significance of the signal, using the distraction to score another goal. Bill glanced at Anne. The happiness in his eyes was gone, replaced with sudden wariness.

Samantha instinctively took a step towards her little boy, taking a moment to ruffle his hair and congratulate him on his goal, as her eyes searched the clouds for any sign of impending death.

That was the reality of their world.

While they lived their lives, the cold war rumbled on, the threat of sudden nuclear annihilation always hanging over their heads. Usually they just ignored it, because there was nothing they could do about it, they were powerless to prevent it. They just had to hope it would never happen.

The siren faded away. A moment of silence followed, which was swiftly filled by birdsong, as nature resumed its normal rhythms.

It was just a test. They happened sometimes. The only way to make sure the alarm system still worked was to use it. Bill scooped up the football, bringing the game to a sudden end.

'There's a café over there,' he said, nodding across the park. 'Who wants a slice of cake?'

'Yeah!' yelled Dean excitedly, already dashing ahead.

'Sounds good to me,' Samantha added.

Within a moment, normal life had resumed, as if nothing had happened.

# CHAPTER ONE
*Enlisted*

A **BRITISH** Army Land Rover tore through the streets of London.

Brigadier Alistair Lethbridge-Stewart sat behind the steering wheel, his eyes fixed on the road ahead, as he raced between the red buses and black taxis, responding to a summons that had come down from the highest possible levels.

It was one of those tricky moments, where he had to respond as if the fate of the entire country was at stake, while also keeping his actions completely covert. It could be an awkward balance to keep, particularly in the crowded streets of central London.

He was currently doing fifteen miles an hour over the speed limit, hoping it was fast enough to meet the needs of the crisis, but not fast enough to draw any unwanted attention from the public, press or civil authorities.

Captain William Bishop was in the passenger seat beside him, clasping a mobile radio transceiver handset, desperately trying to get more information on the situation. All they knew was that something had happened in the Palace of Westminster, at the very centre of government, and that their presence had been urgently requested. Beyond that, information had not been forthcoming, largely because everyone was panicking.

'You must be able to tell us something?' Bishop asked.

The small speaker in the handset hissed static. 'Nobody is telling us anything more,' responded a flustered Corporal Anderson, his voice sounding tinny on the airwaves. 'I can confirm that B Company are on their way from the Loony

Bin. RAF Northolt have scrambled fighters, which are coming into strike range of Westminster Palace now, ready to commence a bombing run on your command.'

Lethbridge-Stewart blinked. 'Who the blazes authorised that?'

The radio crackled. 'No idea, sir. I'm just passing on the information we have.'

Lethbridge-Stewart shook his head in dismay.

Bishop turned his attention back to the handset. 'Our CO is currently against the bombing of any iconic London landmarks,' he stated.

'Particularly when I'm about to go into them,' Lethbridge-Stewart muttered, noticing the familiar visage of Big Ben's clocktower looming up on the skyline in front of them. 'I shouldn't imagine it would do much for our reputation as a covert unit either. People do rather insist on having such things explained.'

Bishop laughed.

Lethbridge-Stewart did not smile. His moustache didn't even twitch. 'Keep those fighters in a holding pattern for now.'

Bishop nodded, his laughter evaporating instantly. 'Yes, sir,' he said, before repeating the order to Corporal Anderson.

Passing the famous clock tower, Lethbridge-Stewart navigated his way between the last few cars, and brought the Land Rover bumping up onto the curb outside a pair of black wrought-iron gates, which served as one of the entrances to the Houses of Parliament.

He climbed out of the vehicle, allowing Bishop to take the wheel.

'Be as quick as you can, Captain.'

Bishop nodded. 'Yes, sir. One scientific advisor coming up.'

Lethbridge-Stewart watched the Land Rover depart and then, with swagger stick under his arm, he strode toward the gates. A lone policeman stood sentry. He had the pale, nervous look of a man who had been told to hold his post, while others had been fleeing. It was a credit to the man that, despite his palpable fear, he was still doing his duty. Lethbridge-Stewart gave the policeman a nod, both of approval and introduction.

'Brigadier Lethbridge-Stewart,' he stated.

'You're expected, sir.' The policeman opened the gate,

letting him through into the main yard. 'I believe they're waiting for you in the Members' Lobby.'

'Thank you, Constable. Can you tell me what you have seen?'

The policeman swallowed nervously. 'I've been told, rather pointedly, that I've not seen anything, sir.'

'Very good.' Lethbridge-Stewart nodded. 'Tell me then, what haven't you seen?'

The policeman paused, momentarily conflicted on whether he should say anything, but then let the words surge out, clearly desperate to give voice to everything he had witnessed.

'Two dozen MPs fleeing the House,' he said, giving a nervous chuckle. 'Saying they'd seen something. A monster, some of them said. An alien, one claimed. Utterly ridiculous, right? Preposterous.'

He looked at Lethbridge-Stewart, with pleading eyes, wanting him to dismiss it all as nonsense.

'Obviously,' Lethbridge-Stewart said, faking an eyeroll. 'Most likely a student prank, or simple mass hysteria. Happens all the time. And you know how flighty these political types can be, don't you? They're not made of the same stern stuff that we are.'

'No, sir.'

'You can take my word on it, there's nothing to worry about. I'll most likely be in and out in a jiffy.'

The policeman looked visibly relieved.

Lethbridge-Stewart wished he could share the sentiment. 'I'll have some troops arriving shortly. They'll sort this mess out in no time. Do be sure to let them straight through, won't you?'

'Yes, sir.'

As Lethbridge-Stewart strode away, heading through the building's open door, he took his service revolver from its holster and checked that it was loaded. He would take no chances. Until his men arrived, he was on his own.

It was at such moments that he missed Samson. Before his death, his old friend and colleague would have been there, walking blindly into danger beside him. He had been told to recruit a replacement for Samson, but he hadn't quite got around to it, feeling it would be impossible for anyone to ever take Samson's place.

It was a foolish sentiment. The greatest honour he could have paid the man, would have been to recruit the finest possible replacement, rather than pretend he could manage without him.

There was no point lingering on such thoughts now.

Samson was gone, and Lethbridge-Stewart was on his own. He would just have to do the best he could. Besides, Sergeant Maddox had already begun to move into the 'inner circle'...

The sound of his bootsteps rang through the corridors, echoing among the high vaulted ceilings. The opulence and grandeur of the building felt oppressive, designed to remind any visitor that they were just a lowly servant, there at the behest of the British public and the pleasure of Her Royal Majesty.

Ahead of him, he could see two figures waiting in the Members' Lobby. They were standing beneath a towering bronze statue of Sir Winston Churchill, whose unwavering metal gaze glowered down at them, as if daring them to do anything less than their best.

'Finally!' cried the first of the two men, throwing his arms up in the air, as he spotted Lethbridge-Stewart approaching.

'I came as quickly as I could, Minister.'

He knew the man. Bertram Greaves, MP. He was tall, with hawkish features, dressed in an impeccably neat navy-blue suit.

'It's been hours,' the politician seethed.

'Unfortunately, it takes time to fly from Edinburgh to London, Minister.'

Greaves snorted with obvious disdain.

Lethbridge-Stewart cocked an eyebrow, but kept his opinions bridled. It was not his place to fight such battles. Fortunately, the second man in the room had no such reservations.

'Typical southerner!' he growled angrily, in a broad northern accent. 'Why don't you stop moaning and just let the fella get on with his ruddy job!'

He was a little man, dressed in a shabby suit, with a loud red tie. Lethbridge-Stewart recognised him from the television. Stanley Carter, MP. A politician from the opposite side of the benches. As a relative newcomer, who had never held a cabinet position, he could have absolutely no idea of what Lethbridge-Stewart's job entailed.

Greaves' eyes narrowed, with obvious hostility. 'Perhaps, Brigadier,' he hissed, 'you'd like to start by removing this half-witted troglodyte from the building?'

The smaller man's face reddened with anger. 'I've every right to be here, you pompous windbag!'

This was Lethbridge-Stewart's idea of hell. He was trapped between two men who would rather spend a lifetime bickering, than ever doing anything bold or decisive.

'Perhaps one of you gentleman would be kind enough to show me the cause of the problem?' he suggested, looking at each of them in turn. 'Some kind of monster, I believe?'

The politicians fell silent, their anger and confidence draining away, as they both glanced at the main doors to the House of Commons. It was quite clear that both men were far happier fighting with each other, than they were facing whatever lay on the other side of the doors.

After a pause, Greaves spoke first. 'I'll show you.'

'It's this way,' cried Carter, immediately shoving his way to the front, instantly emboldened, determined to outdo his rival.

Advancing towards the door, both men ran a hand across the shoe of Winston Churchill's statue, in what Lethbridge-Stewart could only assume was some kind of superstitious ritual to gain good luck. It was an oddly primitive act, particularly for two such educated men, yet both seemed to momentarily swell with pride and bravery.

They opened the large double doors together.

It was a familiar scene. On either side of the room there were five staggered tiers of wooden benching, covered in well-worn green leather, staged so that the two opposing sides were forced to face one another. Above them were cramped viewing galleries for the press and public, tall gothic windows, and a massive arching oaked beamed ceiling, filled with rows of tiny skylights.

What was unusual, was the sphere that was levitating in the centre of the room, emitting a strange bluish glow. The object wasn't solid, it seemed to be composed of perpetually shifting light and shadow, rotating around a central axis. In the darkest areas, it was possible to glimpse something moving, but the images would change before it was possible to discern much detail. For a moment there was a huge tentacle-like limb writhing in the gloom, followed by a vast blank, black eye staring out at them.

Lethbridge-Stewart felt the hairs rise on the nape of his neck. He raised his revolver and aimed it at the sphere.

He waited for it to react.

It did nothing.

He considered taking a shot, but quickly dismissed the notion. Whatever it was, it looked very much like the type of thing that would prove to be invulnerable to normal bullets, and not worth provoking.

Greaves cleared his throat. 'Any idea what it is?'

'Or what it wants?' Carter added.

'Is it hostile?'

'And, if so, how do we get rid of it?'

Lethbridge-Stewart didn't respond. They were all good questions. He had none of the answers, but he didn't want them to know that, fearing the uncertainty would only send them scuttling away in panic, to drum up more trouble.

Greaves glared at him. 'You must give us answers!'

Carter grunted. 'On this matter,' he said, chewing his words, finding them obviously distasteful, 'I am in full agreement with my right-honourable colleague.'

Lethbridge-Stewart sighed. If their arguing had been unhelpful, their sudden ability to find unity through fear seemed infinitely worse, as it meant their hostility was now focused solely on him. Lethbridge-Stewart lowered his revolver, returning it to its holster.

'I have an expert on the way,' he told the two politicians, trying his best to sound reassuring. 'I'm sure he will be able to provide all the answers you need.'

He only hoped it was true.

Bishop pulled up outside a run-down comprehensive school.

Inside was just the man they needed. En route to London, it became clear they'd need some scientific help, and so after a quick call to Scotland, Anne (who had an important meeting with some American chap) had recommended Professor Arthur Grey. It wasn't the first time Bishop had heard his name; she had suggested him as just the all-rounder the Fifth would need when she stepped down. But something had prevented him taking the post. Bishop still didn't know what it was. Curious, he had, however, looked Professor Grey up.

A highly qualified expert in numerous scientific fields, Grey had seemingly upended his career at a high-profile university, to go on to teach O-level Chemistry to ordinary teenagers. To Bishop, it seemed like an odd change of job. The man did still occasionally publish academic papers, but they were widely mocked by the scientific community, because their content was frequently bizarre, although that did not mean his theories were wrong. One such paper, ridiculed for its outlandish speculation about the London Event, had been dangerously close to the truth; showing the mist over the city should never have endured given the prevailing weather conditions, speculating that it was therefore deliberately manufactured and maintained, most likely the work of some foreign intelligence agency. A failed attack. He was dismissed as a crackpot.

But none of that told Bishop why Grey had been rejected for the post of Head of Science & Research at the Fifth. Bishop had meant to ask Anne, but the past year had proven to be rather hectic, and it had eventually slipped his mind.

He found himself staring at the school building, as if hoping it may offer him some additional clues to the man's background, but he could see no reason why anyone would choose to end up there.

The building showed signs of severe neglect. Several windows were boarded up. Many of the walls were defaced by graffiti. There was rust visible on every metallic surface, from the front gates to the fire escapes. It was not the type of place he would have expected to find a genius.

Bishop made his way through the school's corridors, noting the peeling paintwork and water-damaged ceiling tiles, following the signs towards the science lab. When the bell rang, he took his chance and pushed his way through the door, dodging around the exiting pupils.

He didn't know what type of man he expected to find in the classroom, probably a bumbling old professor, in the mould of Anne's father, with a grey beard, thick lensed glasses and a drab suit; but the man he encountered defied all of these expectations.

He was lean and tall, with dark brown skin, a neatly trimmed afro, mutton-chop sideburns and a thick moustache. He wore a garish yellow shirt, brown bell-bottomed trousers and a pair of extravagant leather cowboy boots.

'Arthur Grey?' Bishop ventured, closing the lab door behind the last of the pupils.

The man nodded. 'Arty to my friends,' he said, gesturing around the school lab, which was littered with tripods and test tubes. 'I think it's supposed to be a joke, given the field I work in.'

'I'm Captain William Bishop. Bill to *my* friends, despite my best efforts.' He offered a smile. 'I'm here on behalf of Her Majesty's Armed Forces, because we need your help.'

'Really?' Arty chuckled, sitting himself down on a lab stool, while looking Bishop up-and-down, taking in the details of his uniform. 'I'm just a humble school teacher. What could I possibly do to help the army?'

'You're a man with an exceptional mind.'

Arty raised a sceptical eyebrow. 'Well, that much is true, however...'

'I'm part of the Scots Guards Special Support Group.'

Arty laughed. 'I see. A second attempt then?'

'Something like that, sir, yes. You have come highly recommended.'

'Yes, I was last time, too. I doubt it's on file, but I'm fairly sure my recruitment was blocked due to unspecified reasons,' he said, waving a hand in the general direction of his face. 'So, things must be pretty dire if you're turning to me now.'

Bishop very much doubted it had anything to do with the colour of Arty's skin. If that had been the case, the Brig would have fought against it. Racism was not something either he or Bishop had time for.

'Why should I possibly consider helping you now?' Arty

enquired.

'Perhaps you don't fully understand what we do?'

Arty grinned and shook his head. 'Oh, I do. I have my own… contacts. You're not quite as covert as you like to think. Once I became aware of your operation, it was not difficult to keep tabs on your antics. The mistakes you've made. It's such a wasted opportunity.'

Bishop blinked. 'What do you mean?'

'After everything you've learned, after everything you've encountered, do you know what you've added to the grand sum of human knowledge?' Arty paused briefly. 'Absolutely nothing. You locked it up. Kept it secret. Hid it away. Leaving the world as ignorant and endangered as when you started. What's the point of being involved with anything like that?'

'Civic duty, sir. If you know what we do, you know we keep this country safe.'

'Civic duty?' Arty scoffed. 'Do you know what this country has done for me? Nothing. Worse than nothing, it's stopped me helping.'

Bishop sighed. He could tell from the passion in the man's voice that his opinions were deeply rooted. This was a lost cause. He needed to move on. Find someone else. But Anne had recommended him, and she wouldn't have done that without reason.

'Is there anything I can say to change your mind?' Bishop tried, making one last desperate plea. 'There is a situation happening right now, and we need someone to help us make the right choices, to make sure everything works out for the best, for everyone.'

Arty grinned. It was a broad flash of white teeth. 'Don't get me wrong, Bill. I'm not saying no. I'm very definitely in.'

Bishop shook his head, utterly confused. 'But everything you just said…'

'All true. I just wanted you to understand my reasons.' Arty sprang up from his stool and began pulling on a sheepskin coat. 'Look at me. I'm a secondary school teacher, not because I want to be, but because it's the only half decent job I can get. The world doesn't offer people like me amazing opportunities every day, so I'd be a fool to turn them down when it does. But I'm not doing it for the sake of civic duty,

12

I'll be doing this for me, for my own curiosity.'

Bishop nodded. 'I'll brief you on the way.'

'You do realise I'm going to be difficult, disobedient and unpredictable, don't you? Completely unlike anything the military is used to.'

Bishop shrugged. 'To be honest with you, *Arty*, that's exactly what we *are* used to.'

'Hey, that's right! You used to work with Anne Travers!'

Bishop grinned. 'Still do. On a consultancy basis, at least.'

'I haven't seen her in quite some time. Great gal.'

'I've always thought so.'

'I'm sure she had a crush on me.'

'Luckily for me she's now spoken for.'

'She's...' Arty smiled. 'You and her?'

'Engaged,' Bill said, indicating the ring on his finger. 'In fact, she's the one who recommended you.'

'Ah. She would.'

'We really should hurry,' Bishop said, gesturing at the door.

Arty nodded, glancing at the bell mounted on the wall as it began to ring, signalling the end of breaktime. 'Good idea. Let's scarper before the kids get here.' He grabbed a gym bag from behind his desk and followed Bishop out through the door. 'Right little monsters, the lot of them. Trust me, whatever you guys are up against, it can't be worse than them!'

# CHAPTER TWO
## *Handshake*

LETHBRIDGE-STEWART SEALED the room.

Once the three truckloads of men and equipment arrived, the vehicles were stashed in the underground car park beneath the Palace of Westminster, out of sight of the public. Two soldiers now stood on guard in the Member's Lobby, stopping anyone who was not part of the Fifth from entering the House of Commons. Otherwise, everything outside the chamber appeared to have reverted to a normal, unremarkable day.

It was, of course, an illusion.

The usual cover story had been released; gas leak, etc. For safety reasons, or so they claimed, the House of Commons had been cleared, while engineers worked to fix the problem. By managing to maintain their cover, it enabled Lethbridge-Stewart to feel as if he had regained some control over the situation, but deep down he knew it was untrue. He still had no idea what he was facing.

The sphere continued to glow and spin, hovering impossibly in the space between the green leather clad benches, seemingly unconcerned by anything happening around it. He had a dozen armed men stationed in the room, their weapons trained on the mysterious object, all too professional to be phased by the insanity they were witnessing.

So far, the sphere had done nothing. Its only crime was existing. Given its location, they could not ignore it.

'Is this really all you do?' Greaves asked. 'Point guns at things?'

Lethbridge-Stewart bristled. 'I consider pointing a weapon at it to be a significant improvement on running away.'

Carter grunted. 'But we didn't run away, did we? We stayed, even though it's not our job to deal with such shenanigans!'

Greaves nodded. 'You're the chap who's responsible for dealing with these matters. Whereas, the Commons has other, more important, *real-world* issues to discuss. Northern Ireland. Joining the EEC. The Immigration Act.'

'Gentleman!' Lethbridge-Stewart cried, his temper finally snapping. 'Look at it. It's right in front of you. I assure you this is as *real-world* as it gets. I do apologise if our attempts to protect the safety of our planet have in anyway inconvenienced your debating schedule!'

The two politicians stared at him, shocked by his outburst. Both drew breath to retaliate, but before they could muster their words, the room's main doors opened, as two new arrivals were granted access. It was a timely interruption, for which Lethbridge-Stewart was exceedingly grateful.

'This is Professor Arthur Grey,' Bishop declared, introducing the second man, as they entered the room. 'I brought him up to speed on the way over.'

'It didn't take long,' Grey added, as he stared wide-eyed at the sphere in the centre of the room, an expression of awe written across his dark features. 'It seems you don't know much.'

Lethbridge-Stewart looked the man up and down. He liked to believe he was a quick and shrewd judge of character.

The man was lean and fit, with a confident swagger, which seemed incongruous given he had just walked into a room filled with unknown dangers. He had a comfortable-looking sheepskin coat and a fine moustache, both of which Lethbridge-Stewart thoroughly approved, but he also noted the presence of his garish yellow shirt and ridiculous boots.

Professor Grey, finally moving his eyes from the sphere, glanced around the room. 'Boy, that's a lot of guns,' he observed.

'Purely defensive,' Lethbridge-Stewart told him.

'Sure, but to an untrained eye it might look a little hostile.' Grey put down his gym bag and shrugged off his sheepskin coat. 'Very easy to confuse the two. It just goes to show, it's best not to make snap judgements.'

He locked eyes with the two MPs, who were staring at him with obvious scepticism. He moved before they spoke. He reached into his bag, producing a white lab coat, pulling it on with a distinct flourish, moving more like a performer on *Top of the Pops* than a scientist. If anyone in the room had been judging the man on his skin colour, they were now also seeing the white lab coat, with all the associations of trust and knowledge that it held.

Lethbridge-Stewart nodded approvingly, unable to stop a smile from sliding across his face. The man did not need a lab coat. It was a uniform. It was camouflage on a battlefield. He had a feeling he was going to like this chap. He reached out, offering a handshake.

'Brigadier Lethbridge-Stewart,' he said, as the man clasped his hand. He had a firm, but not over-powering, grip. 'Welcome to the team, Professor.'

'Glad to be part of it.' Grey turned his attention back to the glimmering sphere. 'Tell me, has this disco-ball actually done anything?'

Lethbridge-Stewart shook his head. 'Nothing.'

Grey scratched one of his sideburns thoughtfully. 'Yet we've fled in fear and pointed guns at it. Why don't we assume, just for the moment, that the most dangerous thing in this room is us? You could back off a little, give it some space, do your best to not make it feel threatened.'

Lethbridge-Stewart shook his head. 'I'd rather not. Our mandate is to defend the United Kingdom against outside threats, which is not done by underestimating them. We must proceed with the utmost caution.'

'Have you tried talking to it?'

Lethbridge-Stewart shuffled his feet, and nodded. 'No response.'

'Ah, but it's always worth a go.' Grey stepped back towards his gym bag and started to rifle through the contents. 'But perhaps it requires something more tangible than spoken words. I've seen eyes and tentacles, but no ears.'

He pulled an exercise book from his bag, filled with hand-written notes, most of which seemed to be equations for basic chemical reactions. He tore out a page, folded it into a

16

crude paper aeroplane, then hurled the dart at the sphere.

Lethbridge-Stewart watched, open-mouthed. 'I rather feel you may have misunderstood what I meant by *utmost caution.*'

The paper dart glided across the room, vanishing into the sphere with a flash of blue light.

Professor Grey shrugged. 'Nothing ventured...'

Behind them, the soldiers moved nervously, waiting to see if the sphere would react. After a sufficiently long and uneventful pause, Lethbridge-Stewart placed his hands on his hips and sighed.

'Well, surprisingly, it would seem this creature does not communicate through the medium of paper planes.'

'Give it a minute,' Grey advised, leaning closer to the sphere, as the light and shadows within began to shift.

The fleeting images of the creature were replaced by flashes of numbers and letters, forming as dark swirls suspended in the light, beneath which were ghostly geometric shapes. Then, suddenly, the images were gone. And, with a blaze of blue light, a tiny paper plane launched itself out of the glowing sphere. It flew fast and straight, to hit Grey in the chest, before dropping harmlessly into his hands.

'I stand corrected,' stated Lethbridge-Stewart, suddenly feeling extremely glad he had resisted the urge to put a bullet into the thing. 'Is that the same plane you threw?'

Grey hurriedly deconstructed the plane, glancing at the front and back of the paper, evidently confused by what he was seeing.

'Similar, but not the same. This is not my handwriting. These are not my notes. It's mostly molecular equations, showing the reactions between various chlorofluorocarbons and trioxygen.'

Greaves coughed. 'Could it be a threat?' he asked, leaning forward in his seat.

Grey stared at the page, his brown eyes flitting across the numbers and letters. 'Potentially,' he conceded. 'Earth does have a protective ozone layer. These equations could represent a means to destroy it.'

Carter nodded. 'This is serious,' he observed, his plump

face becoming stern, but then added nothing more, seeming to have no idea what to do with the new information.

Grey stared at the page. 'Ignore the message though. What's important is that it's chosen to reply. Its open to communication. And do you notice how it's doing it? It's following our example. I gave it notes from my chemistry class, it responded with something similar, showing us that it understands. More than that though, it's mirroring us.'

The man had intoned his words as if they were a eureka moment, but as Lethbridge-Stewart had no idea what he was talking about, he could not match the man's enthusiasm. It was not an uncommon feeling for him, particularly when the boffins started gabbling on about science, but he optimistically hoped it meant they were making progress.

'I see,' he said, not wanting to reveal his ignorance. 'Do elaborate.'

'Do you have children, Brigadier?'

The question took Lethbridge-Stewart by surprise. Only recently he and Fiona had learned they were pregnant, but it was not something they wished to share with anybody, especially after the previous complications.

'No,' he stated bluntly, making it clear that such personal enquiries were unwelcome. Even to his own ear the response sounded unnecessarily defensive, so he added a little more, to blunt the sharpness of his reply. 'Not yet.'

'What about you, Bill?' Grey pressed.

'Same.' Bishop shrugged, looking equally uncomfortable and perplexed by the question. 'We're in no rush.'

'Shame,' Grey mused. 'I think Anne will make a terrific mother, don't you?'

'Is this relevant?' Lethbridge-Stewart thundered, unhappy with the personal nature of the questioning.

'Yes. I was trying to find a reference point for you.' Grey shrugged. 'Mirroring is how children learn. They copy actions. They copy language. They copy behaviour. It's how they learn to communicate. It's how we learn the social norms of the world around us. It's why a parent or teacher can't mutter a swear word without a kid yelling it out later just to see what impact it has. Even as adults in high-pressure social situations, like a job interview or a date, people often copy the body language of the other person, so as not to cause offence. It's so innate to us, that our blinking, breathing and even our heart rates and other biological functions can often become synchronised with those around us, without us even knowing it.'

Lethbridge-Stewart nodded. These were concepts he could understand.

'This creature is not trying to threaten us, or frighten us, it's doing all it can to put us at ease,' he surmised. 'It did not put itself in the middle of a military facility, it chose to arrive in a room dedicated to discussion. It is making every effort to communicate with us, in a way it thinks we can understand, by emulating what we give it?'

Professor Grey nodded encouragingly. 'Yes! Exactly! We just need to give it something more substantial to work with. Tell me, has anyone touched the sphere?'

There was a low, nervous chuckle from the men in the room. Lethbridge-Stewart remained stone-faced, treating the question with deadly earnestness.

'Why would anyone possibly do that?' he asked.

'Think about it, Brigadier. One of the first things you did when you met me, was shake my hand. For us, it's a tradition that goes back three thousand years, so old that it appears in *The Iliad*. It serves all kinds of functions. It shows trust, recognition and a desire for peace, without needing one word of common language. It shows you don't hold a weapon. It closes the distance between the two parties, allowing them to see and hear each other clearly. The act itself is a form of mirroring, showing that there is a commonality of purpose and a willingness to communicate.'

'I see. And you think we are being offered such a gesture?'

'Yes, I do. I think this sphere is exactly that, it's a handshake, and we just need to reach out and take it. Someone just needs to touch it. Show it that we want to communicate. It will doubtless extrapolate information from such contact, enabling it to better understand us and start a proper dialogue.'

As the man spoke, Lethbridge-Stewart could feel his right eyebrow edging ever higher, lifting on an ever-rising tide of scepticism. 'I would remind you that your original paper plane did not return.'

'Didn't it?' Grey waved the piece of paper clutched in his hand. 'Arguably, it came back improved, with a wealth of new information.'

Lethbridge-Stewart glanced around the room. The two MPs shuffled nervously, suddenly staring anywhere but at him. None of his soldiers made eye contact. He couldn't see any of them volunteering for such a role.

Improved also meant changed. If any of them touched it, they may never be the same again. What one man considered to be improvement, another may see as detrimental, or worse. Given everything the Fifth had encountered, none of his men were likely to trust such a judgement to a glowing ball of tentacles. Although, he supposed, that was very much the point.

Trust.

'Sir!' The cry came from Bishop, who had moved over to the back of the room to check in with the rest of the troops, quietly and dutifully getting on with his job, while Lethbridge-Stewart had been focused on the sphere. Bishop was now clutching the telephone handset attachment of a portable radio transceiver to his ear. 'HQ has some updates.'

Lethbridge-Stewart nodded, glad for any extra intel. 'What can they tell us?'

Bishop listened intently to the voice in his ear, before repeating the message in a condensed form. 'Jodrell Bank have detected an unidentified object entering high Earth orbit.'

That was not unexpected. Where there was an extra-terrestrial, there was usually a ship.

Bishop paused, as he continued to listen to the report. 'The British Ambassador to the US has seen a second sphere in Washington, inside the Capitol Building, at the very centre of the House of Representatives.'

Lethbridge-Stewart frowned. 'There are more of these things?'

Grey nodded. 'That's logical,' he mused, shoving his hands into the pockets of his lab coat, as he paced thoughtfully around the sphere. 'If they are targeting such locations, stretching out the hand of friendship and attempting to start a dialogue, there is absolutely no reason why they should limit themselves to the United Kingdom. In fact, we're far from the most likely target. If there's one in Washington, there may well be others in similar locations around the world.'

Lethbridge-Stewart felt a large pit open in his stomach. There was a thought in his head, so dark and terrible, he could barely give it voice. But he had to.

'Moscow?'

Grey looked up, meeting his gaze. He nodded.

It was after midnight when a fist hammered on the front door.

When the KGB wanted someone, they were not disposed to call ahead, or wait for a civilised hour. They could show up anywhere, without warning, and would always leave with whatever or whoever they wanted. Those were the rules.

Zoya was accustomed to them.

Having hurriedly pulled on some clothes, she opened the front door, to find two smartly dressed military officers standing on the doorstep. Their uniforms were identical to those of regular service men, except for the distinctive royal-blue piping, which marked them out as members of the state security service.

'Your presence is required,' one stated, gesturing towards a car behind them.

Knowing there was no way to refuse them, she pulled on her red winter coat and stepped out into the street. The vibrant colour of the garment was a deliberate choice. It meant that while she could never be mistaken for a member of the military, she still had a bold and commanding presence, with the revolutionary red loudly proclaiming her loyalty to both her country and to the party.

The two soldiers accompanied her to the car, a black Volga, fresh from the Gorky assembly lines. They opened a rear door for her, then closed it once she was inside.

Most people would have been intimidated by the soldier's behaviour, but she had become numb to it, knowing their lack of communication was often due to them knowing little themselves. They had been told to collect her. Nothing more. She had no reason to fear them. She was a faithful servant of the state.

Over the last couple of years, those in charge had relied upon her scientific expertise in moments of unexpected crisis. So much so, it had given her sway. She knew secrets. She knew that Earth was being visited by an ever-increasing number of extra-terrestrials. She had been present for several such encounters. Now, if she were needed somewhere, it was likely that there had been another such incursion. She did not resent being dragged out of bed for such emergencies; she very much wanted to be there for them.

The Volga sped away, moving swiftly through the dark streets of Moscow. To her surprise, they headed across the Bolshoy Moskvoretsky Bridge, directly into the heart of the city. The colourful onion domes of Saint Basil's Cathedral, gloriously illuminated by the lights of Red Square, flashed past the window.

Despite her previous confidence, Zoya felt a shiver of fear run through her, as she realised where they were headed.

The red brick battlements of the Kremlin loomed out of the darkness.

If some alien threat had penetrated there, within the ancient fortress that symbolised the might of the Soviet Union, then nowhere was safe.

The driver took them through the main gatehouse, stopping outside the Grand Kremlin Palace. The lavish building's white and gold walls towered above her. During the day, its hallways would have been bustling with political activity, as a meeting place for the Central Committee, but currently its many hundreds of windows were dark, showing no signs of occupation. There was one exception. A single window filled with a soft blue glow.

One of the soldiers led her into the building. He guided her through the grand marble-floored hallways, up the stairs and delivered her to an unremarkable door. He then turned on his heel and marched away.

Hesitantly, she opened the door.

Inside was a simple meeting room, with a long wooden table, surrounded by two dozen chairs. Above it hovered a ball of light, turning slowly, as its shifting depths showed fleeting images of an unknown creature. She glimpsed tentacles and blank, black eyes.

A lone man stood at the edge of the glow, staring up at the sphere.

She knew him.

Colonel Rostov was a dour-faced man, with a permanent hang-dog expression. She had never seen him smile. She doubted his sagging face was even capable of such an expression. However, his stern disposition had not hindered his rise to prominence.

After an encounter in the Aegean Sea, in which the Soviet Union had lost one of their nuclear submarines, he had been assigned to a small team in charge of supervising their response. The discovery that a previously unknown species was behind the incident had sent shock waves through the upper echelons of the Central Committee, making them realise that there were threats to the Soviet Union far greater than their human enemies. In the months that followed, an increasing number of specialist military units had been set up to look for similar occurrences within the Soviet Union, which rapidly uncovered an alarming number of incidents.

As the scope and scale of the threats became clear, so Rostov's role had grown, the resources under his command swelling into a major military operation.

However, for all his importance, Rostov remained an unremarkable figure.

He was a small, squat man, in his mid-forties, with dark hair that had already given way to a significant amount of grey. He was wearing an aging regimental uniform, with half a dozen medals pinned beside his left lapel. They were the only sign that he was anything other than an ordinary soldier. They were badges of honour which Zoya had helped him earn. Whenever his military teams confronted something unusual, she would often be called in to help, serving as a scientific advisor.

When they killed the legendary Vodyanoy, a frog-headed creature dwelling in the Lena River, it was she who used sonar to discover its underwater lair, where they discovered a hundred other such monsters living in an underwater cave system. When Soviet botanists had begun experimenting with a batch of mysterious seedpods, accidentally unleashing a species of large plants capable of uprooting and relocating themselves, it was she who had insisted on burning the crops throughout much of the Voronezh Oblast, successfully destroying the thousands of seeds that the wandering monstrosities had released into the wild. When loggers found a wooden cabin in the Dvinsky Forest which could not be opened, it was she who had suggested that they dig beneath the structure, uncovering two vast articulated metal legs buried beneath the ground. She had no idea what it was, or where it had come from, but it had exactly matched the description of Baba Yaga's hut from the Slavic folklore tales which her grandmother had told her when she was a little girl.

The events were hushed up.

The evidence disappeared, shipped off to a remote military facility in Siberia. She had no idea whether such discoveries were taken to be studied, stored, or simply destroyed. Despite numerous requests, she had always been denied access to the base, the work undertaken there deemed too secret to be revealed to anyone outside the military.

The world remained ignorant of their activities; and while Zoya received no formal recognition for her work, Rostov had slowly amassed his medals.

Zoya stepped closer to the sphere, peering curiously into its murky depths. A vast eye rose from the shadows, but it did not seem to register her presence.

'Has it shown any hostile behaviour?' she asked, skipping straight to business, knowing the man had little patience for social niceties or small talk.

'No,' he replied, his Russian tinged with a rural accent, rather than the more sophisticated tones of urban Moscow. 'Not yet.'

'Whatever this thing is, it must know we are here,' she mused, as she walked around it, shedding her red coat and rolling up the sleeves of her blouse. 'It can hardly have chosen this location by accident.'

Before Rostov could respond, the image in the sphere abruptly changed. The creature vanished, with black shapes appearing in the light, in the form of numbers and letters, set against a backdrop of twisting, flickering shapes.

24

Rostov frowned. 'That is not Cyrillic script.'

Zoya nodded. 'They're American or European. But they are more than that. It's chemistry.' She frowned. 'Basic chemistry, not unlike that you would teach a school child.'

Rostov nodded. 'Is it attempting to communicate with us?'

Zoya's frown deepened. 'I do not think so. I think it is pattern matching. Someone, somewhere, has provided it with information.' She nodded approvingly, as she realised what she was seeing. 'If you are trying to create a method of communication with something that shares no common cultural framework, then mathematics and science would be a logical place to start; as the principles are universal and recognisable, regardless of culture or language.'

Rostov bristled, clearly uncomfortable with the implication that the entity might be communicating with someone in the West.

'This thing cannot be allowed to communicate with our enemies. We must intercede.'

Zoya nodded. 'Agreed. If there is a conversation, we must be part of it.'

Rostov's eyes narrowed. 'More than that. If we cannot find a way to communicate with it, that conversation must be terminated, by any means necessary.'

Zoya shifted uncomfortably. She knew exactly what that meant.

She was not squeamish; during her service she had been responsible for the deaths of numerous, non-human, intelligent lifeforms; to ensure the safety and security of the Soviet Union. However, contemplating killing a creature, purely for having contacted their international opponents, seemed excessively aggressive.

Rostov glared at her. 'They are already trading scientific secrets,' he growled.

'That is textbook science for children. Nothing we do not know.'

Rostov shook his head. 'But where does it end? What secrets might it give them?'

There, reluctantly, she had to agree with him.

She nodded. 'We will respond,' she assured him. 'I will find a way.'

Rostov gave her an approving nod.

The image in the sphere suddenly shifted, the letters and numbers abruptly fading away. In their place was an image of a man.

He was tall, dressed in foreign military fatigues, with a neatly clipped moustache.

'I know that face,' Zoya stated, studying the image. 'That's the British military officer that Major Bugayev encountered in the Aegean. I recognise him from the photographs in the files.'

Rostov snorted. 'The British. Will they never learn their place?'

'I doubt it. They're almost as proud as we are.'

Rostov shook his head. 'I suppose, if anyone should be one step ahead of us, it should not surprise us that it is him. Our intelligence suggests the British may have had a handful of extra-terrestrial encounters of their own, nothing of major consequence, but certainly the London Evacuation had all the hallmarks of being a cover up for such an incident. This man, Brigadier Lethbridge-Stewart, is invariably involved in those reports.'

Zoya leaned in closer to the sphere, noting how the British officer's arm was stretched out towards them, his fingertips splayed out and flattened as if they were pressed against a piece of curved glass.

She smiled. 'Well, you will be pleased to hear, he has already made his first mistake. He has just shown us how they are communicating with this lifeform. Based on the image in front of us, I would say he has made physical contact with a sphere.'

# CHAPTER THREE

*Face of the Enemy*

LETHBRIDGE-STEWART LIFTED his hand and touched the sphere. In the end, there had been no other choice. Who else could have done it? It had to be him. It was his responsibility, his duty.

And there was no time for debate. If their speculation was correct, and there was an identical sphere in Moscow, they had to move with urgency.

Time seemed to slow. Everything around him faded away. The grand room, along with his men, was replaced by an empty white void. He felt the presence of another mind, huge and utterly alien, swirling around him.

It slipped inside his head.

Instinctively, he tried to let go of the sphere, but his hand didn't respond.

He panicked, tried to step back, tried to cry out; but nothing happened. It was as if he was utterly disconnected from his physical body.

He could feel the creature sifting through his thoughts and memories, raking through every aspect of his identity, peering into the dark corners of his soul. Too late, Lethbridge-Stewart realised what a terrible mistake he had made. He felt like a child who had sucked a finger and plunged it into a power socket, curious to see what would happen.

Suddenly, Samson was standing beside him, staring at him with large brown eyes.

No. It couldn't be. Samson was dead.

Lethbridge-Stewart knew what was happening.

The alien was burrowing into his mind, using whatever it dug up to attack him, toying with memories and emotions it did not understand. He squeezed his eyes closed, trying to banish the ghost from his sight, but it remained visible. A phantom of the mind.

He steadied himself, breathing slowly, trying to regain his professional detachment and composure.

'No. Stop it. Get out. You have no right to rummage through my mind like this.'

He felt the intruder recoil, letting go of him, receding back into the nothingness that surrounded them. He suspected he had driven it out through sheer force of will. He continued to focus on calming himself. He needed to be rational. He needed to be strong. He needed to be ready for the next attack.

'What are you?' he asked

Samson continued to stare at him.

'What are you?' Samson repeated.

Lethbridge-Stewart frowned. 'What do you want?' he pressed.

'What do you want?'

A moment later, footsteps echoed in the emptiness.

The ghost of Samson abruptly vanished, his form dissipating like a mist, dissolving into the bright glow of the void.

Another figure stepped out of the light. Lethbridge-Stewart didn't recognise him.

He was a stout man, wearing a Soviet military uniform, with numerous medals pinned to his chest. The three golden stars on his epaulettes marked him out as a colonel. His face was set with grim determination, but his eyes were alive with curiosity.

Lethbridge-Stewart instinctively reached for his revolver. He had no idea if the weapon in his hand actually existed, but he felt far more confident having it in his grip. He was fairly sure his real body was still standing in the House of Commons, with whatever form he was now perceiving being little more than a dream, a facsimile designed to help him understand what he was experiencing.

'Hello?' Lethbridge-Stewart ventured. 'Who are you?'

The stranger glanced at the weapon in Lethbridge-Stewart's hand. He spoke in Russian. *'Ya ne govoryu po angliyski.'*

*Angliyski.* English. The man didn't speak English.

The Soviet officer shook his head, then reached out, offering a handshake. Lethbridge-Stewart stared warily at the hand, then reluctantly clasped it in his own. This was hardly the time or place to cause a diplomatic incident.

'Rostov,' the man stated.

'Lethbridge-Stewart.' He glanced at his right hand, realising that when he had accepted the handshake, his revolver had vanished. He found it back in its holster.

Colonel Rostov glanced about. He spoke several sentences in Russian. The first few, directed at Lethbridge-Stewart, sounded pithy and dismissive. The remainder of the Russian officer's words were shouted into the void, evidently directed at the alien mind, calling out to it, angrily demanding its attention.

'What are you doing, Colonel?' Lethbridge-Stewart asked. 'Whatever it is, stop. This thing is dangerous. We can't trust it. We have no idea what it is, or what it wants.'

Even as he spoke the words, he knew they were wasted. Rostov couldn't understand them, and neither did he seem to have any interest in listening.

An odd look filled the colonel's face, his eyes widening, his jowls trembling. There were a thousand emotions there. Fear. Doubt. Excitement. Awe. Horror. Hope.

A new phantom formed in the nothingness.

An old man, with a stooped frame and a scraggily beard.

Rostov took hold of the elderly man's hand. They exchanged several words in Russian. Rostov waved dismissively in Lethbridge-Stewart's direction.

Abruptly, he felt himself falling away, becoming detached and remote from the events he was witnessing. He tried to shout out, but his voice was powerless, too weak to be heard.

For a moment, there was nothing but light, then nothing but darkness.

Lethbridge-Stewart awoke, lying flat on his back, in the centre of the House of Commons, staring up at the tiny square sky lights in the ceiling.

'He's awake!' someone cried.

The faces of his soldiers suddenly crowded over him, all bearing worried expressions.

'Are you all right, sir?' asked Bishop, pushing the others aside, reaching down to help him to his feet. 'You had us worried for a moment.'

Clasping the outstretched hand, Lethbridge-Stewart pulled himself to his feet. 'I'm fine, Captain,' he muttered, despite feeling as if he had been torn to pieces. He straightened his jacket and cap, trying to give the impression that such small actions were all that was required for him to pull himself together, then cleared his throat for good measure. 'How long was I gone?'

'Only a few minutes,' Professor Grey replied. He stood a short distance away, his white lab coat pushed back, to allow his hands to rest casually in his trouser pockets, as he stared upwards at the sphere. 'About thirty seconds communing with this thing, the rest of it napping on the floor.'

'It seemed much longer,' Lethbridge-Stewart muttered.

The sphere pulsed, the blue light brightening and dimming as the tentacles suddenly squirmed with an increased ferocity. Grey took a step back, removing his hands from his pockets, his face filled with alarm.

'With the greatest respect, we don't have time to worry about you right now, we need to know about them. Were you able to communicate with them? With the aliens?'

Lethbridge-Stewart rubbed a hand against the back of his neck, feeling slightly anxious, aware of the two MPs still sat on the front bench, staring at him with judgemental eyes.

'Yes,' he stated. 'I made contact, after a fashion, although I'm not sure I understood everything that happened.'

'Tell us about them.'

Lethbridge-Stewart frowned, not quite sure how to respond. 'Well, it's not a question of *them*,' he muttered. 'There is only one, I think.'

Professor Grey's eyes lit up with curiosity. 'It told you that?'

'Not in so many words.' Lethbridge-Stewart frowned, unsure how he had gained the knowledge, but feeling certain of it anyway. 'There was only one mind there.'

Greaves rose to his feet, straightening the jacket of his navy blue suit as he strode in among the huddle of concerned soldiers. 'I must insist you answer our most pressing question. Is it hostile?'

Lethbridge-Stewart paused, considering the question, then gave his verdict. 'Yes, I believe so. We must regard this creature as a threat to the national security of the United Kingdom.'

The MP blinked. It was clearly not the response he had

wanted.

Carter rose to his feet, straightening his red tie, and hurriedly pushed his way to his colleague's side. 'Why would you say that? Did something happen? Did it do something?'

As he spoke, the image in the sphere shifted, momentarily showing the face of Colonel Rostov, before it began to contract, the light appearing to crumble inwards. It spun faster, its shape distorting, and the glowing material drained away through a central point, vanishing like water swirling down a plughole. With a final blaze of light, it vanished from existence, leaving behind a hushed, empty space.

Professor Grey broke the silence. 'What happened? Where'd it go?'

Lethbridge-Stewart cleared his throat. He tried to find the right words, but they eluded him. No matter how he phrased it, it would never sound good, so he just gave them the stark, unpleasant truth.

'To the best of my understanding, the Soviet Union has successfully established communication with this creature, and the United Kingdom has been frozen out from any further contact with it.'

A new day dawned in Moscow.

Zoya made her way to Red Square, to wait for events to unfold, knowing that she was about to witness a historic moment.

An early morning winter fog lingered in the air, laying between her and everything else, making the distinctive buildings around her seem pale and inconsequential. The domes of the cathedral and the towering battlements of the Kremlin were just faded silhouettes lurking in the gloom. The sky above her was overcast, the freshly risen sun appearing as nothing more than a white smudge, glowing behind the banks of thick January cloud.

The entrance roads had been blocked with barricades, each one manned by a dozen uniformed soldiers, there to prevent any civilians from wandering into the square. A trio of heavy tanks, with huge gun barrels, sat directly outside Lenin's Mausoleum. Four platoons of soldiers, over one hundred men, were standing in neat lines beside them.

There was more than enough firepower to wage a small war.

She hoped it was unnecessary.

If a single shot was fired that day, she suspected it would end badly not just for the Soviet Union, but for all of humanity.

Rostov stood in the centre of the square, looking directly up at the clouds. Every other man there was wary and cautious, yet his normally dour face was lit with a broad grin, his eyes gleaming with excitement. His behaviour had been markedly changed since he'd interacted with the sphere. The coldness was gone, seemingly replaced by an almost child-like sense of excitement.

She didn't trust it.

Zoya approached him cautiously, the sound of her footsteps the only noise in the eerily quiet square, utterly silent despite the presence of so many soldiers.

'Not long now,' Rostov announced, his breath fogging on the cold air. 'The ship is in descent. It will arrive in a few minutes.'

Zoya frowned. 'How do you know this?' she asked, unable to stop herself from sounding suspicious. 'Is the creature still in contact with you?'

Rostov chuckled. It was disconcerting to see the once dour man so happy. 'No, Miss Volskaya. I do admire your wariness, it is so Russian, but it is not necessary.' He glanced at her, his saggy face aglow with happiness. 'I merely know what is to come. Today is the beginning of a new epoch. Mankind is no longer alone. We are to be given a wealth of knowledge and access to technology beyond our wildest dreams. Do not allow yourself to be consumed by fear, not on such a momentous and glorious day.'

Zoya looked up at the pale, empty sky. 'None of our previous encounters have yielded such positive results.' She shook her head sadly. 'Your optimism feels unfounded and misplaced. There will be a price. There always is. I would feel much easier if I knew something, anything, about this creature. We don't even know what it is called.'

Rostov shook his head. 'You are thinking in very human terms, Miss Volskaya. What we are dealing with here is vastly different to us, better than anything we can ever aspire to be. It is a true patriot, seeking only to serve, just as I do.'

If his words were supposed to reassure her, they failed. She was terrified by the unbridled eagerness in his eyes.

She said nothing, maintaining a neutral expression.

From above them, there came a noise, like the boom of a supersonic jet.

Rostov took hold of her arm, his fingers closing around the red sleeve of her coat. Instinctively she flinched, feeling uncomfortable at being manhandled, before realising he was attempting to move her to safety.

'It is time for us to stand out of the way of history, Miss Volskaya,' he informed her. 'Whether you fear it, or welcome it, the future is on its way.'

She let herself be guided across the square, until she stood in front of the line of troops, where Rostov stopped and turned to look back up at the sky.

It was at that moment she noticed the bulky film camera, mounted on a tripod, standing between the tanks. It was manned by soldiers, rather than members of the state media, presumably because they were deemed more trustworthy. Everyone in the Central Committee and military, other than Rostov, were clearly still feeling circumspect about this event. They still wanted full control of any record of it. The camera lens was pointed down the length of the square, angled so the troops and tanks would be out of shot, but Saint Basil's Cathedral would appear as the backdrop to the events about to occur.

Above them, the white clouds lit up, as if a second much larger sun had appeared in the sky. A moment later there was a sound like thunder as a large circular shadow grew behind the light.

She was in no doubt that a large craft had just fired an engine to slow its descent. She watched, open mouthed, as it dropped through the clouds.

The vessel had a sleek, circular design. Its surface was a flawlessly smooth, polished metal, reflective enough that it seemed almost colourless. There were no doors, windows or any other utilitarian features. There were no visible engines, just a white light burning below it, which was creating enough thrust that the mist beneath it was blasted away.

The updraft whipped at her hair. Rostov held onto his cap.

With the mist gone, Zoya had a clear view across the square, as she watched the vessel descend. Despite everything she had seen, such sights still filled her with awe. Returning cosmonauts still crashed their re-entry capsules into the sea, the technology to make such a controlled vertical landing from orbit, like the one they were witnessing, was still decades beyond their capability. If the creatures were prepared to share such technology, they would be leaping ahead perhaps fifty years of technological progress, giving them a distinct advantage against their enemies.

Rostov was nodding to himself.

'We may have lost the race to the moon, but with the gifts we are about to be given, we shall easily win the race to Mars. Not that we will need to view the Americans as a rival anymore. Imagine what our airforce will be capable of with technology such as this.'

The vessel came to a halt, hovering a few feet above the ground.

Four silver legs slid out of its base, reaching down to plant themselves on the paving stones of Red Square, and the light beneath the ship faded away.

She heard the quiet hum of its engine dwindle to nothing.

As they watched, an entrance way opened in the side of the craft, which was slightly larger than would be necessary for even the tallest man. From the opening, a long silver ramp slid outwards, descending to the ground, creating a walkway that would give them easy access to the craft.

Rostov strode directly towards it.

'Please join me, Miss Volskaya,' he said, his words sounding more like a military order than an optional invite. 'Someone of a scientific background must witness this. I would have you by my side.'

Zoya nodded. She was nervous, worried about how events were unfolding, but there was no way she could resist the opportunity to see inside the craft.

Behind her, she could hear the soldier manning the film camera hurriedly detaching it from the tripod. Glancing back, she saw the young soldier hoist the heavy piece of kit onto his shoulder, then proceed to follow them towards the ship.

Rostov made his way up the ramp, stepping into the gloomy interior of the craft. She swiftly followed, not wanting to miss anything, despite her trepidation.

'Hello?' Rostov called into the darkness. 'I'm here. Are you there?'

The words seemed strangely inauspicious for their first official contact with another intelligent species; she had expected something more grandiose from the ambitious military officer, but the unpretentious greeting seemed oddly appropriate given the circumstances. It was perhaps best to keep things simple, given that any complication could cause a disaster.

Ahead of them, something moved in the darkness.

A large form slithered out of the shadows, rolling forwards on countless twisting tentacles, until it loomed over them, fully revealed in the shaft of light that fell through the open entrance. It slunk its head downwards, so that it was level with their own, as it stared at them with eight large black eyes.

It was hideous.

Zoya instinctively took a step back. Rostov held his ground.

Despite her fear, Zoya could not contain her curiosity. Ignoring the trembling in her knees, she quickly retook the step she had lost, so that she was close enough to study the creature, keen to see what information she could glean from studying its physiognomy.

It was unlike any lifeform she had seen before.

There was no discernible torso, it was just a mass of squirming limbs, which seemed to be actively branching and merging into new shapes as required. On closer inspection, the limb which she had assumed to be a head, appeared to be nothing more than a clump of eyes. The appendage possessed no visible mouth, or ears, meaning there was no guarantee that it had heard or understood any of the words they had spoken. It was possible the creature had no understanding of verbal communication at all.

More intriguingly, there was no skull cavity, no space to house its brain. Wherever the creature's intellect dwelt, it was somewhere other than the eye-covered limb.

If they needed to stop the creature, she would be hard pressed to advise a soldier where to aim their bullet, as while destroying the limb may blind it, it was unlikely to kill it. Even then, the creature appeared to be able to grow new limbs in an instant, meaning it may quickly recover from such an injury. There were no other visible weaknesses; no obvious location for a heart, no indication that it had lungs, or any structure akin to a spinal cord.

She shook her head, reigning back her thoughts.

She had spent too long working with the military, she was considering ways to eliminate the creature before she had even established if it was a threat. As a scientist, she should be trying to understand what stood before her, rather than determining the best way of killing it.

Rostov reached out a hand towards the creature.

'I am ready,' he stated, a tremor of nervousness in his voice. 'Let us begin.'

The alien creature reared up, lashing out with numerous tentacles, wrapping them around Rostov's wrists and neck.

The soldier behind them gave a cry of alarm. Zoya heard him backing away.

'Stand your ground, soldier!' she shouted.

She had no authority to issue orders, but the man instinctively obeyed, hurriedly bringing his panic under control. He kept the camera focused on what was unfolding in front of them. The creature clung onto Rostov for several seconds, then slowly loosened its grip, letting go of him, the tentacles retracting into the roiling mass.

Rostov steadied himself, drawing several calming breaths.

He glanced at her, with an odd look in his eyes, then straightened his uniform and stared directly down the camera lens. She could hear the film ticking around, capturing every moment for posterity.

This was the speech, she reasoned, there was no way an ambitious military officer like Rostov would miss an opportunity to claim the glory of this moment. Something needed to be said, which would endure with the same tenacity as Neil Armstrong's famous statement, '*One small step for man, one giant leap for mankind,*' which was burned into the memory of every human being alive.

He spoke.

Zoya did not understand a word of it.

It was in English.

This was particularly disconcerting, because having worked with the man for two years, she knew that up until a moment ago, he could not speak anything other than Russian.

It was immediately clear that their visitor was already influencing and changing Rostov's behaviour. Despite Rostov's earlier words, Zoya had been right to fear the arrival of these aliens.

# CHAPTER FOUR

*Gathering the Troops*

LETHBRIDGE-STEWART SAT, cap in hand, outside Major General Hamilton's office.

He felt like a troublesome schoolboy, hauled up and sent to see the headmaster. He was rarely called in to account for the Fifth Operational Corps' activities, as they understood he needed a certain amount of latitude to get the job done, but rarely had things gone quite as badly as they had in Westminster.

In the official report, he had been brutally honest, stating that while his team had failed to establish communication with the alien lifeform, he believed the Soviet Union had stolen a march on them and successfully opened a dialogue with the creature. He would never lie, or try to obfuscate the facts, it was important that they knew the truth. Unsurprisingly, he had been swiftly summoned to see the top brass.

He'd brought Professor Grey with him, in case they needed to discuss the scientific side, in the vague hope that he may be able to deflect any criticism by impressing them with technical gobbledegook.

The man was currently lounging in a chair, humming something tuneless. He did not seem to have a care in the world. Why would he? He was not the one they would hold accountable.

The door to Hamilton's office opened, and a young female communications officer emerged and shot them a wry look, as if to say, *Good Luck. You're going to need it.*

'They're ready for you,' she said, gesturing towards the open door.

Rising to his feet, Lethbridge-Stewart made his way into the office, with Professor Grey sauntering in behind him.

Nothing in the room was as he expected.

The blinds had been pulled closed, even though it was still daylight outside, with the room lit only by a single office lamp. There was a hefty film projector sat on the general's desk, with its lens aimed at a large white screen at the far end of the room. General Hamilton stood beside it, holding a sheaf of papers, which judging by the manilla cover and red 'Classified' stamp upon it, was the report Lethbridge-Stewart had submitted a week ago.

They also had an unexpected guest.

Mr Peter Grant, from the Ministry of Defence, was sitting in a corner, idly flicking through a photocopy of the same report. It seemed logical to have their contact with the Ministry present, given the political ramifications of the latest encounter.

'Brigadier,' Grant said, looking up. 'I'm not sure if *good* is right, but it's nice to see you again.'

Lethbridge-Stewart said nothing. He just stood before Hamilton's desk and waited for the general to speak.

'This is unacceptable,' General Hamilton stated, dropping the report onto his desk, dismissing it with a wave of his hand.

Lethbridge-Stewart bowed his head. 'I can only apologise, sir.'

'You misunderstand, Brigadier,' Grant said, waving his copy of the document in the air. 'It's not a criticism of your work, but of the situation. We've got ourselves in a right ol' pickle now, haven't we? The Soviets alone now have access to this thing. And whose fault is that? Not yours. You've been dealing with events of global significance, with only the resources of the Fifth at your disposal. This was bound to happen sooner or later.'

Lethbridge-Stewart raised an eyebrow in surprise.

Hamilton reached into his desk drawer, taking out a large stack of colour photographs, which he dealt out onto the desk, so that each one was clearly displayed.

'The Americans have been good enough to share these images with us,' he informed them, as Lethbridge-Stewart studied the sequence of pictures. They showed a silver craft passing from space, through the thin blue arc of the stratosphere, heading eastwards over the Baltic Sea. 'One of their reconnaissance satellites tracked this unidentified object as it descended from orbit, entered Soviet airspace, and disappeared somewhere near Moscow.'

Lethbridge-Stewart felt his stomach sink. To speculate that the worst had happened was one thing, to have it confirmed was quite another.

'If we required any further proof, this morning the following film was anonymously delivered to Whitehall,' Grant said, gesturing towards the reel mounted on the projector, 'which leaves no room for doubt.'

He flipped a switch, causing the reels to begin to spin, but no image appeared on the screen. He frowned.

Professor Grey coughed politely. 'You need to turn on the projector light,' he advised, leaning in to flip a second switch. 'Luckily, you've got a technical expert on hand. When I was a student, I used to work part-time at the Odeon.'

A bright beam of light shone through the lens, projecting a washed-out image of Red Square on the white screen. The colours were muted, but the elegant domes of St Basil's Cathedral were clearly visible. After several seconds had elapsed, a silver craft dropped into view, the image becoming momentarily blurry as the cameraman tried to refocus on the new object, as it descended towards the ground. Once it landed, two figures approach the vessel's entrance. One was a dark-haired woman, in a red coat, that Lethbridge-Stewart did not recognise. The other was a small grey-haired man, wearing a Soviet military uniform.

His face was familiar.

'General Rostov,' Lethbridge-Stewart muttered.

On the screen, Rostov and the unnamed woman had advanced into the unlit interior of the ship, the images becoming grainy, as the camera struggled in the low light. In the shadows loomed something inhuman, a mass of squirming tentacles, with eight eyes that glinted in the darkness. After a brief interaction with the creature, Rostov glanced at the woman with a questioning expression, then turned to face the camera.

'Mankind is no longer alone in the universe,' he declared.

'The Soviet Union has a new ally, who freely offers us access to their advanced technology, to help us usher in a new age of peace, prosperity and unity for the world.'

To the untrained ear the words might have sounded benign, but to Lethbridge-Stewart they were a clear threat. Delivered in English, they were obviously intended for an international audience, to inform them that they no longer had any say in the shape of the future.

The picture abruptly vanished.

The film had run to the end of it spool, its untethered end flicking noisily against the metal reel, until Grey turned off the tiny motor.

Lethbridge-Stewart composed himself, looking at the three men around him, choosing his words carefully, not wanting any of them to underestimate the severity of his next statement.

'Gentleman, it is my recommendation that we must find a way to force the Soviet Union to give us access to this creature. In my opinion, there has never been a greater threat to our national security. That our enemies have sole access to this alien, and the technology it offers, is simply unacceptable.'

Grey nodded. 'Lethbridge-Stewart is right,' he said, sitting himself on the edge of the general's desk. 'Within a decade, this will transform the socioeconomic balance of our world, inevitably leading to the collapse of western civilisation. All without a shot being fired.'

General Hamilton snorted. 'A decade? The military implications will be far swifter. Ten years ago, the Americans were so terrified by the prospect of missile bases in Cuba, that it almost resulted in a nuclear war, yet now the Soviets have access to a spacecraft, which must surely be capable of deploying such weapons from orbit. Not to mention the possibility that this creature may have brought other, far more advanced, weapons with it. The balance of global geopolitical power has changed overnight. We must act now, before they can find a way to use such weapons against us. We have but a moment, a brief window of opportunity to act, or we shall surely pay the price.'

Grant raised his hands, attempting to calm the room. 'Gentlemen, I am glad we are all in agreement about the severity of the situation, but it is academic; the Soviets are never going to give us access. They have absolutely no reason to do so.'

Lethbridge-Stewart bristled. 'If they will not accept a diplomatic solution,' he declared, 'perhaps we must consider a military one.'

There was an awkward silence.

'The stakes are too high,' Grey muttered, glancing around the room, evidently alarmed that nobody else was objecting. 'That could end very badly for everyone.'

Lethbridge-Stewart shook his head. 'To run with your gambling analogy, the stakes are already on the table, the hands have already been dealt and we are set to lose.'

Grey laughed. 'So, your solution is to up-end the table? Bring the game to an end?'

Lethbridge-Stewart paused, silenced by the professor's words, feeling the comparison was starkly appropriate. As ever, the solutions he could offer had a finite range, he needed some lateral thinking from his scientific advisor.

'I'm sure we would all welcome another option if you have one.'

'I do.' Grey nodded thoughtfully. 'Let's change the way we phrase what we need. The Soviets will never agree to a demand for access, it's not in their nature to bow to intimidation, so let's offer to help them instead. Let's give them the chance to consult with the Fifth Operational Corps, on neutral territory, no strings attached. Offer them an exchange of information, tell them what we've learned over the last few years, show them that we have the skills, experience and knowledge that they need. Let's put our cards on the table, be honest with them, so that we can convince them that they need our help.'

Lethbridge-Stewart had to admit that Grey's suggestion was something he would never have considered. It was a complete betrayal of the founding principles of the Fifth Operational Corps.

General Hamilton looked outraged. 'May I remind you, Professor, the Fifth Operational Corps does not officially exist.'

Grey shrugged dismissively. 'In name, perhaps not, but it

*does* exist, and they *know* it. And you know that they know. Based on the reports I've read, they've known ever since the incident in the Aegean. And we have proof they've acquired a UFO, even if they've not officially admitted it, so why continue to play these ridiculous spy games? Why keep up the pretence of lies when everyone knows the truth?'

His words were met by stunned silence.

'I know our enemy,' Hamilton stated. 'No matter how well intentioned such an offer may be, there is no way the Central Committee or the Soviet military would ever accept British assistance.'

Grey tapped the metal film reel on the camera. 'Well, someone over there wants to talk. As much as this film was obviously crafted for the West, we're not supposed to have it yet, otherwise it would have arrived through more conventional channels. Can you imagine how difficult it was for them to get this film out of the Soviet Union? So, let's give them a chance to speak to us. Propose the meeting, see who takes the bait.'

Grant shrugged. 'We could perhaps set something up in West Berlin,' he suggested tentatively. 'See how they respond? See who they send?'

Hamilton shook his head. 'Even if such rebel elements existed, there is no reason to suppose they would be part of any official Soviet delegation.'

Lethbridge-Stewart nodded, stroking thoughtfully at his moustache. 'Out of curiosity, have MI6 been able to identify the woman in the red coat?' he asked Grant.

'No. There was no clear picture of her face. Is she important? She's just a civilian.'

'Exactly. So why is she there? Right at the heart of events? What is her role?'

Grey's eyes immediately lit up with excitement. 'A scientific advisor, perhaps? If so, she may be more open to a constructive dialogue. Logically, if we emphasise that this is a scientific meeting, rather than political or military, they may include her as part of their delegation. If we can convince her that they need us, and if she has the necessary influence, she might be able to persuade the others to give us the access we want.'

Hamilton mulled over what he had heard. 'It feels like a lot to risk, with little chance of success. We could play our hand and gain nothing.'

Lethbridge-Stewart nodded. 'It is a high-stakes game, sir. That is what makes the gamble worthwhile.'

Hamilton sighed, then reluctantly nodded his agreement. 'Fine,' he said, as he opened the blinds, letting dazzling sunshine into the room. 'Gentlemen, it seems we have the beginnings of a plan. Let us propose this meeting, see if we can lure this mysterious woman out into the open, in the hope of convincing her that they need our scientific expertise, getting us access to both the creature and the ship. Brigadier, you will assemble a team, representing the very finest that the Fifth Operational Corps can muster, particularly on the scientific front. I want you in Berlin within seventy-two hours.'

'Yes, sir.'

Grant moved towards the door. 'I'll contact the Foreign Office,' he said, 'we'll make a formal approach. I'll let you know how the offer is received.'

As they all began exiting the room, Hamilton shot Lethbridge-Stewart a sideways glance, subtly tilting his head, silently conveying another message to him: *Stay back a moment, there is more to discuss.*

Lethbridge-Stewart paused, letting the others exit the room ahead of him, then turned back to Hamilton, who leaned in close, speaking in a low voice.

'Be in no doubt, Stewart, you must eliminate this threat, by any means necessary. Make sure, as subtly as you can, that your team has the relevant skillset to achieve that end. Is that understood?'

'Yes, sir.'


Major Bishop parked his pale blue Ford Cortina by the curb outside his Edinburgh home.

He sat for a moment, pondering the task ahead of him, as rain drummed on the windscreen. He had shed his uniform and put on civvies, but he was still a soldier, he still had a job to do. Lethbridge-Stewart had tasked him with the most impossible mission imaginable.

He had to *tell* his wife that she was being reactivated as a member of the Fifth. The emphasis was very much on it being *tell*, not *ask*, as she did not have a choice in the matter. Under the Emergency Powers Act, a subclause of her old contract had been activated, meaning she was being conscripted.

Anne would be furious.

She would do everything in her power to resist, despite the inevitability of her compliance. For some reason, the Brig had decided that this information was best delivered by her husband, although the logic of that reasoning escaped him. Bishop saw it very differently; he knew it would put an unnecessary strain on their fledgling marriage, by making it appear as if he was somehow culpable. Being newly-weds (four months still counted, right?) was not as easy as he had imagined, everything had changed so quickly, particularly after the birth of their first child.

Bishop was not sure Lethbridge-Stewart really understood such relationships. To him such matters were not a priority. It was not a sentiment that Bishop shared. His relationship with Anne, and baby Samantha, were the most precious things in his life. He would do anything for them. He did everything *because* of them.

He rather suspected Lethbridge-Stewart had given Bishop the task, regardless of the effect it had on his marriage, so that the Brig himself would not have to deal with Anne's response. He wanted to keep himself away from any tears and arguments, so that his judgement was not clouded by emotion. He doubtlessly believed that he needed to remain a cold and aloof authority figure, above such petty emotional concerns, if he was going to lead his team through the difficult days ahead. So, inevitably, it had fallen to Bishop to break the news to his own wife.

He would rather have faced a hoard of Yeti.

He glanced through the rain splattered window at their little Edinburgh townhouse. It was a very ordinary three-bedroom Victorian terrace, with little more than a smudge of garden, yet they had both fallen in love with it, mostly because it was so ordinary; it was a slice of normality, a world away from the craziness of his work for the Fifth Operational Corps.

44

It had given them enough space for a nursery, which Anne had painted and decorated, building up her dreams of having a normal family life.

Now he was going to tear that away from her.

He turned off the Cortina's engine, climbed out of the car and walked to his front door, the cold rain driving him rapidly down the path despite his reluctance to face what lay ahead.

'I'm home,' he announced loudly, as he entered the house.

Anne immediately appeared in the hallway, holding their baby in her arms, with a warm smile on her face. 'Look,' she cooed, 'Daddy's back!'

She was a picture of normal, suburban, family bliss. Anne had taken so naturally to motherhood, that it had surprised him, turning her back on her beloved scientific career with surprising ease. He was sure the interest would resurface again given the least provocation, but as she stood there holding three-month-old Samantha, it was clear she did not have a thought for anything else in the world.

'I have some news,' he said, leaning in to kiss her, a gesture which she instantly reciprocated. 'Bad news.'

Anne instinctively took a step backwards, holding Samantha ever so slightly tighter. He tried to explain to her, letting the details of the last few days spill from his lips, but with each word she retreated further away from him, her face darkening with anger.

'I know where this is going,' she stated bluntly.

'Anne, we need you.'

'No,' she said, turning away, as if to shield Samantha from his words. 'Bill, we have a baby now, I can't just drop everything and go.'

Bishop sighed. 'It's in your contract. Clause Twelve.'

She frowned at him. 'You think I could abandon our child, because of the small-print in a contract? You think I give one jot about the rules?'

Bishop hung his head. 'Your country needs you. What's happening is bigger than us.'

He tried to reach out and touch Samantha's fingers, but Anne carried her another step away. 'What can I possibly do that would make any difference?' she asked. 'Do you think I can solve the Cold War?'

She kept her voice low and steady, making it quieter as she became angrier, hiding the hostility from Samantha's young ears.

'Nobody expects you to fix the Cold War.' Bishop sighed, raising his hands placatingly. 'Even you have your limits.'

'Really? Because I can do it,' she seethed, her voice beginning to rise. 'Pointing nuclear weapons at each other is mad. We all know it. That's why it's called Mutually Assured Destruction, because the acronym is mad. Nobody wins. All we need to do is stop. Start co-operating. Stop wasting money on weapons that must never be used, start spending it on making a better world for everyone, so that we have less to fight about. See? Simple. I've fixed the Cold War. Yet nobody does it. Why is it so impossible, when everyone just wants peace?'

Samantha began to cry. Anne bounced her in her arms, trying to soothe away the distress.

'That's what we're trying to do,' Bishop replied. 'We're trying to bring the Soviets to the table to talk. And if we can, we need you there, so that we can make co-operation a reality.'

Bishop was wary, he had turned her own argument against her, but he'd been involved with Anne long enough to know that being right was never enough to win an argument.

Anne scowled at him. 'If I refuse?' she asked.

Bishop winced, knowing how his answer would sound. 'They'll put you on the plane anyway, or in prison.'

Anne shook her head sadly. 'If that's the country we live in, where armed soldiers will drag a screaming mother from her child, what are we even trying to protect? We're no better than the other side.'

Bishop nodded. It was an unpleasant image. He could not imagine Lethbridge-Stewart actually going through with such a threat. The whole system worked on the very British basis that nobody would ever want to create such a fuss, so everyone would just quietly comply with the demands of the law.

For once, he was not sure that would happen.

Anne may refuse. If she did, Lethbridge-Stewart may send armed men to collect her. Inevitable steps of escalation, between two irreconcilable parties, which could only lead to a horrific conclusion. It was a miniature Cold War that threatened a destructive resolution, with his marriage as one of the casualties.

'Please, Anne,' he begged. 'It'll only be a few days. Once we have the access we need, we'll get you home in no time.'

Anne's eyes were like glass; hard and emotionless. 'Who would look after Samantha?'

Bishop breathed a sigh of relief. The blunt, thoughtless hostility had stopped. She had accepted the inevitable outcome. She did not want it to end in disaster. She would negotiate; try her best to find a tolerable compromise.

'My sister could look after Samantha. You know she's itching to spend time with her namesake.'

He didn't doubt it was difficult for Anne. It was more than he could ever have imagined asking of his wife, yet she had not disappointed him, giving everything that was required, despite her better judgment. It was why he loved her. She gave more than anyone could be expected to give.

Having only recently returned to Edinburgh, Lethbridge-Stewart spent most of the evening driving back south.

He did not have long to assemble his team. While Bishop was more than capable of dealing with the tricky business of talking to Anne, there was another more difficult role to fill, which he wanted to deal with himself.

There had been a hole in his team since Samson Ware had died. He could not help but wonder if it had cost them the difference between success and failure in Westminster. If so, that was his fault, for failing to face up to the task of replacing him.

He would never find someone who knew him as well as Samson, but he could find someone just as bold and reliable. Someone who had the skills he needed. He'd finally looked through the personnel files waiting in his in-tray, and found a hefty selection of capable men, plus several wildcards. His people knew him well enough to put something unexpected into the mix.

Having looked through the skills and talents they all offered, he had quickly identified the most qualified candidate for the mission at hand, but he wanted to meet them in person, before formally recruiting them. Working for the Fifth Operational Corps was not for everyone, and he liked to believe he had become good at recognising the type who had what it took.

He had arranged to meet them outside the Beacon Barracks in Staffordshire.

Shortly after starting his journey, he noticed a pair of headlights in his Land Rover's rear-view mirror, trailing about fifty feet behind him, never getting too close. They followed him from the A702, onto the A74, and then on to the M6. If he slowed, they slowed. If he sped up, they would keep pace.

He had a tail.

Studying the unremarkable Ford Granada in his rear-view mirror, he saw an assault rifle in the hands of the man sat in the passenger seat. Both occupants were heavy set men, with humourless expressions, whose eyes were permanently locked on the Land Rover.

Given the circumstances, it could be anyone; the Soviets, the Americans, or even elements of the UK's own security services. Although he liked to believe British agents would be considerably better at running a surveillance operation.

At least for the moment, they had done nothing aggressive, so not wanting to delay his schedule, he decided to keep his appointment. Presumably, the men behind him wanted to know where he was going and who he was meeting before they took more precipitous action. It gave him an opportunity to turn the tables on them.

If they were a threat, he could not have them lurking in the background, they had to be confronted and neutralised.

Having reached the gate of the Staffordshire base, he slowed the Land Rover down, turning it to face back the way he had come. He kept the engine running, as he watched the other vehicle slow to a halt, waiting halfway down the approach road. They turned their headlamps off, making themselves invisible in the darkness, but he knew they were there.

There was a knock on his passenger-side window.

'Brigadier Lethbridge-Stewart?' enquired the officer outside.

He glanced at her. Regimental Sergeant Major Margaret Marsh threw him a salute. He returned the gesture, leaned over and popped the door open. She was wearing a service cap, with a neat green blazer and skirt, which were thoroughly impractical for a combat situation. Compared to the women he had known, she struck him as surprisingly unfeminine, with noticeably broad shoulders, a squarish chin and short cropped hair.

'Are you carrying a small arm, Sergeant Major?'

Marsh frowned. 'No, sir.' She shrugged, one hand reaching to where a revolver holster would sit on her hip, but then using it to smooth down her skirt, highlighting the absence of any weapon.

Lethbridge-Stewart grunted. 'Then you're driving.'

He opened the driver's door, then hurried around to the passenger side, pulling his revolver from its holster. He landed himself in the passenger seat, just as she was buckling herself into the driver's side.

'Drive,' he instructed.

'Yes, sir,' she replied, instantly pushing a polished shoe down on the accelerator. She glanced around, checking mirrors and windows, searching for any sign of danger.

The Land Rover sped back up the road, passing the other vehicle, which was still sitting unmoving in the darkness.

She glanced at it as they went past.

'Is this part of the interview, sir? I'm a fully qualified driver. I spent two years working in the logistics corps, I'm quite good behind the wheel of an HGV, even if I do say so myself.'

Lethbridge-Stewart nodded. 'You may get a chance to prove your skill in a moment,' he said, watching in his sideview mirror, as a pair of headlamps flashed on behind them. 'But tell me, I understand you're also competent with explosives?'

'Yes, sir.' Marsh shrugged. 'I did a year with the Royal Engineers. I can wire charges and a detonator. And honestly, if you have enough explosives, demolishing something is easy.'

Lethbridge-Stewart nodded, still watching the lights behind them, as the other vehicle resumed its pursuit. 'And I understand you also speak some Russian?'

'Yes, sir. More than a little.' Marsh glanced up at the rear-view mirror, her eyes narrowing with suspicion. 'My mother was Russian, sir. I've honed my skill over the last four years, working in Communications and Intelligence Analysis. I wanted to make myself useful.'

'Are you fully fluent?'

'*Da, Ser!* Best you'll get this side of the iron curtain, anyways.' She glanced again at the rear-view mirror. 'Are you aware we're being followed, sir?'

'Yes.'

'Is it something I should worry about, sir?'

'Yes.'

'Good to know, sir.' Her eyes moved back to the road. Beyond the small stretch in front of them, which was illuminated by their headlamps, there was only darkness. 'There's a junction ahead, sir. If you want me to try and lose them, that's the place to do it.'

Lethbridge-Stewart shook his head. 'To the contrary, I'd rather like to know who they are.'

'I can do that too, sir. Hit the brakes. Block the road. There's nowhere for them to go, but back to the base. They'll be trapped.'

'My thoughts exactly.' Lethbridge-Stewart looked at her, searching for any sign of fear on her face, but finding none. 'Are you ready to do more for your country, Sergeant Major?'

Marsh grinned. 'To be honest, I've always felt wasted working in support roles, sir.'

Lethbridge-Stewart nodded. He disengaged the safety on his revolver.

'Then, Sergeant Major, I think it's time we caused some trouble.'

'Yes, sir.'

# CHAPTER FIVE
*The Edge of Treason*

THEY'D BEEN summoned back to the Kremlin. Questions were being asked. Answers were expected.

Zoya stood waiting in one of the reception halls of the Grand Kremlin Palace. The floor beneath her heels was made of marble. Glittering chandeliers hung from the ceiling. Everything around her was so excessively opulent, far beyond the needs of any human being, that it seemed utterly vulgar to her senses. It was a relic of the era of the Tzars, long before the revolution, preserved and repurposed for modern governmental use, to inspire awe in any citizen privileged enough to walk within its halls.

There were soldiers standing by the door. Leaving was not an option.

General Rostov stood beside her, pacing irritably, unimpressed by their summons, his face once again locked into its familiar scowl.

He only ever seemed to be happy when he was in contact with the creature, but it had been taken away by the authorities. The vessel had been relocated to the remote Siberian base, where all such finds were deposited, never to be seen again.

The fact they had taken such action was a relief for Zoya. Someone, somewhere, had listened to her warnings. The Party had moved swiftly, taking away his access to the creature, bringing Rostov to heel.

'I have no time for this,' he seethed. 'We have so much to do, we cannot keep bending to the Central Committee's whim.'

Zoya gave a shrug. 'We hardly have a choice.'

Rostov snorted, shaking his head. 'Don't we?'

The hall's gilt-covered doors suddenly opened, allowing entrance to an elderly man in a black suit, who moved with the distinctive swagger of someone high enough in the Party hierarchy that they never had anything to fear.

'Minister Gorbenko,' Rostov declared, giving the man a nod of recognition, suddenly transforming his entire countenance into one of feigned cordiality, with a thin, forced smile. 'It is good to see you again.'

The two men shook hands.

'General Rostov,' the white-haired minister growled in response. 'We are greatly concerned by how things are proceeding. None of our other experts have been able to forge a bond with our visitor. You must inform us how you were able to accomplish this task.'

Rostov shook his head. 'Unnecessary. I am happy to serve as the intermediary.'

The old man shook his head. 'We cannot be reliant on you alone, General.'

'Yet you must.'

Gorbenko's eyes bulged with irritation, his bushy white eyebrows rising in outrage at Rostov's show of defiance. 'I would remind you that your own wishes are irrelevant, you are required to do whatever is in the best interests of the state.'

'I am!' Rostov thundered, making no attempt to hide his frustration. 'I know the future we face. If we do not follow my plan, the Soviet Union will fall. The Berlin Wall will be torn down by our own citizens. The flag, which we fly so proudly, will become nothing but a relic of a fallen empire. We will lose our status, our power, our pride, everything! We will be unable to prevent the terrible events that lie ahead. We cannot allow that to occur. You must give me full control of the situation, so that I may guide not only the Soviet Union, but our entire world, to a better future.'

Zoya stared at him.

She quietly took a step to the left, sidling away, wanting to distance herself from any association with the man. He sounded mad. She could see the wide-eyed look of disbelief in the eyes of the minister.

'We will do no such thing, General,' he said, choking back outraged laughter. 'It is a ludicrous suggestion. The days of Stalin are behind us. The fate of our nation must never again lie in the hands of a single individual; to do so would be a complete betrayal of everything the Soviet Union represents. Power resides with the

Politburo for that very reason. You are a soldier. You answer to us. You will do as you are told.'

Rostov snorted with disdain. 'You will lead us to our destruction.'

Gorbenko shook his head, turning his eyes towards Zoya. 'Miss Volskaya, will you be any more compliant? Or must I have you both arrested?'

She swallowed.

It was not an idle threat.

If they believed she was not co-operating, it was well within their power to make her disappear. Forever.

She heard the gentle tread of boots behind her, as the two guards moved quietly away from the door, advancing towards them, ready to intervene if necessary.

'I wish I could offer more,' Zoya said, choosing her words carefully, knowing her future hung in the balance. 'It is my belief that the general has formed some kind of symbiotic link with the creature, meaning they are now connected, so we are unlikely to get anything from it without him.'

Gorbenko grunted. It was not the answer he wanted.

'The British have been hammering on our door. They have freely offered their own scientific expertise, proposing we send a team of five to meet them in West Berlin for an exchange of scientific information on encounters with extra-terrestrial lifeforms. Their proposed delegation includes members of the Scots Guards Special Support Group. Given that our own people are proving so difficult, perhaps we should accept their offer.'

The comment was meant to be outrageous, the prospect of asking for foreign assistance being utterly unthinkable, but instead of dismissing it, Rostov nodded encouragingly.

'The offer must be accepted. The Fifth Operational Corps, as they are more correctly known, are by equal measures both a threat and an asset, which must be brought into the fold, contained and controlled. Brigadier Lethbridge-Stewart is an asset that must be secured.'

His statement was met by a confused stare from Minister Gorbenko.

'Even if we were inclined to listen to your proposals, which we are not, it would already be too late for Lethbridge-Stewart. SVR Agents have been dispatched. Given his initial contact with our visitor, it was deemed prudent to eliminate him.'

Rostov's expression darkened. 'This charade has gone on long enough. You jeopardise everything. If Lethbridge-Stewart dies, we will all pay the price for it in the years to come. I cannot allow you, or your ilk, to remain in control any longer. It seems I must make it clear to you, the balance of power has changed, your days are done. I am here to reshape the future. The Chairman must be persuaded to resign, or be removed by force. I am the only one that can save us.'

Gorbenko laughed, shaking his head in dismay. 'You have clearly taken leave of your senses, General. You have condemned yourself with your foolish words.' The old man glanced at the two soldiers, waving a dismissive hand at General Rostov. 'This man is to be placed under arrest.'

The two men did not move. They both glanced at Rostov.

Zoya remained still, not uttering a word

'By a twist of fate,' Rostov stated, 'I have served with both of these men before. They, like many others, are loyal to me.'

Gorbenko glanced at the two soldiers. Their faces were set, nervous but determined, their hands resting on holstered revolvers. It was a clear statement of intent, but it left open the possibility of them stepping back from the brink, in a way they never could have done if their weapons had been drawn.

Gorbenko scowled at them. 'Consider your actions very carefully, any attempt at a military coup will be considered as treason. None of you will survive it.'

'Neither would you, Minister.' Rostov shrugged. 'So do not let it come to that. Follow my guidance. Call off your assassins. Let me meet with the British. Give me access to the base in Siberia. Allow me to communicate with our visitor again. Do not interfere with my plans any further. Let me prove I am right. If within a month I have not transformed this world for the better, I will resign my commission, and you may charge me with whatever you deem appropriate.'

Gorbenko hesitated. Zoya watched him.

The suggestion sounded reasonable. It would defuse the immediate situation. In the moment, he had little choice.

'I could perhaps accept most of these terms. However, both myself and Miss Volskaya must be part of any delegation that meets with the British, as both science and politics must have a part to play in any such meeting. The British have specifically emphasised that this is a scientific, rather than military, conference.'

Rostov frowned. 'Fine.' He shrugged.

Gorbenko nodded. 'And, regrettably, it is too late to recall the SVR agents.'

Rostov sighed. 'No matter.' He shook his head sadly. 'I doubt they will succeed. In almost all the futures I have seen, Lethbridge-Stewart lives to see retirement.'

Gorbenko stared at him. 'You genuinely know the future?' It seemed to Zoya, that now Gorbenko was finally entertaining the general's outlandish claims, he was desperate to reassure himself that he had not made a deal with a madman.

Rostov smiled. 'I know what the future was, but I am changing it.' He shrugged again, then turned to look at Zoya, tilting his head in an almost apologetic gesture. 'The minister and I have much to discuss, Miss Volskaya. Some changes to the hierarchy will be necessary. In the meantime, you are dismissed. I shall send a car for you tomorrow, as there is much you must know before the meeting in Berlin; assuming, of course, that Lethbridge-Stewart survives his assassins.'

Zoya nodded, mutely.

She did not dare speak, knowing any misplaced word may have fatal consequences. Her attempt to stop Rostov had failed, but at least he did not suspect her involvement.

The Land Rover's tyres screamed.

Mags Marsh turned the wheel, while yanking on the handbrake, setting the whole vehicle into a dangerous turn. Lethbridge-Stewart placed one hand on the dashboard, bracing himself through the manoeuvre. Mags could feel the sweat on her palms, forcing her to grip the steering wheel tighter, for fear of it slipping through her fingers.

The car behind them barrelled forwards, the driver suddenly finding he had nowhere to go, with the Land Rover coming to an abrupt halt, blocking both sides of the road.

Glancing past Lethbridge-Stewart and through the passenger side window, Mags could see nothing but the oncoming headlamps rushing out of the darkness towards them. She had expected the other driver to brake, but instead they were accelerating, intent on ramming into their flank. She winced, expecting a collision.

Beside her, clearly having realised that the car was not going to stop, Lethbridge-Stewart hurriedly rolled down his window. He aimed his revolver, took a shot. The tyre on the Ford Granada's passenger side exploded, causing the vehicle to suddenly veer off to one side.

They both watched as the car flew off the road, careering through the beams of the Land Rover's headlamps, to come crashing down in a ditch. It slammed to a halt, its front-end crumpling on impact, the windscreen exploding inwards.

In the light of the headlamps, Mags could see two figures slumped forward in the front seats, neither moving.

'Oh, bloomin' heck,' she muttered, staring at the wreck. 'We're sure they're bad guys, right, sir?'

Lethbridge-Stewart did not answer her question. 'Stay here, Sergeant Major.'

He released his seat belt, opened his door and hurried outside.

Mags watched him as he surveyed the accident, leaned into the car, picked up a couple of objects, then hurried back towards her. He tapped on her window, which she hurriedly wound down.

'Definitely not tourists,' he stated, passing a rifle and ammunition pouch through the open window. 'AK-47, a standard issue assault rifle for the Soviet Union's armed forces, with a GP-25 grenade launcher, commonly only given to specialist units. One shot from that and we would have been toast.'

Mags placed the items carefully into the back of the vehicle, feeling an overwhelming sense of relief that the occupants of the other car were not just random civilians.

'Are they alive?' she asked.

'They need urgent medical attention. Get on the radio, contact Beacon Barracks, get them to send assistance.'

'Yes, sir. Given the circumstances, I'm kind of surprised you want to help them.'

Lethbridge-Stewart frowned. 'They're soldiers, Sergeant Major. Doing their duty, as ordered, on behalf of their country. Whatever you think of the people that sent them, or the methods they employ, don't forget that. Should the roles be reversed, I like to think they would extend the same courtesy to us, in accordance with the articles of the Geneva Convention. That is, after all, what they're for.'

She gave him a sceptical glance, then made the requested call, while he grabbed a First Aid Kit and hurried away to provide help to the men who had intended to kill him.

Once assistance was on the way, she turned the Land Rover's engine off, but left the headlamps on, then hurried over to join him.

She peered into the half-lit car. She could smell the blood.

Lethbridge-Stewart was doing his best to patch up the man in the passenger seat. The driver was in a far worse state.

His legs had been crushed when the front of the car crumpled, the steering column forced up into his rib cage, his head dangling across it at an unnatural angle. He was not going to live.

His eyes flickered open. Only semi-conscious, he began burbling incoherently in Russian, blood-filled spittle spilling across his lips with every word. She only understood one sentence.

'*Skazhi moyey zhene, prosti menya.*'

She crouched down beside him, holding the man's hand, watching as the light faded from his eyes.

'What did he say?' Lethbridge-Stewart asked, not looking up, as he continued to try and stem the flow of blood from the other man's wounds.

'Tell my wife, I'm sorry,' Mags said.

Lethbridge-Stewart nodded.

Within a few minutes a military ambulance had pulled up alongside the crashed car, producing a team of medics who swarmed around the remaining wounded man, unsubtly ushering them out of their way.

Lethbridge-Stewart exchanged a few words with the lead officer, then turned and strode back towards the Land Rover, climbing into the driver's seat. Following his lead, Mags took the passenger side.

While the interior light was on, she could see there was a smear of blood on his left cheek, trailing down to the top of his upper lip. He pulled his door closed and re-started the engine.

'Will he live?' Mags asked.

'There's a good chance.'

'I'm glad.'

Lethbridge-Stewart glanced at her. 'I'd like to officially offer you a position in the Home-Army Fifth Operational Corps,' he informed her, as he put the Land Rover into gear and began driving them away from the crash.

'I'm not familiar with the name, sir.'

'More commonly known as the Scots Guards Special Support Group.'

Mags had heard stories about that unit, but she never really believed.

'Don't worry, Sergeant Major, all will become clear once you're read in on the Official Secrets Act.'

Mags swallowed. 'Yes, sir. Well, if that was the interview, I can't imagine what the job involves.'

A smile lifted one side of Lethbridge-Stewart's lips, just below the splatter of blood. 'Things beyond the imagination,' he said, driving off down the dark lane. 'You'll be brought up to speed on the way to Berlin.'

'Berlin?'

'Yes, we're hoping to meet with some representatives from the Soviet Union. Tensions have been escalating over a classified incident.'

She stared at him incredulously. 'You're going to a meeting with the people who just tried to assassinate you?'

'Yes.' Lethbridge-Stewart nodded, his eyes on the road ahead. 'It might be a bit awkward, but when the bullets start to fly, the greater the need for words. Now, more than ever, is the time to sit down and talk, while we still can.'

Anne sat in the passenger seat of the Cortina, gently rocking Samantha in her arms, while Bill sat silently beside them. He was back in his Fifth uniform.

The atmosphere was palpable and awkward. There were no words that could be spoken which would make the situation any better, so they sat and waited in silence for Bill's sister to arrive. She and her husband, Jarryd, were coming to collect Samantha. It would be good for Samantha to spend some time with the Brooks, for her cousins to get to bond with her, but still… Through the rain splattered windscreen, Anne could see the vast grey metal bulk of the waiting Hercules transport plane on the nearby runway, which would soon be carrying her and Bill away.

Samantha gurgled, wide-eyed and innocent, unaware of what was happening.

The rain drummed relentlessly on the roof.

'What happens if we don't come back?' Anne asked, desperate

to break the quiet.

'We always come back,' Bill replied. 'It's just a meeting, and by our normal standards it's a walk in the park. We'll be on our way home in no time. Maybe a week or two, if we can actually convince them to give us access to the creature.'

Anne snorted. 'If things go to plan.' She shook her head. 'You know things never go to plan. So, tell me, if we don't come back, what happens to Samantha?'

Bill sighed, clearly reluctant to indulge her in such a bleak conversation. 'Sam and Jarryd will manage.'

'For sixteen years?'

Bill nodded. 'They have experience, Anne. Michelle will help, maybe even Dan, too. Even Alun is on hand if needs be.'

Anne knew her brother and Bill's siblings would, of course, help, but that didn't make this any better. Anne sniffed, then looked out through the window, doing her best to conceal the tears that were brimming in her eyes. 'They shouldn't have to manage. Samantha should be with... She isn't old enough to even remember us.'

Bill put a hand on her knee. 'We *are* coming back,' he stated, making it sound like a fact, rather than an opinion. 'I won't let anything prevent that.'

Anne smiled at him, but she didn't give voice to her response. *Neither will I.* Her priorities had changed...

On the other side of the airfield, she could see Lethbridge-Stewart's Land Rover driving up the entrance road. The little green vehicle cut swiftly across the tarmac, slicing through the puddles, circling to approach the Hercules from behind. It bumped up the cargo ramp, disappearing into the interior of the gigantic plane, to join a number of other passengers that they had seen arriving in the last few minutes. She and Bill would be the last to board.

A moment later another car slipped quietly onto the airfield. It was Jarryd's white Morris Minor. It drew up alongside them, while Bill got out of the car, moving to greet his sister and brother-in-law. Anne watched as hugs and kisses were exchanged.

She didn't join them. It felt wrong.

'I'm sorry,' she whispered, staring down into Samantha's wide hazel eyes. 'If I had a choice, I wouldn't do this.'

There was a knock on the window beside her. The door was

opened from outside.

She found herself looking up at her in-laws, huddling together under an umbrella, as they both looked down at her with sad, sympathetic eyes.

'We'll take good care of her,' Sam said in a warm voice, trying to sound reassuring. 'She'll be in safe hands.'

Anne nodded. 'I know.'

Sam held out her hands.

Anne rose to her feet, climbing out of the car and joining them under the canopy of the umbrella, to gently place Samantha into her aunt's out-stretched arms. Bill fetched a bag from the back seat, containing nappies and other daily necessities, which he handed to Jarryd.

Goodbyes were exchanged, and Anne's in-laws returned to their car. With her daughter. Anne watched as they climbed into the little Morris Minor, departing with a brief flurry of waved hands and weak smiles, before driving away into the rain. Anne suddenly became aware they had taken the umbrella with them and that she was rapidly getting soaked.

Bill locked up the car, then returned to her side, opening another umbrella above her. 'Ready?'

She shook herself, trying to clear her head. 'Yes,' she replied. 'Let's go and end the Cold War, shall we?'

She turned on her heel and strode towards the waiting plane.

Bill hurried along beside her, trying his best to keep the umbrella over her head. Their shoes clattered noisily on the metal loading ramp, as they made their way up into the Hercules, to find Lethbridge-Stewart waiting for them.

His face was impassive, his chin angled to give him an air of aloof indifference. He held his swagger stick at a perfect ninety-degree angle, tucked neatly under one arm. It was a look Anne knew well, it was the cold mask of authority he used whenever he did not dare show his emotions for fear of undermining himself as their leader.

'Good to have you aboard, Dr Bishop,' he stated.

She shook her head. 'I'll never forgive you for this, Alistair.'

# CHAPTER SIX
*Meeting the Enemy*

THE HERCULES touched down at Gatow airfield, in the British Sector of West Berlin.

They stayed overnight in the officer's barracks at the RAF airbase but, after only a few hours of sleep, they relocated to a hotel in the centre of the city. Having installed themselves in a set of rooms on the third floor, Bishop swiftly changed into his regimental dress uniform, then set out to meet with their guests at the border.

RSM Marsh drove, perfectly at ease behind the steering wheel of Lethbridge-Stewart's Land Rover, as she navigated her way through the busy and affluent streets of West Berlin. The buildings and parks were well tended, a showcase for a Western lifestyle, which far outstripped the reality of the Edinburgh suburb where he and Anne had recently bought their first home together.

While she drove, Marsh was grilling him for information, seemingly keen to verify the claims Lethbridge-Stewart had made about the Fifth Operational Corps' previous missions, which he imagined would sound outrageously implausible to any outsider.

He felt uncomfortable talking about their past assignments. As part of a covert unit, he had become accustomed to keeping secrets, not dishing out the truth.

A sign flashed past his window, telling them they were crossing the boundary of the British sector, moving into the area of the city controlled by the Americans.

Marsh was shaking her head in disbelief.

'We're privy to the most profound discovery in human history, Major, that we are not alone in the universe, but we're not allowed to tell anybody. Presumably, because someone thinks the public couldn't handle it, or because they think we can gain some kind of advantage out of it over our international rivals?'

Bishop nodded. 'That's about the size of it, Warrant Officer. You are okay with that?'

Marsh shook her head. 'Honestly, Major? No, I'm not. It seems like an awfully big responsibility to be left to just a handful of men. That's the reason this has got you all so rattled. You've lost control of the situation. If the Russians go public, the cat's out of the bag, suddenly everything changes.'

Bishop shook his head. 'I doubt they'll do that. They'll want to keep control of this as much as we do. And the Soviet government is good at keeping secrets.'

Marsh grunted. 'Well, at least you've got that in common with them then, but in my books, that's not something to be proud of. Supressing the truth is suppressing the people, who if I'm not mistaken, we all signed up to protect. Sir.' She slowed the Land Rover, hitting the indicator, eyeing up a parking space. 'We're here.'

Bishop glanced out through window, glad of the distraction, trying to ignore the fact that the opinions the RSM had voiced made it clear that she was a security liability. She had been employed in a hurry, not properly vetted.

'Such views won't sit well in the Fifth,' he said, unable to stay silent. 'You'd do well to remember that, Warrant Officer. And perhaps train yourself to stop thinking of the Fifth as *you*, and instead thinking of it as *we*. You're part of it now, you've signed the Official Secrets Act, so you are now sworn to secrecy.'

'I can believe one thing, but do another,' she said, manoeuvring the Land Rover into the narrow space. 'We can work together, for the benefit of all, without having to share the same views. That's the point of this meeting, sir. That understanding is what separates us from the Soviets. They try to stamp out any voice of dissent. We allow free speech. So, let's try to remember it's okay for us to disagree, because if we don't, we'll already have lost what we're trying to protect, and we really will end up with a Thought-Police.'

Bishop grinned. '*1984*,' he said, recognising the reference. 'George Orwell.'

'Bloomin' heck! A soldier that reads. The Fifth really is full of surprises.'

'Yes, it is. And outspoken NCOs, it seems. A word of advice, though, Warrant Officer, the Brig is happy to hear the views of his troops, but be careful to remember where the line is. Chain of command is important, especially in the Fifth.'

Marsh nodded sharply, turning the engine off. 'Understood, sir.'

Directly in front of them stood the Berlin Wall.

For such a famous structure, as the physical manifestation of the dreaded Iron Curtain, it seemed surprisingly utilitarian. It was composed of simple concrete breezeblocks, rising to just above head-height, topped by threads of barbed wire, which were so old they had created long orange stains of rust on the wall beneath them.

'This is Checkpoint Charlie,' Bishop told Marsh, as he climbed out of the Land Rover, gesturing towards a small security hut and a narrow gap in the wall. On top of the little cabin was a large sign, declaring it to be the *Allied Checkpoint*, which bore pictures of the American, British and French flags. 'All visiting diplomats have to use this entrance, so the House Guests will have to pass through here.'

Marsh nodded. 'So, what do we do, sir, just wait at the security hut for them?'

Bishop smiled. 'No, Warrant Officer,' he said, pointing in the opposite direction. 'The Café Adler. The *Eagle* Café. From the upstairs windows you can see right across the top of this wall, into no man's land, and over the top of the other wall on their side. Meaning, we'll be able to see them coming. And, I don't know about you, but I could really use a brew.'

Marsh gave a nod. 'That sounds like a smashin' plan, sir.'

Anne opened the door to the conference room, surveying the space they had requisitioned for the meeting, marvelling at how ordinary it seemed.

There was a large wooden table, with five leather-backed chairs on either side, each with a notepad in front of it, embossed with the hotel's logo. It was the kind of setting she expected for a business conference, rather than a meeting where the greatest classified military secrets of the age would be exchanged. She had been expecting James Bond glamour, not practical reality.

Lethbridge-Stewart stood beside a radio transceiver base station, wearing a freshly pressed dress uniform, waiting for a message from Bill. The hotel was only a short drive away from the checkpoint so, once that signal came in, they knew they would not have long to wait.

'We've received some additional intelligence from the Americans,' Lethbridge-Stewart stated. 'There have been ructions within the Soviet Government. A cleansing of party ranks, with much of the old guard swept away. We're not entirely sure who is in charge over there anymore.'

Anne shrugged. 'Does it make a difference?'

Lethbridge-Stewart stared at her. 'I guess not.'

There was a disturbed quality to his voice, indicating that despite his statement, he very much felt to the contrary. Lethbridge-Stewart was a terrible liar. Anne regarded that as his greatest strength; he could normally be relied upon to voice the hard truth, but now even he was stooping to half-truths.

Arty, having mooched into the room behind her, slumped himself down into one of the chairs. Anne had been delighted by their reunion on the Hercules; they had been good friends at Cambridge, and being able to spend some time reminiscing with him had at least distracted her from the anger she felt at being separated from Samantha.

'I think it makes a big difference,' Arty declared, swinging his feet up onto the table. 'If we need to convince them to give us access, the conversation isn't just about what we can give them, it's also about what they need. So, we have to figure out who we're dealing with, so we can determine what they want. Right now, we're flying blind.'

Anne shook her head. 'Can we not just take this meeting at face value, as a free and honest exchange of scientific knowledge, mutually beneficial to all? An olive-branch. An offer of friendship.'

Lethbridge-Stewart stared at her. 'No, we cannot. Professor Grey is correct. We know why we proposed this meeting, but we don't know why they accepted it. I'm sure our offer intrigued them, but do not doubt they will have an additional angle; they will already have a vision for what they want to achieve from this meeting. For all we know, they may be coming here to lay out their new capabilities, to give us an ultimatum, to lay the groundwork for the surrender of our country.'

Anne blinked. His tone shocked her. She could hear the fear in his voice. She'd never known him to be afraid before. He had always been fine with the other-worldly threats they had faced, taking them all in his stride, but dealing with such a real-world threat had clearly shaken him. This time he truly understood how indomitable and powerful the enemy were.

She threw her hands up. 'Can we at least hope for the best?'

'And plan for the worst?' Lethbridge-Stewart nodded. 'Yes, Anne, that is exactly what I am doing.'

The transceiver speaker crackled. Bill's voice cut through the static.

'Mayhem Three to Mayhem Leader, are you receiving? Over.'

Lethbridge-Stewart immediately grabbed the base station's microphone. 'Mayhem Leader to Mayhem Three, I can hear you loud and clear. Is there news? Over.'

The speaker crackled again. 'The House Guests have arrived. We'll be on our way shortly. Over.'

'Thank you, Mayhem Three, we're ready to receive them. Over and out.' Lethbridge-Stewart put the microphone down

He glanced around the room. 'Any last questions?' he asked.

Arty nodded, swinging his legs off the table. 'Are there any guidelines on what we can tell them about the Fifth's previous encounters? And what we can't?'

Lethbridge-Stewart gave a non-committal shrug. 'As little as possible, but as much as you need to.'

Anne sighed. 'Well, that's as clear as mud.'

'Then I shall be clearer. We cannot leave this meeting without an agreement. We must convince them to give us access to the creature and its ship. I can assure you the only other alternatives are too terrible to contemplate.' His tone was no longer fearful, but harsh and dark, in deadly earnest. 'Be in no doubt, the freedom of our country is at stake here. This may be the day the Cold War ends, with us on the losing side.'

The Soviet delegation had arrived.

Bishop watched the cavalcade of vehicles pass through Checkpoint Charlie. There were four sleek black cars, of a design he had never seen before, with tinted windows that obscured the occupants from view.

Abandoning their perch on the upper floor of the café, Bishop and Marsh hurried downstairs and out into the street, where Marsh began a conversation with the lead driver.

Not being able to speak Russian, Bishop didn't understand a word of it.

'Warrant Officer,' he said, halting the conversation. 'Have you asked why so many? We agreed to five-a-side.'

'One moment, sir.' Marsh spoke to the lead driver. She nodded. 'Drivers, security staff, interpreters, sir. What shall we do?'

Bishop didn't like this at all. 'We don't have much choice, do we? Very well, as you were, Warrant Officer.'

Marsh finished her conversation and she and Bishop returned to their Land Rover.

'Based on what I've been told, sir,' Marsh said as she started the vehicle, 'we're lucky they turned up at all.'

'I don't feel that lucky.'

As they approached the hotel, the last two Russian cars veered away, disappearing into a side road.

'Some of our friends are taking a detour,' Bishop observed.

Marsh's eyes flicked to the rear-view mirror. 'Where are they going? They're not supposed to just drive off like that.'

'I don't think they care much about our rules.'

Marsh nodded, as she brought the Land Rover to a stop outside the hotel. The remaining two cars pulled in behind them.

'Let's go and say hello,' Bishop said, and climbed out of the Land Rover, putting a hand on his holstered revolver, drawing some reassurance from its presence. It didn't matter that they were meeting for diplomatic talks, he could not help but view them as the enemy; he had been trained to regard them as such, and everything that was happening was only hardening that view.

As they approached the first car, the rear doors opened, with two men swiftly stepping out. Much to his surprise, Bishop recognised one of them.

'Captain Bugayev!'

He threw the man a salute, even though there was no need

to do so.

The Russian glanced at him, then tapped a hand against his epaulette. '*Major* Bugayev,' the man corrected him, returning his salute. 'Do I know you, Major?'

Bishop shook his head. 'We didn't meet, but I was there during the Aegean Incident, when you assisted Lethbridge-Stewart.'

Bugayev frowned, with an expression of disapproval. 'You mean, I think, when he assisted me.' He spoke perfect English, with barely a hint of an accent. 'Most of the soldiers deployed in those battles, putting their lives at risk, were Russian, not British.'

Bishop shifted uncomfortably, feeling he had already unwittingly caused offence, with the one man who might have been a natural ally in difficult negotiations.

The Russian grinned, then laughed. 'Do not fret, Major. We all write our own histories, do we not?' He clamped a hand down on Bishop's shoulder. 'We are all the hero of our own story. It is natural for you to magnify your nations own achievements, to take pride in them, by diminishing the contribution of others. I think your countrymen often forget the eight million Russians who died fighting in World War Two. You do your best to ignore all our achievements. You focus on the Americans putting an astronaut on the moon, rather than us putting the first cosmonaut into space. Only the weak rely on such bluster and self-deceit. The strong have no need of such self-aggrandisement. I am sure, if you asked Lethbridge-Stewart, he would not diminish our involvement in the Aegean in the way you have just done.'

Bishop flustered. 'Sorry, sir.'

Bugayev shrugged, dismissing the matter as if it were nothing. 'The past is the past, we are here to discuss the future,' he said, gesturing towards the man approaching from behind him, who had made his way around from the other side of the car. 'Please, allow me to introduce General Rostov.'

Bishop saluted. 'Welcome to West Berlin, General.'

The little man nodded his head in greeting. 'Thank you, Major,' he said, his English even more perfect than that of Bugayev. 'I feel honoured to have the chance to meet Lethbridge-Stewart's team.' He gave Marsh a curious look. 'You're new, I assume?'

Bishop saw a tiny frown appear on Marsh's face. Rostov was oddly well informed, or extremely shrewd.

'Yes, General, she is. May I ask what happened to the other two cars that crossed the border?'

Rostov grunted. 'My security team. They will establish a perimeter.'

Bugayev gave a nod. 'In case of misunderstandings.'

'Completely unnecessary, I assure you,' Bishop said.

Rostov shook his head. 'I feel safer knowing they are there. It puts me at ease. Given we all desire a productive meeting, you can hardly deem such reassurance as unnecessary, can you?'

'No, sir.'

General Rostov glanced over his shoulder, to look at the second car, from which three other figures were emerging. One of them was a dark-haired woman, in a long red coat, carrying a large maroon shoulder-bag. It was the woman from the film, whom his superiors had hoped would attend, in the belief that she may be more malleable than some of her military companions. It seemed as if, so far, their plan was working.

Rostov waited for the woman and her two companions to reach him. 'My team are ready,' he announced, gesturing towards the large glass doors of the hotel lobby. 'Please, show us the way.'

Lethbridge-Stewart waited patiently, sitting at the conference table.

The moment the door opened, he immediately rose to his feet, ready to meet the new arrivals. His own colleagues stood up alongside him, following his lead. They all watched as Major Bishop held the conference room door open, allowing their guests to file into the room, taking their places on the opposite side of the table.

He noted the presence of Major Bugayev and the woman in the red coat, but kept his eyes fixed on General Rostov, very aware of the etiquette and protocols for such situations.

Lethbridge-Stewart leaned forward, offering Rostov a handshake across the table. The general smiled. He shook the outstretched hand, clasping it warmly with both of his own. Lethbridge-Stewart felt his right eyebrow twitch, an involuntary gesture of surprise, bewildered by the man's overt friendliness.

'Nice to see you again,' Lethbridge-Stewart ventured, keen to establish a connection. 'I see you have been promoted, several times, since our previous meeting.'

Rostov's face immediately soured. 'No,' he stated, suddenly retracting his hands. 'You are mistaken. I've held the rank of general for several years. If this is any indication of British Intelligence, perhaps we are wasting our time here.'

Lethbridge-Stewart frowned. 'I must say, your English is excellent,' he said, ignoring the misunderstanding, hoping a compliment would smooth over any confusion, but unable to stop himself from adding an additional probing comment. 'After our previous meeting, I was under the impression you didn't speak a word of it.'

A sly smile crossed Rostov's face. He raised his hands in a gesture of surrender. 'There you are correct,' he said, as they all took their seats. 'It is a gift from our alien benefactor, a skill taken from your own mind when you first attempted to make contact with it.'

Lethbridge-Stewart shifted awkwardly in his chair. He knew the creature had been rooting around in his head, but to be told that some of that information had been shared with the enemy sat in front of him, left him feeling distinctly uncomfortable.

'It took that knowledge without my consent,' Lethbridge-Stewart declared, risking a quick glance around the table, briefly making eye contact with the other members of the Soviet team. 'I'm sure we can all see the danger in that.'

Rostov laughed. 'Hardly classified material. Do not fear the creature, just because its methods are alien to you, when the purpose and results are merely to facilitate easier communication. See it as a boon, which will enable us to conduct this meeting in a common language.'

'You're happy to conduct proceedings in English?'

Rostov nodded, with a friendly smile. 'I imagine my English is significantly superior to your Russian.'

'So it would seem.'

'Allow me to introduce my team.' Rostov gestured to the uniformed officer sat to his right-hand side. 'I believe you already know Major Bugayev.'

Lethbridge-Stewart gave the man a nod of recognition.

'Indeed, a fine officer, who I have been honoured to work alongside.'

Bugayev returned the nod.

General Rostov turned to the dark-haired woman sitting on his left-hand-side, who had shed her red coat and hung it on the back of her chair, with her maroon bag slung over the top of it.

'This is Miss Zoya Volskaya, one of our scientific advisors.'

The woman gave a small, nervous wave.

The general moved his hand on, gesturing to the elderly man sat beside her. 'This is Minister Gorbenko, a representative of the Central Committee. Neither he, nor Miss Volskaya, speak English, so the last member of our team, Warrant Officer Petrov, will be interpreting on their behalf.'

Lethbridge-Stewart glanced at each of the strangers in turn, meeting their eyes, giving all of them a moment of his time. 'Allow me to introduce the Scots Guards Special Support Group.'

Rostov gave a shrug. 'We are familiar with you, Lethbridge-Stewart, and with Miss Travers.'

Anne gave him a thin smile.

'Mrs Bishop now, actually,' she corrected him, showing him the diamond ring on her hand.

Rostov hesitated, looking momentarily perplexed, then nodded his head. 'Congratulations. We know you have considerable experience, *Mrs Bishop*, but what of these others?' He gave a gesture towards Professor Grey and Marsh. 'We have no interest in meeting new recruits.'

Lethbridge-Stewart nodded. 'Sergeant Major Marsh is here merely as an interpreter, as we assumed it would be necessary, but given your new-found familiarity with English, she may indeed be surplus to requirement.'

He glanced at her. She did not even blink.

Professor Grey leaned forward. 'Whereas I am currently the Group's senior scientific advisor. Arthur Grey. Arty to my friends. And I can assure you, I'm the most qualified man in the room, sir.'

He briefly glanced at Anne, who let the sexist comment pass. They all knew what he was doing. He was testing Rostov's prejudices, trying to get the measure of him, seeing how he responded.

General Rostov tilted his head, considering the dark-skinned man sitting in front of him, still wearing his sheepskin coat. 'This is also a surprise.'

'And why's that?' Grey asked, peering at the general.

Rostov flashed a smile. 'Do not think me a racist, Arty. I am working with a creature from another world, completely unlike anything we have ever known, I welcome the contributions of all. I may once have held other views, but my mind has been opened to a more enlightened perspective.'

Grey leaned back, clearly thrown by the response. 'Then why are you surprised?'

'We have no intelligence file on you.'

'Good. I am part of a covert military unit, after all.'

The general nodded, accepting this answer. He seemed both pleasant and reasonable.

And Lethbridge-Stewart didn't trust it at all.

In his experience, a smooth charm was usually just a veneer, used to disguise an unscrupulous personality. Just because he knew the right words to say, it didn't mean any of them were genuine.

Rostov leaned forward, studying him curiously, evidently trying to determine what he was thinking. Lethbridge-Stewart remained stone-faced, giving nothing away.

'And where is the final member of your team?' Rostov asked.

Lethbridge-Stewart glanced at the empty chair at the end of the table. Bishop was missing.

When the Soviet delegation had entered the room, he had seen Bishop lingering outside in the corridor, meaning he had deliberately chosen not to follow them inside. They had worked together long enough that Lethbridge-Stewart knew there must be a very good reason for his absence, something which caused him to try to surreptitiously slip away.

'He's running an errand for me. He will join us shortly.' It was perhaps an unnecessary lie, but he did not want to look weak or disorganised in front of his opponent. 'We can proceed without him.'

Rostov nodded, seeming to accept the words at face value. 'Then let us begin.'

# CHAPTER SEVEN
*Negotiation: Impossible*

ANNE LOOKED at the faces on the opposite side of the table. They were the enemy, or so she had been told. She felt disappointed with herself. In her head, the word Soviet had long been synonymous with monster, yet the people in front of her were nothing but human. The faceless enemy were suddenly just a set of people, displaying recognisable human emotions.

Minister Gorbenko was cynical and wary. Warrant Officer Petrov looked nervous. Miss Volskaya seemed restless. Major Bugayev was detached and calm, patiently listening to everything. General Rostov appeared intensely curious. Eager, like a dog waiting to be fed.

Lethbridge-Stewart attempted to begin the discussion. 'Perhaps you should start by telling us about your new visitor?'

His request was met by silence.

Arty hurriedly intervened. 'Or perhaps we could start by telling you what we already know?'

Trust was in short supply, so if the other side were not prepared to make the first move, they would need to do so instead. Anne approved.

Rostov gave a nod.

Lethbridge-Stewart's eyes narrowed, begrudging the fact that he was being compelled to reveal his information first.

'We are aware that, ten days ago, the Soviet Union established contact with an extra-terrestrial lifeform. Using a reconnaissance satellite, we were able to track its vessel as it descended from orbit and entered Soviet airspace. We know the ship landed in Red Square.' His statements were bold and confident. He didn't mention that the satellite was American or make any reference to the leaked film. So, while every word was true, the spaces between them were crammed with lies of omission. 'As a starting point, we respectfully request that you admit this lifeform exists, and disclose its nature and intentions.'

Rostov gave another swift nod. 'The Soviet Union hereby confirms the existence of the extra-terrestrial visitor.'

He glanced sideways at Miss Volskaya, who then answered the second part of the question, her words being interpreted by Petrov. 'It is a Delta class lifeform, with a level nine technological capacity,' she stated, as she removed a selection of handouts from her bag, sliding them across the table. 'This document will show you what those classifications mean. We call it the Kerensky Scale. This is how we categorise any lifeform we encounter, so our scientific teams can quickly and easily understand the nature of any new species. I assume you have a similar system, but we find this has worked well for us, and we would like to use it as the basis for future discussions.'

Anne flicked through the pages.

To have such a method of categorisation was such a simple idea, necessary when working with several independent scientific groups, yet they had never done it. Which implied that, while the Soviets may have set up their operation much later than the British, it now had far vaster resources. It also implied there had been previous encounters.

She glanced at Arty, who was staring at his own copy, obviously impressed.

'Yes,' he stated, 'we find this acceptable.'

'Delta class,' Anne announced, reading the listing aloud. 'A lone entity or intelligence, with a physical form. Level nine technology; access to faster-than-light travel, capable of traversing intergalactic distances.'

Her mind boggled. The alien was on its own, it had access to technology beyond their imagination, and it had allied itself with the Soviet Union.

Lethbridge-Stewart nodded thoughtfully. 'That just leaves the last part of my question,' he said, leaning forward. 'What does it want? What is its purpose here?'

'It is here to help us,' Rostov replied.

Lethbridge-Stewart shook his head. 'That is not an answer, General. Why would it do that? What does it get out of the deal?'

'Nothing. It doesn't want anything.'

Lethbridge-Stewart rolled his eyes. 'General, that is naïve. I am sure you must know the old adage; if something seems too good to be true, it probably is.'

Anne nodded. Everything about the discussion made her feel nervous, her fears only compounded by the mysterious absence of her husband. She glanced at the empty seat beside her.

Bishop had taken the lift back down to the lobby.

Something felt wrong.

His instincts were screaming at him, telling him they were in danger, even though none was apparent. Perhaps it was just nerves, perhaps it was something more, either way he had opted to scout their surroundings, double-checking for trouble.

As the lift doors pinged open, he knew his instincts had been correct.

There were four men, wearing identical trench coats, loitering in the lobby. They all had sturdy builds and buzzcuts. From their position, they had an eye-line on both the lift and the stairwell. There was a large military kit bag lying on the floor among their identical boots. They all glanced at him, then looked away, pretending not to have seen him, but all keeping him in their peripheral vision.

They were military men, unskilled in espionage, trying and failing to look inconspicuous.

He walked past them. They didn't stop him.

He made his way back to the Land Rover, restarting the engine. He drove around to the back of the building, noting the presence of a Russian-built car parked at the rear of the hotel, with two more soldiers lurking beside it, both openly holding assault rifles. From their position, they had an eye-line on the building's rear doors and fire escapes.

He drove past them, momentarily drawing their stares. He pressed down on the accelerator, hurriedly disappearing into a side road, before they could decide how to respond.

He parked up in an alleyway, where the vehicle would remain hidden, unless anyone conducted a methodical search for it. He considered what he had seen.

The general had openly admitted his men were forming a security perimeter, so their presence was no surprise to Bishop, but their positioning worried him. They were not watching the approach roads. They were watching the exits.

They weren't there to stop people going in, they were there to prevent them leaving. The teeth of a trap, waiting to be sprung.

Mags sat quietly at the end of the table, seemingly forgotten by everyone else, listening to her colleagues describe some of their previous otherworldly encounters. A few days ago, it would have all sounded like implausible nonsense, more suited to an episode of *The Twilight Zone* than to a high-level scientific and military conference in West Berlin, yet it was all conducted with serious faces and earnest voices.

Petrov was doing a reasonable job of interpreting, but sometimes got stuck on the more complex discussions; Mags had almost laughed out loud at his mangled attempt at retelling Lethbridge-Stewart's account of the earthquakes in England caused by a disembodied entity living in the void between worlds.

She didn't correct his mistakes. She said nothing. She was doing her best to become invisible.

Lethbridge-Stewart's statement that she was 'surplus to requirement' had sealed the deal. It had been a deliberate pre-agreed ploy, not an idle slight, designed to make her seem irrelevant to the proceedings.

Three hours into the discussion, Zoya Volskaya excused herself from the table, taking her bag and leaving the room, intent on using the conveniences. Rostov and Lethbridge-Stewart continued their conversation, barely acknowledging her departure.

Rostov seemed particularly interested in the latest tale.

'This man, your father, was involved in a war on another world? He had access to their weapons and aircraft? Did the British Government not gain access to any of this technology?'

Lethbridge-Stewart leaned back in his chair. 'Briefly, yes. That is the point, General. We have experience with such alien artifacts. If we could examine the ship you have acquired, we may be able to give you advice on it, use our combined knowledge to reverse engineer the technology.'

Rostov shook his head. 'That is not necessary. Our guest is freely sharing their technology with us.'

Mags could see Lethbridge-Stewart's mounting frustration; his teeth were clenched, the corners of his eyes flaring with anger.

'And how do you know you can trust this creature? That ship could be capable of anything. My team can help you spot the dangers, they can help you neutralise any threat.'

'This creature is our ally. My trust is absolute.'

Arty shook his head, interceding in support of Lethbridge-Stewart's cause. 'The threat may be unintentional. An accidental biological contagion, for example, could spread around the world in months.'

Beside him, Anne nodded vigorously. 'You do not have the right to make such decisions for the whole human race.'

Rostov shook his head. 'I have every right. The visitor came to us. To me.' He spread his hands, indicating their arguments were hopeless. 'You have no say over the policies of the Soviet Union.'

They were so engaged in the debate, they didn't notice Mags quietly leave her seat, or make her way over to the door. Lethbridge-Stewart kept arguing his case, keeping their attention focused on him, with a verbal assault designed to distract them from her departure. When they had discussed it, he had referred to it as 'covering fire'.

Nobody looked at her as she opened the door and slipped quietly out of the room.

She hurried down the corridor to the women's lavatories, to find Zoya Volskaya standing by a basin, staring at herself in the mirror, touching up her make-up, perfecting the image she presented to the world.

They had always known that the Soviet team would present a united front, so if they wanted to speak to Miss Volskaya on her own, this was the only way to do it. Back in the conference room, beside her comrades, she could not speak freely.

'Miss Volskaya,' Mags began cautiously, using the woman's native tongue. 'I wondered if we could talk, away from the others.'

Zoya turned to face her, a wary expression haunting her eyes. She stepped back, away from the mirror, hurriedly checking all three toilet cubicles were empty.

'I am not authorised to talk to you outside of the meeting,' Zoya stated bluntly, glancing around the room, as if expecting to find something terrible lurking in every corner.

'We were hoping, as a scientist, you might be prepared to share additional information with us. If you have any concerns about what is happening in your country, now is your opportunity to tell us. The only opportunity you're ever likely to get.'

Zoya stared at her. 'You are talking about treason.'

'I know.'

Mags had expected the woman to decline and walk away, but instead she hesitated, meaning she was at least prepared to consider talking.

'If I betray my country, will you offer me asylum in the United Kingdom? Can you get me out of here? Can you keep me safe?'

Lethbridge-Stewart had discussed this possibility with Mags, leaving her in no doubt as to the answer.

'No,' she replied, shaking her head. 'We can't do that. If we put you on a plane here in West Berlin, we have to leave via the official air corridors through East German airspace. We doubt that plane would ever be allowed to reach NATO territory. Which would mean we would have moved from a cold war to a hot one. Something we hope everyone is keen to avoid. The situation is too precarious. We can't risk starting an armed confrontation, not for you.'

Zoya nodded, swallowing nervously. 'You understand the risk I am taking then? You understand that if I speak to you, and they find out, I will lose everything?'

Mags nodded. 'We understand, but we also know there are people in the Soviet Union worried about what is happening. People that are brave enough to put both national loyalties and self-interest aside, to do what is right, for the good of everyone.'

Mags was uncomfortable with her own words. She was being deliberately manipulative, trying to get the information they needed, regardless of the consequences it would have for the woman.

Zoya paused, glancing at herself in the mirror, as if trying to judge the worth of the woman staring back at her. She shook her head in disgust, seemingly appalled, unable to empathise with the woman in the reflection.

'This is everything I can give you,' she said, as she reached into her bag, pulling out a folder crammed with documents,

77

which she placed into Mags' hands. 'I stole them from General Rostov's office. These dossiers were created by a specialist unit under his command. Analyse them, see what you make of them. See if they terrify you, as much as they terrify me.'

Mags quietly scooped up the folder. 'You're worried about Rostov's intentions? You think he is misusing the alien and its technology?'

Zoya laughed, humourlessly. 'Misusing? I've seen the plans. The advancements in missile technology. The tanks already under construction. I am sure those alone would terrify you. But, from my perspective, that is not misuse. No, I am not worried that *he* is using it, I am worried *it* is using him. I fear he has been compromised. He has changed since he encountered the creature. He was always a reliable, rational man, but now his moods and actions swing wildly for reasons I do not understand. I worry who is pulling the strings, what end they are intent upon, and just how far they are prepared to go to get what they want.'

Zoya looked away.

She was agitated, but she was not done. She was still trying to find the strength to divulge more. Trying to figure out if she would be able to live with the woman in the reflection if she gave away too little, or too much.

'Can you persuade General Rostov to give us access to the creature?' Mags pressed.

Zoya gave her a sour smile. 'He will offer you access of his own free will,' she replied. 'However, it is an offer you must not accept. If you cross the border with him, you will never be seen again. He sees the Fifth Operational Corps as a threat. A danger to his plans. An asset to be controlled. He seeks to contain and use you. Right now, he is using this meeting as an opportunity to get as much information from you as possible, because he believes you will be less compliant once he has detained you.'

Mags shook her head. 'We're here to get access to the creature; we can't just turn it down if it's freely offered.'

Zoya shrugged. 'Under armed guard, there is little you will be able to achieve. He will make use of you, but he will never give you the access to the creature you want.' She tapped a finger on the folder in Mags' hands. 'While you remain free, armed with this information, you will be able to take a much broader range of action. That is what he fears. That is why it is the right move. Still, it is your choice. The freedom to choose is something you take for granted, but it is a luxury which you will not be afforded later. As, I assure you, your choices are narrowing by the hour.'

Mags nodded.

Zoya returned her make-up pouch to her bag, then zipped it closed and slung it over her shoulder. 'He will, of course, not let you leave. He has armed men around the building. Right now, they are keeping their distance because he does not want to spook you, but once you reject the offer, the troops will move in. You will have to play your hand carefully. If you fail, I fear for the fate of us all.'

Mags felt a cold shiver run through her. She suddenly understood how the other woman felt.

Zoya was living in fear, with no way out.

They were now trapped in the same predicament. If they turned down the general's offer, they would find themselves confronted by armed men. If they accepted it, they would find themselves imprisoned on the other side of the Iron Curtain. There were no good choices.

Zoya strode towards the door. 'I must return to the meeting, before they notice we are both absent. Give it several minutes before you follow.' She glanced back, her eyes wide and worried, windows through a made-up face into a fear-filled soul. 'Do be careful with those files, if he finds out I gave them to you... I am dead.'

She exited through the door, letting it swing closed behind her.


Anne sat and listened to the discussion with growing frustration.

Lethbridge-Stewart was behaving like a soldier. He was giving the Soviet delegation as little as he could, not daring to say anything that might compromise them, or reveal too many of their secrets. He was treating it like a firefight, only risking leaning out far enough to take a shot, before hurriedly ducking back behind his defences. Any progress they were making was so painfully slow that they were essentially getting nowhere.

She needed to move things forward, or the entire trip would be wasted.

'Tell me, General, has anyone else on your team interacted

with the creature?' she asked. 'Or do you remain the only one to communicate with it?'

Rostov raised an eyebrow. 'I do not require assistance.'

'You alone represent the Soviet Union?'

'Yes.'

'You alone represent mankind?'

'I do so for the greater good of all.'

Anne shook her head. 'The greater good is very subjective. I suspect everyone around this table would hold quite different views about what it entails.'

Rostov nodded. 'We are only human, Mrs Bishop. We have our fallibilities and petty grievances, but our guest has no such failings, it can discern clearly what is best for all of us.'

Anne shot him a disparaging look. 'So, if we think of this all-powerful, highly advanced creature as being God-like, that makes you its Pope, does it? The voice of God on Earth.'

The general's eyes widened. The comment was deliberately antagonistic. Angry people talked. They never left anyone in doubt as to their thoughts and feelings.

Lethbridge-Stewart let the comment fly. He kept his face passive.

Much to her annoyance, Arty raised his hands in an apologetic gesture. 'Anne, show some respect,' he hissed, stepping in as the senior member of the scientific team, clearly thinking she had gone too far. 'I think what she means, General, was to question whether it is wise to rely on just one point of contact.'

Rostov remained calm, showing no signs of having taken offence. 'I think she meant considerably more than that,' he said, his gaze remaining locked on Anne. 'I think she intended to be provocative. We are, after all, not here to trade banalities.'

Behind him, Zoya Volskaya quietly re-entered the room, retaking her seat at the table. The general glanced sideways, his brow furrowing, as if only just registering that she had been absent.

Lethbridge-Stewart slammed a hand against the table.

The act was so violent, so unexpected, that all eyes immediately turned in his direction.

'Damn it, General, surely you can see how unacceptable this is to us? Surely you can see we must be allowed access to this creature, if for no other reason than to be comfortable with what is happening? Trusting your government to act responsibly is one thing, because its many members will moderate any impulse towards rash action, but to trust a lone individual is frankly impossible!'

At the far end of the table, the white-haired old man in the black suit cleared his throat. Petrov, swiftly shifting gears, began interpreting his words.

'I believe there is some merit in having a secondary contact. If nobody else on our side can connect with this creature, perhaps the British should be allowed to try to re-establish their link. They did, after all, have some success making the initial contact.'

The statement surprised Anne. She hadn't expected the other side to give any ground. Their ranks were not as unified as they had assumed.

Lethbridge-Stewart immediately pounced on the weakness. 'It would seem the representative of the Central Committee shares our concerns, that this matter should not rest solely within the hands of one officer in the Soviet military, that others must be allowed their say. And, respectfully, the Scots Guards Special Support Group are the most likely to succeed in that role.'

During his tirade, RSM Marsh returned to the room. Paying her no attention, remaining focused solely on Lethbridge-Stewart's statement, Rostov shook his head.

'You failed to connect with our guest.'

'And why was that?' Anne asked, her curiosity piqued. 'What did you do that we didn't? Will you tell us that?'

General Rostov shifted uncomfortably in his seat. 'We are kindred spirits. It is more attuned to our Communist ideals than it is with the principles of your Capitalism. Surely you understand, it would be sheer arrogance for you to assume that any advanced lifeform would favour your ideology over ours?'

Anne gave a non-committal shrug. She should let the matter go. She'd done her job, she had managed to tease some useful information out of the general, she had broken their united front, she should just step back and let the others sort out the rest. She should go home to Samantha.

She didn't want them to succeed in their mission. She didn't want to be invited beyond the Iron Curtain, to meet the creature and sink herself deeper into danger.

She just wanted to go home.

Yet, as much as she knew her own mind, there was a tiny part of her that would not be silenced, that demanded she do more, because it was the right thing to do.

'There are other concerns,' she began. 'There have been other visitors to this world which have grievances with one another. The United Kingdom has worked with one, on a handful of occasions, which we have codenamed the Cosmic Hobo. This means that we need to start co-ordinating our efforts, before we officially ally ourselves with such lifeforms, as otherwise we risk choosing different sides in existing conflicts; turning our planet into a battlefield for someone else's war, with ourselves on opposing sides.'

Anne was aware of Lethbridge-Stewart staring at her. She had just given away their biggest secret, to their most dangerous enemy.

Rostov nodded. 'I knew there had to be something else,' he muttered, staring at Lethbridge-Stewart, 'to account for your success.'

Anne leaned forward, staring the general in the eye. 'It is clear to us, that with or without our knowledge and consent, these creatures are already visiting our world. So, let us choose our friends and enemies wisely. Let us choose them together. Work with them together. Fight them together. It is the only safe way to proceed.'

Having made her case, she sat back, waiting to see how they would react.

Gorbenko spoke first. 'The British make a compelling argument.'

Beside him, Major Bugayev nodded in agreement. 'We have co-ordinated operations with the British before. It may not have been included in all of the official reports, but it was a successful partnership.'

Rostov sighed. 'I can see the logic of it,' he muttered. 'It is important we act together.'

Lethbridge-Stewart's eyes ignited with unexpected hope. 'We have a deal then?'

'Fine.' Rostov sighed again, glancing at his colleagues. 'It does, regrettably, seem prudent. The Soviet Union hereby cordially invites the British Special Support Group to join us in our research efforts.'

He stood and reached across the table, offering Lethbridge-Stewart a handshake, which was swiftly taken up.

'Thank you, General. On behalf of Her Majesty's Armed Forces, I accept your offer.'

Rostov smiled. 'Have your driver follow us to the border, once on the far side we will lead the way to Schönefeld Airbase, from there we will fly you to a classified location, where you may assist us with our scientific programme. This way, please.'

He turned to face the door, expecting them to follow.

Out of the corner of her eye, Anne saw Lethbridge-Stewart glance at Marsh, causing the woman to give an almost imperceptibly small shake of her head, her eyes filled with panic. No words were spoken, but it was enough for Lethbridge-Stewart to suddenly switch tack.

'We shall join you in the lobby shortly, General. I just need a moment with my people. I'm sure you understand.'

Rostov paused on the threshold, pulling his military cap back on. 'Of course.' He nodded, frowning. 'Don't take too long. I need to be on my way.'

Rostov swept out of the room, his cohorts following in his wake.

Lethbridge-Stewart quietly pushed the door closed. 'Well, spit it out, Sergeant Major. We don't have long.'

'We have a problem, sir.'

She explained what she had learned from Zoya, and Anne felt her heart sink. They had been hooked in, and the trap had been sprung.

*Samantha*, she thought, fearing she would never see her daughter again.

# CHAPTER EIGHT
*The Berlin Event*

**THE R/T** in the Land Rover crackled into life.

'Mayhem Leader to Mayhem Three.' Lethbridge-Stewart's voice sliced through the static. 'Are you there? Over.'

Bishop scooped up the handset.

'Receiving. I'm parked about a quarter of a mile away. Apologies for going AWOL, sir. The House Guests have men on all the exits. The whole situation feels off to me. I wanted to make sure our transport was secure, but I didn't dare risk using the radio to tell you, not while you were meeting with them. Over.'

He paused, waiting for a response, half expecting a reprimand for letting his paranoia get the better of him.

'Good man,' Lethbridge-Stewart said. 'We've got trouble this end. We're going to try and exit the building. We expect considerable resistance. Over.'

Bishop frowned.

That didn't sound sensible. Lethbridge-Stewart and Marsh may have been able to handle themselves in such a situation, but his wife was also part of the group. Anne had some basic self-defence training, and knew how to fire a gun – but she always found it difficult to pull the trigger. They wouldn't be a match for the troops he'd seen.

'They've got four men in the lobby, plus two around the back. Best guess, there's at least one more carload somewhere, but I don't know where. Over.'

The transceiver was silent for a moment, presumably while the others discussed the situation. A minute later, Lethbridge-Stewart's voice returned to the radio.

'Contact RAF Gatow, get them to send support. Regardless, we're coming out the back ten minutes from now. Rendezvous with us there. Mayhem Four will lead the others out, I will provide suppressive fire if necessary. If the House Guests act with hostility, you may need to neutralise them. If anything goes wrong, your priority is to get the others away. Is that understood? Over.'

Bishop made a note of the time on his wristwatch.

Lethbridge-Stewart was speaking in military terms, as if it were all just strategy, but it was clear that he was intent on putting his own life on the line, so that he could be sure everyone else got away. That was what made him such an exemplary superior officer; behind the cool, aloof exterior, there dwelt a very human heart.

'Yes, sir. For clarification, if necessary, am I authorised to fire on the House Guests? Over.'

There was a long pause.

'Try not to shoot first, Mayhem Three. Over and out.'

Bishop swallowed nervously. They seemed to be sliding headlong towards an armed confrontation, and if anyone were foolish enough to pull a trigger, there was no telling where it would end.

It only took one bullet to start a war.

Bishop switched the frequency on the mobile transceiver, changing from long-wave to short-wave, so that he could reach the airbase.

'This is Mayhem Three to RAF Gatow,' he declared. 'Urgent assistance required.'

He let go of the sending switch, expecting an immediate response. Static abruptly roared out of the speaker. It was far too loud to be normal interference. He hurriedly switched frequency again, but the screaming static filled every channel.

He couldn't even contact Lethbridge-Stewart.

The airwaves were being deliberately overloaded, making it impossible to transmit. It was a basic military strategy, used before an armed assault, to disable an opponent's communications, so that they could not co-ordinate their response. Regardless of any action he took, things were already escalating.

It meant that there was every likelihood that someone

had been listening in on their previous conversation.

He checked the time on his watch. He had eight minutes.

Bishop restarted the Land Rover engine, pushing his foot down on the accelerator, heading back towards the hotel.

The atmosphere in the lobby was tense.

Zoya stood quietly among the soldiers. She glanced at the glass doors, desperate to leave before the situation spiralled into violence, but forced to remain in place to maintain the pretence that she believed the British would be willingly coming with them.

'They will be useful assets to our team,' she told Rostov. 'I believe both scientists can be objective, putting the research above their own national interests.'

General Rostov ignored her. He glanced at his wristwatch

'What is taking them so long?' he muttered, glancing at the lift's display panel, which showed it had not yet been summoned back to the third floor.

Major Bugayev approached from outside. 'They know. I've jammed their signal.'

'How could they know?' Rostov scowled.

Zoya said nothing. She did not dare move, or blink, or breathe, for fear that some minor tell would reveal the fact she had betrayed her motherland.

Bugayev shrugged. 'Paranoia,' he suggested. 'They're not coming down. They're going to try and exit through the back.'

Rostov turned his head, looking directly at Zoya, his eyes burning with irritation. She could not stay quiet any longer. To avoid suspicion, she needed to react.

'Paranoia implies a fear is unfounded,' she stated. 'They have every reason to fear us. If they are scared, a fight or flight response is instinctive; it is hardwired into our biology. A frightened animal reacts, without thought, using one of the two strategies most likely to ensure its survival. Attack or flee.'

Rostov sighed. 'Detain them, Major.'

Bugayev nodded. He made a gesture towards the four men in trench coats, who immediately unzipped the military kit bag at their feet, each taking out an assault rifle.

Zoya stared at the weapons. 'Were you not listening, General?' No matter the risk to herself, she had to try to stop what was happening, make them step back from the brink. 'Fight or flight. They will not surrender. It is basic behavioural science. If you corner them, they will lash out. This will escalate. People will die.'

Rostov shook his head. 'We are not animals, Miss Volskaya. We are soldiers, engaged in a game of strategy, like two Grandmasters playing chess. Pieces are moved. Pieces are sacrificed.' He turned away, locking eyes with Major Bugayev. 'Remember, I need Lethbridge-Stewart alive, the others are dispensable.'

Bugayev gave him a brief nod, then moved towards the lift, signalling for three of the armed men to follow him.

Zoya watched them leave.

'Perhaps I should wait in the car,' she suggested.

Rostov gave a nod. 'That would seem wise,' he said, glancing across the room towards Minister Gorbenko, who sat quietly in a chair by the window. 'Perhaps you would be kind enough to escort Miss Volskaya to safety?'

The old man grunted. 'Of course,' he muttered, rising to his feet. He stepped forward, looping an arm through hers, guiding her towards the glass doors. 'Come, my dear. We had best leave them to it. They have no need for science or politics here anymore. This is a military matter now.'

She could hear a defeated tone in the old man's words.

He had no more power than her. They were just pawns. This was Rostov's game; and he was playing to win, no matter the cost.

Anne glanced through the stolen files.

'I can't understand much of this, most of it's in Russian. But there are dates, global co-ordinates, scientific formula and technical diagrams, mostly referring to people and events over the last ten years.' She frowned, bewildered by what she was seeing. 'And for about thirty years into the future.'

Marsh shrugged. 'First chance we get, I'll translate it for you, but for now you just need to hang on to them. She has risked her life by giving them to us, so they must be valuable.'

Anne nodded, closing the folder, tucking it under one

arm. She focused on the situation at hand.

Lethbridge-Stewart stood by the conference room door, his eyes fixed on the face of his wristwatch, watching the seconds count down.

'Right, time to go,' he announced to the room. 'Major Bishop will arrive in six minutes.' He unclipped his holster, pulled his revolver and opened the door.

Arty shook his head. 'I'm not going anywhere.'

Lethbridge-Stewart glared at him. 'It's not up for discussion, Professor. We're going.'

Arty sat down. 'We can't just dismiss their offer. One of us should go with them, make sure that woman was right, not just paranoid. I'll stay. If nothing else, I can slow them down; every moment they're dealing with me, they won't be looking for you.'

Anne stared at him. 'Arty, that's madness.'

'Maybe.' He shrugged, leaning back in his chair and smiling. 'But sometimes you've got to take crazy chances, right? Give the other side the benefit of the doubt, no matter how many times they've let you down.'

Lethbridge-Stewart shook his head in despair. 'Brave, but foolish. We don't have time to debate it. I can't stop you. The choice is yours, as are the consequences.' He stepped through the door, into the hallway. 'The rest of us are going. Move, Anne! Come on, Sergeant Major!'

Anne shot Arty a parting smile. 'Good luck.'

He gave her a mock salute and a wink.

Anne stepped away, knowing that she might never see him again.

Lethbridge-Stewart led them down the hallway. He made his way to the lift, glancing at the control panel, which showed an illuminated upward arrow.

'Someone is already on their way up,' he muttered. 'Stairs, now!'

He moved swiftly forward, pushing open the door to the stairwell. The moment they were through, he eased the door closed, leaving only a one-inch gap, through which he could observe the hallway. He pressed a finger to his lips, indicating they should both be silent.

Anne heard the distinctive ping of the lift arriving, followed by the sound of the metal doors rolling open. Lethbridge-Stewart eased the door to the corridor closed.

'Bugayev and three soldiers,' he whispered. 'There is at least one more in the building somewhere. Come on!'

He led the way down the stairs, trying to descend both quickly and stealthily, but unable to prevent the clatter of their footfalls echoing on the floors above. Reaching the ground floor, he pressed himself up against the door, to peer through a narrow window that looked out into the reception lobby.

'Rostov and one soldier,' he informed them, his eyes narrowing.

His trigger finger twitched, his brow furrowing.

Anne could tell he was considering a dangerous, desperate move. She placed a hand on his elbow, pushing the revolver slightly to one side, making him turn his attention towards her.

'Don't do it,' she said.

'I could take him out now. Eliminate him. It might be our only chance.'

Anne shook her head. 'You'd just get us killed,' she said, gesturing in the opposite direction, towards a green fire door at the base of the stairs, which she presumed had been their original target.

It led out to the rear of the building, to where Bill would shortly be arriving with the Land Rover, offering them a real chance of escape, if they could find a way around the two soldiers outside. There were no good choices, but she knew she wanted to live, so she needed Lethbridge-Stewart to stay focused on the option that was most likely to ensure that outcome. It was simple self-preservation.

'I need to get home to my baby.' She hoped her emotive plea would make him see sense.

He glanced at her. His eyes were cold. She knew immediately that she had used the wrong approach. He was only thinking of his duty as a soldier, any emotional concerns were unimportant.

He shook his head. 'There is far more at stake here than your child.'

Marsh moved towards the fire door, placing her hand on the security bar that would release the lock.

'With all due respect, sir, Rostov is just a man. The alien creature is the real threat. Our duty is to get the intel in those files out of here. If you attack the lobby, you are jeopardising our most valuable assets, throwing away our one real hope of dealing with this crisis.'

Lethbridge-Stewart blinked. 'You're absolutely right, Sergeant Major. We must stay on mission.' He gave a brisk nod, accepting her strategic assessment. If she had been wrong, he doubtless would have told her, but confronted by a well-reasoned and logical argument, he had listened and adapted.

Anne smiled grimly. That had been her once; the one with the reasoned arguments that could talk Lethbridge-Stewart down, but now... She had been changed in ways she'd never expected.

Lethbridge-Stewart strode towards the fire door. 'Once outside, there will be two enemy operatives. I will lay down suppressing fire. You must both run. If you see the Land Rover, go towards it. If you don't, try to lose yourself in the alleyways. Are you ready?'

Anne tightened her grip on the folder in her arms.

It was not much of a plan. She was far from ready, but there was no time for any delay. Lethbridge-Stewart didn't wait for their answers.

He pressed on the release bar, popping open the fire door, then stepped outside.

'Go! Go! Go!' he yelled, aiming his revolver high, firing a round into the sky.

Anne fled.

After the dim electric lights of the stairwell, the sky outside seemed dazzlingly bright. Anne moved fast, trying to comprehend her surroundings as she ran through them. There was a large black automobile parked across the back of the building. Two large men, dressed in trench coats, were scurrying for cover behind the vehicle, each clasping an assault rifle.

She focused on her feet, wishing she were wearing more

practical shoes, as she raced across the uneven ground. There were shouts in Russian. A second shot sang out from the revolver, then a third.

'Left!' Marsh yelled from behind her. 'Go left!'

Anne wheeled about, blindly obeying the instruction, to see the Land Rover racing towards her. She glimpsed Bill's face behind the steering wheel, his eyes wide with alarm.

The vehicle sped past her, turning and braking, kicking up a wave of dirt and dust as it slammed to a halt between her and the gunmen. There was another shout in Russian, answered by another two shots from Lethbridge-Stewart's revolver.

Marsh was suddenly beside her, bundling her into the back of the Land Rover. Through the front windscreen, she saw Lethbridge-Stewart fire one last round, blowing out one of the Russian car's front tyres. He pulled the trigger again, but the gun clicked uselessly, its last round expended.

In front of him, the two soldiers rose from their hiding position behind the car, their assault rifles held ready.

There was no way Lethbridge-Stewart could make it to the Land Rover.

'Go!' he yelled, making no attempt to run. 'Get out of here! That's an order!'

Still clasping his empty revolver, he raised his arms in a gesture of surrender.

Anne could see the horror and indecision on Bill's face.

He was obligated to obey the order he had been given, getting them to safety, but he also could not bring himself to abandon his commanding officer. He hesitated.

There was a noise from behind them, a hissing thunk, like the sound of an air rifle being fired. The black vehicle was suddenly consumed by a flash, the whole car bucking as it was torn apart, disintegrating into chunks of burning metal. Both gunmen were knocked from their feet, thrown backwards, slammed into the dirt.

Anne glanced over her shoulder.

Marsh stood behind the Land Rover, holding a rifle, still aimed at the burning wreckage of the car. The woman's hands were trembling, her face pale with shock, clearly stunned by the result of her own actions.

She gave a little shrug, looking uncertainly at the weapon in her hands.

'Took it from one of the spies in the UK,' she muttered. 'Left it in the back by accident. The grenade launcher packs a bit more welly than I thought.'

'Get in!' Lethbridge-Stewart yelled, sprinting towards the Land Rover, yanking open the door and swinging himself into the passenger seat. 'Don't stand there yakking!'

Marsh immediately obeyed, pulling herself into the back alongside Anne.

Infront of them, one of the soldiers was rising to his feet, staggering slightly as he tried to unscramble his senses. The other soldier remained on the ground, surrounded by an expanding pool of blood. The rear door of the building was suddenly thrown open, with another soldier rushing out into the backstreet, his rifle raised.

Bill threw the Land Rover into reverse, then stamped on the accelerator.

'Get down!' he yelled, looking back over his shoulder, his eyes fixed on the road behind them as they tore backwards.

Anne ducked down, closing her eyes and putting her hands over her head.

She heard the thundering rattle of an assault rifle. She heard the plink-plink-plink of metal rounds punching holes through the bodywork of the Land Rover. The front windscreen shattered, blowing inwards, showering them with shards of glass.

Bill turned the steering wheel, spinning them about. He hit the brake hard, then shifted the vehicle into forward gear, sending them all lurching as he accelerated away.

The sound of gunfire faded.

Anne cautiously opened her eyes. 'Hardly the most successful of diplomatic meetings,' she muttered.

Marsh gave her a wry smile.

Lethbridge-Stewart snorted. 'I'm surprised either of you can find any levity in the situation. RSM Marsh, you disobeyed a direct order, a man is likely dead, and the entire situation has escalated into a major diplomatic incident!' He was seething, making no attempt to conceal his disappointment. 'We were engaged in a game of brinkmanship, where sensible minds were supposed to prevail, steering us away from the edge, but instead I fear we have gone careering across a line from which there is no coming back.'

Beside him, Bill remained silent, focusing on getting them away from trouble. Now, needing further instructions, he looked towards his superior officer for direction.

'Which way, sir?'

'Back to RAF Gatow, Major. Our priority has to be getting those files back to HQ.' Lethbridge-Stewart glanced through the window, watching the streets of Berlin flash past. 'We need to get out of this city as quickly as possible. The gloves are off. There's no guarantee they'll continue to respect the Allied air corridors. We'll be lucky if we get out of here alive.'

Zoya had heard the gunfire and the explosion.

'Should we not leave?' she asked the driver, feeling a growing sense of panic.

The soldier behind the steering wheel shrugged his large shoulders. 'Not until ordered.'

Zoya leaned back in her seat. She had no idea what was happening, but knew Rostov had lost control; it had certainly never been his intention for the situation to end in violence.

She glanced at Minister Gorbenko, who sat quietly beside her.

'How can you let this happen?' she asked him. 'Why are you letting him do this?'

The old man gave a defeated shrug. 'I cannot stop him now. He has somehow outmanoeuvred me at every turn. Now, everywhere I go, I am accompanied by a soldier. We can only hope he knows what he is doing and, if he does, that he is not a madman, or the puppet of that creature.'

Zoya shook her head. 'Does it sound to you as if things are going to plan?' she cried. 'Do you realise how serious the consequences could be?'

Gorbenko looked at her, his eyes dull and hopeless, suddenly seeming like nothing but a world-weary old man. 'Change is never easy. Conflict and revolution are not just part of history, they are an inevitable part of life, which we must do our best to endure and survive. We may take some reassurance from the fact that the Soviet Union is prepared for such times, largely due to the preparations made by Rostov himself. There are advanced armoured units stationed on the border, which could easily be called upon, should the situation here demand it.'

Zoya stared at him, dumbfounded.

The old man did not care about the future. His influence was gone. Most of his days were spent. He was resigned to watching events unfold, more out of curiosity than concern.

Zoya couldn't afford to have such a lackadaisical attitude. She needed to know what was happening. She would rather take a risk, than have others seal her fate in her absence.

She turned her back on the old man, opened the car door and climbed out, striding purposefully back towards the hotel. She could see a plume of black smoke rising from behind the building. She could hear the distant scream of police sirens. She did not want to consider what would happen if the West German civilian authorities found them at the hotel. They needed to go, but there was no sign of Rostov ordering his men to leave.

She found him standing in the lobby, berating one of the soldiers.

'Why did you open fire on their vehicle?' he demanded, his voice shaking with fury. 'I gave strict instructions Lethbridge-Stewart was to be taken alive. Do you have any idea of what the consequences will be if a stray bullet has hit him? No, of course you don't, that's why you're supposed to follow orders!'

The general pinched the bridge of his nose between his thumb and forefinger, bowing his head in despair, seemingly overwhelmed by frustration.

The soldier, foolishly, tried to explain himself.

'They fired on us, sir. Popov is dead. I reacted in the heat of the moment. I thought I might die.'

Rostov rolled his eyes. 'Then you should have died. Your life is insignificant. The mission is all that matters.' He waved a hand dismissively. 'Get out of my sight!'

The soldier hurried away.

Zoya had paused in the doorway, watching events play

out, fearful of approaching the furious man. Rostov glanced in her direction.

'Why is Lethbridge-Stewart so important to you?' she ventured cautiously.

Rostov gave a small shrug. 'In the years ahead, he was to be instrumental in defeating various extra-terrestrial threats to this world. That is part of the future I need to keep. I need him to work with us, rather than against us.'

Zoya frowned. 'You have claimed to have knowledge of the future before. How is that possible?'

'Our new ally has remarkable foresight.'

'And how do you know you can trust it? How do you know it isn't lying to you?'

'It's not just words. I have seen it with my own eyes.'

His head abruptly turned to the side, as he became aware of the sound of the police sirens, which had finally penetrated the thick glass windows.

'The civilian authorities are on their way,' Zoya told him, abandoning her questioning. 'We need to return to our side of the border. Quickly. Whatever diplomatic immunity we had, it won't cover what has happened here.'

Rostov shook his head, looking genuinely amused. He reached out a hand, placing it on her upper arm. She supposed it was meant to be a gesture of reassurance, but she was too scared of him to take any comfort from it. She said nothing, having to tolerate his grip, grateful that the thick fabric of her red coat protected her skin from feeling his touch.

'No, Zoya. We need not flee. There is no reason to be afraid. The civilian authorities will not be coming here. They will be responding to events elsewhere in the city.' He smiled. 'We stand on the threshold of a new future, a new beginning for all mankind, which we will have the honour of witnessing. The tide of history is about to turn forever in our favour.'

She frowned at him, unsure what he meant.

'What's going to happen?' she asked, a tremor of nervousness in her voice. She had never been more frightened of him.

'The Berlin Wall is about to fall,' he said, and Zoya was sure she could see a manic gleam in his eyes. 'The entire city will soon be ours.'

# CHAPTER NINE
*Escape from Berlin*

THE LAND Rover raced westwards along the autobahn, weaving through a steady stream of Volkswagen Beetles and Mercedes-Benz sedans, heading towards RAF Gatow.

A cold wind poured through the shattered windscreen.

In the back of the vehicle, Anne was working her way through the stolen files, trying to understand what she was seeing. Marsh was leaning in beside her, translating parts which she thought may be of interest, or any sections Anne picked out.

'They've got a file on you,' Anne observed, looking at a photograph of Lethbridge-Stewart, held by a paper clip to several pages of Russian text.

Lethbridge-Stewart grunted a response. 'If all we've acquired is a copy of my CV, then we really are in trouble.'

Anne looked through a few more pages, having to hold them firmly in place to prevent the breeze from randomly flipping them over. 'There's a file on me too,' she said, as she studied the accompanying photograph. She flipped to the next file. 'And one on Rostov.'

Lethbridge-Stewart shook his head. 'Nothing more useful? Anything about the creature?'

'A list of weaknesses and vulnerabilities, perhaps?'

He nodded. 'Yes. That kind of thing.'

Anne flipped several more pages, looking for anything pertaining to the creature, but found nothing. 'No, I don't think so.' She sighed, opening a large folded document at the back of the folder. 'There's a schematic though, showing the location and layout of a classified military facility, in the forests of Eastern Siberia.'

Marsh's hand shot forward, her forefinger running along a

line of hand-written Russian text, her voice rising with sudden excitement. 'It's where they've taken the ship and creature, sir.'

Lethbridge-Stewart glanced back at them. 'Eastern Siberia?' he said, his eyebrows arching with disappointment. 'I'm afraid that's beyond our reach. Even if we weren't worried about retaliation, there's no way one of our bombers could reach a target that deep in their territory; their airspace is too well defended.'

Anne glanced up from the page, looking at him in horror, shocked that he would even contemplate such action. He caught her look, tilting his head in a questioning gesture, as if daring her to voice her objections, so that he could shoot them down.

When she didn't respond, he turned away, returning his attention to the world beyond the shattered windscreen.

Bill nodded at the road ahead. 'We're coming up on RAF Gatow now, sir,' he reported, as he slowed the Land Rover, preparing to make the turn into the compound.

Lethbridge-Stewart leaned forward, frowning as he observed the entranceway. 'Something's wrong.'

Anne followed his gaze.

At first glance the road ahead appeared unoccupied. There was a small wooden security hut on the left-hand side, with a raised red and white boom barrier, which would normally have been lowered to block the access road.

'Where are the guards?' she asked.

The moment she spoke, she spotted the body of a young man in uniform lying on the tarmac, his eyes staring unblinkingly at the sky. Bill, ignoring the fallen airman, pointed to a black car parked just inside the entrance.

'That's the other Soviet car that crossed the border,' he said, his tone doubtful, as if he could not believe what he was seeing.

Lethbridge-Stewart's frown deepened. 'They wouldn't dare,' he declared, shaking his head in disbelief. 'An armed assault on a British RAF base would be an act of war. They would not dare risk the consequences.'

Bill glanced at his superior officer. 'There's only a handful of them, sir. What can they possibly hope to achieve?'

'Four well trained commandos, catching a base by surprise, could wreak havoc.' Lethbridge-Stewart's eyes narrowed, a look of cold calculation flitting across his features as he considered the enemy's strategy. 'They could easily disable the facility, put it out of action, but for what purpose?'

There was a moment of silence, as he considered the question, which was broken by a series of distant gunshots.

Lethbridge-Stewart's right hand instinctively flew to his holster, his left gripping the door handle, ready to leap into the fray. Anne reached forward, pressing her hand down hard on his shoulder, bringing him to an abrupt halt.

'Have you considered the possibility that this is happening purely to prevent us from leaving?' she asked. 'If we're the threat Rostov fears, your duty is to get us home, not join the battle here. If this way out is compromised, we must find another.'

Lethbridge-Stewart glared at her as he considered her words. He clearly felt torn. On the one hand, he needed to think about the bigger picture, but on the other, it meant abandoning good men to an uncertain fate.

He removed his hand from the door handle. 'Get us out of here, Major.'

Bill nodded, hurriedly turning the steering wheel, bringing them around. 'Where to, sir?'

'Find me a phone box.'

'Yes, sir.'

Bill stamped on the accelerator.

Anne watched from the back of the vehicle as the tall chain-link fence which protected the airfield raced past them. Through the metal mesh, she could see their large grey Hercules transport plane sitting on the runway. It was tantalisingly close. She could easily imagine climbing the fence, racing across the grass and clambering aboard; the mighty aeroplane spiriting them safely home.

The Hercules exploded.

A bright flash erupted underneath the fuselage, causing a cascade reaction, as each of the four fuel tanks beneath the wings blossomed into orange fireballs, spewing vast quantities of black smoke into the sky. The flames raged through the plane, bursting the windows and igniting the rubber tyres, burning with such intensity that the metal fuselage began collapsing in on itself.

'Go! Go! Go!' Lethbridge-Stewart cried.

Bill pushed the accelerator to the floor.

Zoya had left the hotel lobby.

She stood between the sleek black Volga cars that had ferried them to the conference. She could not face returning to her seat beside Gorbenko, feeling only a deepening sense of loathing for the old man, who had so spinelessly allowed himself to become the general's puppet. Neither could she stomach spending any more time around Rostov, or the soldiers under his command, fearing how they would react if they realised what she had done.

It amazed her that Rostov still trusted her, confiding so much in her, continuing to insist on her involvement, when her distaste for everything he was doing must have become apparent to him.

She listened to the West German police sirens, singing out across the city, still hoping some of them were headed towards the hotel; coming to restore law and order. As the minutes passed, that hope died. She glimpsed numerous of the little green and white police cars speeding across a nearby intersection, with flashing emergency lights, all headed eastwards. Towards the Berlin Wall. Towards the border.

'It's time to go,' declared Rostov, as he pushed his way through the glass doors of the hotel. 'Can you make use of this man?'

He gestured towards the figure behind him.

The dark-skinned man, wearing a sheepskin coat, was one of the two scientific advisor's the British had brought to the meeting. He lifted a hand, giving her a small wave, revealing his wrists had been cuffed. He made a statement in English, which she could not understand. Given the communication barrier, there was little chance of them being able to work productively together. However, if she said as much, the man would probably disappear forever.

'It depends on his skills.' Zoya sighed, trying to appear a little reluctant, knowing there was more chance of the man surviving if the general was actively involved in a discussion, rather than just being presented with an opinion. 'What experience does he have?'

'He claims to have been the Chief Scientific Advisor to the Scots Guards Special Support Group ever since Anne Travers resigned, over six months ago, with an in-depth knowledge of every incident they have encountered.'

Zoya rolled her eyes. 'That is a patent lie,' she said, glancing at the British man. He grinned at her, clearly unaware she was denouncing him as a liar. 'We know from the intelligence files that their appointed *head* of scientific research is a man called Jeff Erickson.'

'Why would he lie?' Rostov stared at her, his eyes burning with curiosity.

Zoya shrugged. 'To prolong his life. To make himself seem more valuable than he actually is.'

Rostov nodded, seeming to mull over her suggestion. 'Any other possibilities?'

She frowned. 'The Intelligence files are wrong,' she suggested, her voice tinged with scepticism, not because she doubted the possibility, but because she did not dare offend him by implying the intelligence gathering unit under his command was anything less than perfect.

Rostov's expression darkened. 'The files were not wrong,' he growled. 'Yet nothing is as it should be. Can you use the man, or not?'

'If he has skills, I can use them, if I have something to work on.'

It was another gamble.

She wanted access to their visitor. If she were to have any hope of understanding the threat the creature posed, or what it had done to Rostov, she needed to be able to study it.

With Minister Gorbenko now in General Rostov's pocket, there was nothing to stop him regaining access to the creature. She imagined he was keen to return to it.

The general nodded. 'Then we shall take this man with us,' he said, stepping forward and opening a car door for her. 'I've had word that our forces have successfully struck their first objectives, securing and destroying key targets, giving us clear passage. So, we are heading to Schönefeld Airport, then onwards to the base in the Irkutsk Oblast. You will finally have full access to all the classified secrets that are stored there, just as you've always wanted.'

The last statement stung her.

It alarmed Zoya that he knew her so well, particularly given her recent betrayal. 'I cannot deny I am curious about the place,' she admitted.

'I know,' he said, watching her as she climbed into the back of the Volga. 'I promised you I would make it happen. Now, I am keeping that promise.'

She glanced up at him, puzzled. 'You made no such promise.'

'Did I not?' Rostov rubbed wearily at his eyes. 'Perhaps not. It is so difficult to keep track of what is, what was and what will be.'

He pushed the car door shut.

A moment later, Professor Arthur Grey was bundled into the seat beside her, his wrists still bound by the metal cuffs. He looked terrified. He didn't have a clue what was happening.

She tried to explain, speaking slowly and carefully, using only the simplest of Russian words, which she hoped may have some phonetic resemblance to their English counterparts, as the two languages did share a common ancestry. Every word she tried was met by the same blank expression.

He understood less Russian than a toddler.

He gave a small, helpless shrug. It seemed, for the moment, that even basic communication was beyond their grasp.


Lethbridge-Stewart climbed out of the Land Rover.

He made his way across the street, towards a phone kiosk, leaving Anne and Marsh pouring over the stolen files. Bishop remained at the wheel, engine running, vigilantly watching for any sign of approaching danger. The vehicle was a pitiable remnant of its former self, with numerous bullet holes and broken windows. Given the extent of the damage, it was a miracle it was still running at all.

Lethbridge-Stewart pushed his way through the kiosk's folding doors, picked up the handset and listened to the dial tone. Pushing a few Deutsche Marks into the coin slot, he dialled for the operator, hoping to place an international call to General Hamilton in the United Kingdom. He needed to make sure HQ was up to speed. He needed guidance.

The operators line rang. It kept ringing for much longer than he considered normal.

Abruptly, someone picked up. Nobody spoke, there was just the gentle hiss of an open line.

'Hello?' he ventured.

There was a kerfuffle at the other end, indistinct noises that he didn't understand, then the phone line went dead.

He hammered on the hook switch, attempting to reconnect the line, desperately wanting to hear the reassuring drone of the dial tone again.

Nothing.

Silence.

He replaced the handset in its cradle, his shoulders sagging.

He would never want the others to see it, but as he stood alone in the kiosk, he allowed himself a moment of despair. He wiped a hand across his eyes, drawing a deep breath, hoping that if he calmed his nerves, the situation might not seem so grim. It didn't work. It was bad. Far worse than the others knew.

The Soviet forces had seized control of the main airport and disabled the telephone network. They were hitting strategic targets, crippling their enemy's ability to react, breaking the key supply lines that the Allied military forces were dependent on. These were not just acts of Stasi espionage, they were openly hostile attacks committed by the Soviet military, taking the first logical steps that would be necessary for an invasion of West Berlin.

It was a day he had feared for over twenty years, which in his heart he had always felt would never happen, because both sides were too terrified of the consequences. Now, he feared the Soviet's access to alien technology had destabilised the precarious balance of peace, making them believe they had a distinct advantage, giving them the courage to act with aggression.

If he was right, the world had just crossed a threshold far more dangerous than any in its history. He just needed to confirm the truth with his own eyes, beyond any reasonable doubt, before he could decide how to respond.

Lethbridge-Stewart straightened his cap, then stepped out of the telephone kiosk, banishing any worry from his face. He strode back towards the Land Rover, climbed into the passenger seat and gave Bishop a nod.

'Back into the city,' he instructed. 'I want eyes on the checkpoints.'

'Yes, sir,' Bishop said, already pressing down on the accelerator. 'Trying to cut their agents off at the border, are we?

Turn the tables on them. Stop them going back?'

Lethbridge-Stewart made a grunt, high enough that it could be misinterpreted as a confirmation, but indistinct enough that it could mean nothing at all. He didn't want to answer Bishop's question. He didn't want to scare them unnecessarily.

'I think we've found something else,' Anne said, gesturing at the open folder on her lap, which she and Marsh had been continuing to dissect.

'Good. I could use something to lift my spirits.'

Anne flipped through the pages, a confused look on her face. 'This file is nonsense. It's full of mistakes. Some of the profiles are woefully inaccurate.'

It was less than he had hoped for.

'Are you telling me those files are worthless?'

'Not at all.' Anne glanced up, meeting his eyes, a look of concern crossing her face. She had heard the despair in his voice. He needed to make more effort to conceal his feelings from them. There was a job to do, he needed them focused, not distracted by fear and doubt.

'What then?' he demanded, sounding angrier than he intended.

'I think it's the errors that had Miss Volskaya so spooked. Take Rostov's file for example, it lists his rank here as colonel, just as you said he was when you encountered him via the sphere, despite the fact the man we met claims to have been a general for several years. Unless, of course, you were mistaken about his rank?'

Lethbridge-Stewart mulled this over. He clearly remembered the three gold stars on the man's epaulette, signifying his rank as a colonel, as an indisputable fact of which he had been utterly certain. He had later only presumed he had been mistaken, because he was confronted with undeniable evidence, which was irreconcilable with his original belief.

He should have known better. He had been doing the job long enough to know that such inconsistencies, rather than being errors, were often the very clues they needed to understand an impossible event.

'He was a colonel,' Lethbridge-Stewart stated, every doubt evaporating from his mind.

Anne turned the page. 'My profile is even stranger; they

seem to think I've been continuing to freelance for you. They've got no record of Arthur Grey at all, even though he's worked with you for over six months, while Bill's file, other than his rank, seems entirely correct.'

Lethbridge-Stewart frowned, confused by what he was hearing. 'What about my file?' he asked, unable not to feel curious.

Anne turned another page. 'Seems mostly right, as far as we can tell. Doesn't it?' She glanced at Marsh, as the woman quickly reassessed the page of Cyrillic script.

Her eyes suddenly flicked up and locked onto his left hand, which was gripping the back of Bishop's seat, keeping him steady.

'Where's your wedding ring, sir?' she asked.

Lethbridge-Stewart almost laughed. He glanced at the fingers of his left hand. 'I'm not married, Sergeant Major.' Marriage was not something he ever gave much thought. It was something he was very much in two minds about, simultaneously considering it to be both an inevitable part of life, while also being utterly impossible given his responsibilities. 'When would I find the time for such things?'

Marsh shook her head. She tapped a finger against the open file. 'According to Soviet Intelligence, you got married fairly recently.'

Lethbridge-Stewart frowned. It was a ridiculous conversation. 'To Sally?'

He felt a lump of sadness in his throat. He couldn't imagine ever having married her, but neither could he imagine marrying anyone else.

Marsh shook her head. 'Fiona Campbell,' she said, glancing up at him. 'That's the name in the file.'

Lethbridge-Stewart stared blankly at her. For a moment he could not place the name, although it did feel vaguely familiar to him, until suddenly a memory surfaced from the depths of his mind. There had been a woman with that name, a cousin of an old friend, whom he had met shortly after Sally's death. She was a handsome woman, if he recalled correctly, who had certainly intrigued him, but he had been far too preoccupied at the time to consider pursuing such a matter. Like so many of life's passing events, the day had come and gone, making very little impression on him.

Anne leaned forward. 'Does that name mean something to

104

you?'

'Not really.' He shrugged, feeling uncomfortable discussing the subject with them.

'Well, that's not even the oddest aspect of these files,' Anne continued, glancing down at the page. 'These reports also give an account of future dates. According to the information here, in ten years' time you're apparently going to be retired and teaching mathematics at a private school.'

Lethbridge-Stewart would have laughed, had he felt able to muster a sense of humour. 'Ludicrous,' he muttered.

'There are all kinds of other mistakes, a reference to the first probe landing on Mars, saying it is due to occur later this year, whereas that goal was achieved by the Soviet Union almost three years ago now. Or simple factual errors, like saying the United Kingdom currently has a Conservative government, even though Labour are in power.'

Lethbridge-Stewart shook his head. 'Those files are clearly nonsense,' he declared. 'False intel, designed to distract us. A complete waste of time.'

'I don't think so. I think it's evidence of something far more worrying.'

Before she could explain further, Bishop hit the brake pedal, causing the Land Rover to lurch to a halt.

'Sir!' he hollered.

Lethbridge-Stewart swung around in his seat, once again facing the road ahead of them, to see what had made Bishop brake so abruptly.

They had stopped on one of the city's central streets, facing towards the Berlin Wall, with a clear view down the road towards Checkpoint Charlie. The road was filled with chaos. An American military jeep, parked across both lanes, was ablaze. A dozen green and white police cars were attempting to block the side roads. A handful of soldiers, in British, French and American military uniforms, were fleeing towards them. Some had stopped, using their rifles to fire back the way they had come, in the hope of enabling their allies to escape.

In the distance, a line of Soviet Tanks was trundling through the abandoned checkpoint, impervious to the rifle shots being fired at them. Lethbridge-Stewart stared, not quite able to believe what he was seeing.

The large armoured vehicles were not the standard T-64 design with which he was familiar, they were something new which, despite their vast bulk, were moving with surprising speed and agility. Their main turrets, carrying both a massive main barrel and a hefty machine gun mount, were also covered in an array of metal pods, tubes and other devices that were completely unknown to him.

'What's happening?' Bishop asked, his voice muted with shock.

'They've crossed the border!' Marsh said in a horrified tone. 'But they can't! They just can't!'

Lethbridge-Stewart shook his head. 'They have, they've finally done it,' he said, unable to deny the evidence of his own eyes, as he watched the machine gunner of the lead tank turn his weapon on the soldiers in the road before him. The weapon spat white-hot bullets at the brave men, cutting them down. 'The Soviet Union has plunged us into war.'

Bishop threw the Land Rover into reverse, backing up as fast as he dared, desperate to get them away from the carnage unfolding before them.

'How could they do this?' he asked, turning about in his seat, so that he could see where he was going. 'It's madness! Even if the creature has given them incredible weapons, millions could die.'

'Billions,' Anne quietly corrected him, looking up from the folder.

'It's inhuman.' Bishop brought the Land Rover around, before throwing it back into forward gear and driving off in a random direction.

Lethbridge-Stewart nodded. 'Alien, perhaps,' he suggested. 'This must be exactly what the creature wanted.'

Marsh gave a little snort. 'What easier way to wipe out the human race, than just handing us the weapons and letting us get on with the job.'

Lethbridge-Stewart nodded. 'No wonder the creature chose to ally itself with the Soviet Union rather than Britain. We are far too principled; we would never have allowed this sort of thing to happen.'

Anne laughed. 'Listen to yourselves,' she chided them. 'Such a lack of imagination. You can't imagine anything worse than tanks and bombs.'

Lethbridge-Stewart scowled, turning to look at her, to find her glaring back at him. With his temper already frayed, he was in no mood to tolerate criticism. 'If you can make this appalling situation seem any better, do please speak up,' he thundered. 'Because things look pretty damn bleak to me!'

'Better?' she said, shaking her head. 'Oh no, as bad as you think things are right now, I assure you they're far worse. If I'm understanding this file correctly, our enemy is not just unleashing death and destruction in a chaotic manner, it is in fact a carefully considered and orchestrated plan to subdue and control the human race. Our way of life, every freedom we take for granted, is in the process of being erased forever.'

Lethbridge-Stewart shook his head, his patience exhausted, feeling utterly overwhelmed by everything happening around them. 'What the blazes are you talking about, Anne?'

She waved the open folder in his face. 'These files document a past that never happened, along with a future that can now never be. Isn't it obvious what's happened? I should have guessed the moment Miss Volskaya started rambling on about level-nine technology and faster-than-light travel! Rostov even told us it was sharing its technology with them.'

Lethbridge-Stewart blinked, his mind reeling, finally pulling the facts together even as Anne voiced her conclusion.

'The Soviet Union has access to time travel technology,' she stated, slamming the folder closed. 'They've seen the future. They've changed the past. They're rewriting the reality we live in.' Anne paused, looking at Lethbridge-Stewart, as the enormity of her words sunk in. 'The Cold War is over,' she said slowly, stressing her point, 'because we can't win a game of brinkmanship, not when our opponent knows exactly what is going to happen and can correct their every mistake.'

# CHAPTER TEN

*The Most Dangerous Man in the World*

BISHOP PARKED the bullet-scarred Land Rover in the loading bay of a factory. The fuel gauge was riding close to empty, the engine whining and the axels grinding. If he restarted it, he doubted it would get far. Inside the factory gates, with the daylight dimming, the vehicle was concealed from any enemy forces passing on the nearby road.

Lethbridge-Stewart left them, hurrying off across the yard, saying he was going to investigate an 'option'. Bishop was left behind, to protect Anne and Marsh, as they continued to decipher the stolen files. He gripped a loaded revolver in his hand, but he wasn't sure what use it would be if they were discovered; he could hardly fight off an entire army on his own. He only knew that he was prepared to lay down his life if it meant Anne could get to safety. Samantha deserved to have at least one parent.

Through the broken windscreen, he had a view down over the heart of Berlin, where numerous buildings were ablaze. As the sky darkened, it reddened with the glare of the flames. The world seemed to be burning before his eyes. There were intermittent bursts of gunfire echoing across the city, but any significant resistance had long since fallen silent, crushed by the invading forces.

The sun vanished beneath the horizon and he turned on the Land Rover's interior light, despite fearing it would make them visible from the road.

Anne needed the light to work.

The passenger door suddenly sprang open, and Lethbridge-Stewart clambered back into the vehicle, his face set in an expression of grim determination.

'Right, I have a plan,' he announced boldly, glancing around their worried faces. 'But you're not going to like it.'

Anne shrugged. 'Just as long as you can get us home.'

Lethbridge-Stewart winced. 'Well, that's just it, I don't think I can. As I see it, we have only one option, which is to go on the offensive. Last time I spoke to General Hamilton, his orders were quite clear; if we could not reach a diplomatic solution, then this threat was to be eliminated by force. Everything that has happened, everything you have inferred from that file, has merely reinforced my belief that such a response is required. As we cannot run, I propose we strike directly at the source of the problem. We head into the Soviet Union, with the objective of destroying both the ship and the creature.' His suggestion was met by stark silence. 'If you have any objections, you need to voice them now.'

Anne leaned forward. 'That's insane.'

Bishop was inclined to agree with her, but he did not say so, as he could never bring himself to criticise his commanding officer in such a manner. Heading eastwards was the last thing he wanted to do, but as a soldier he could understand the impulse to strike such a target. They were a military unit, at what was now undoubtedly a time of war. Lethbridge-Stewart's mind had immediately switched gear, deciding on the best military strategy, intent on completing his mission. For him, there were no other concerns.

Marsh unfolded the schematic from the folder. 'We do know the location of the base in Irkutsk, sir.'

Anne shook her head. 'That's what...' She glanced at the fold-out, doing a hurried mental estimate. '...three or four *thousand* miles, through enemy territory, during wartime. We'd never make it.'

Lethbridge-Stewart shook his head. 'This is a covert military unit, already deployed behind the main national borders, we are ideally situated to make such an attempt. We have the skills, the training, the experience. The only question is, do we have the will?'

Anne shook her head. 'You have no back-up, no supplies, no authority to do this.'

'Back-up, no. However, we do have supplies; you'll find a small cache of useful odds and ends in a box in the back with

109

you. As to the authority, our official mandate gives me unilateral power against any threat to the United Kingdom. This situation most certainly fulfils that remit.'

Bishop shook his head. 'The Land Rover won't make it to the end of the road, sir. Besides, it would stand-out like a sore thumb on the other side of the border. And how do we even get out of West Berlin? It would have been difficult in peacetime, let alone now, sir.'

Lethbridge-Stewart nodded. 'I have a plan. It will mean abandoning this vehicle, taking whatever resources we can carry, heading out on foot and acquiring new transport once we're beyond the wall. But once we've begun, there will be no turning back, which is why I need to be sure every member of this team is fully committed to seeing this mission through to the end, no matter the cost.'

He glanced at each of their faces, his blue eyes judging them, daring them to disappoint him.

Marsh responded first. 'Are you ordering us on this mission, sir? Or are you asking for volunteers?'

'It is an order, Sergeant Major, but I need more than just blind obedience. I need to know that you understand what is at stake. I need to know I can rely on you to do your duty.'

Marsh nodded. 'At a moment like this, to protect everything we know, it will be an honour to serve, sir.'

Lethbridge-Stewart nodded, pleased by her enthusiasm. His eyes flicked to Bishop.

Bishop's every instinct was to obey the order, but instead he looked to Anne for guidance. While his loyalty to his country and fellow soldiers was absolute, he could not bring himself to ignore his other responsibilities, particularly with Anne sitting so close. He looked at her with pleading eyes, needing her to comply, saving him from the impossible choice between following orders and protecting her.

Anne's face remained grim. 'I don't need to follow your orders, Brigadier. I'm here under duress. I just want to go home. I need to get back to Samantha.'

Lethbridge-Stewart glanced away, looking out at the burning skyline of the city. 'That's not an option,' he said softly. 'I suppose you may be able to find somewhere to take shelter, avoid the immediate fighting, but I wouldn't rate your chances of getting home, even with Bishop's help.'

Bishop looked away, unable to make eye contact with either of them, desperately hoping neither of them would involve him in their discussion.

Anne shook her head in despair. 'The worst thing is, I know you need me. If you go without me, it will be nothing but blood and thunder, with little chance of success. At least if I'm there, there's a chance you might find a way to deal with the situation.' She wiped away a single stray tear. 'So, really, what choice do I have?'

Bishop bowed his head.

There was the decision, once again seeming inevitable, carrying them further from home and deeper into danger. The decisions seemed to be falling like dominos, toppling in an unstoppable sequence, racing towards an end that none of them wanted.

'Then I can count on you, Anne?' Lethbridge-Stewart pressed.

Anne nodded, the anguish fading from her face, replaced with an emotionless expression as hard as steel. 'Of course.'

Lethbridge-Stewart glanced from her to Bishop. 'And you, Major?'

'Yes, sir. You can always count on me.'

'Good man. Now, grab what gear you can and follow me.'

Raiding the cache of supplies hidden in the back of the Land Rover, Bishop found a surprisingly large array of weaponry, including a Lee-Enfield Rifle. It wouldn't be much use in close combat, but using its telescopic sights, it could be lethal at long range. Given it was in their best interests to move with stealth, rather than risk open confrontation, he hoped it would prove to be a better choice than any of the heavier weapons he was leaving behind.

Tucked in among the other munitions there was a small wooden crate, which had the words 'C-4 Explosives' stencilled in neat black letters on its side.

'Those aren't standard issue,' Bishop observed.

Lethbridge-Stewart gave him a curt nod, as he picked a handful of electric torches out of a small haversack, handing one to each of them.

'I did plan for less-than-ideal contingencies, nothing quite like this of course, but if we had been able to get legitimate access to the ship and creature, I wanted to make sure we had the tools for all eventualities.'

Anne scowled at him. 'If I'd known that was your expectation, I really would never have come.'

'Which is why I didn't tell you. As I said, you represent our hope for the best. My duty was to plan for the worst.'

Lethbridge-Stewart took the explosives and detonator out of the box, placing them in the now empty haversack, which he then hoisted up onto his shoulder.

Bishop glanced around their little group. Under normal circumstances he would have felt they were well enough equipped to take on any opponent, but having seen the vast resources and manpower of the enemy, their little group suddenly seemed woefully inadequate.

'Ready?' Lethbridge-Stewart asked. He did not wait for a response. 'Let's go.'

Professor Grey sat quietly aboard an Antonov transport plane, trying not to draw attention to himself, as his armed guards didn't have the gentlest of dispositions. Any time he did anything unexpected or unwanted, they responded by pushing and manhandling him, forcing him into whatever position they wanted.

On the positive side, nobody had shot him yet. On the negative side, his wrists were still locked in steel cuffs.

The Soviet aircraft was similar in design to the Hercules but, despite being much smaller, seemed to be packed with far more resources. As they had dragged him aboard, he'd glimpsed several pieces of modern electronic equipment, far more advanced than anything aboard its British counterpart.

To his right-hand side there was a small window, overlooking the dark airfield outside, which seemed to be receiving a constant stream of Soviet military aircraft.

Zoya Volskaya had taken the seat to his left, presenting a barrier between him and the soldiers, which he assumed was a deliberate ploy to prevent any accidental hostility breaking out. She had so far proven to be an exceptional shield, as none of the soldiers dared come near her, all of them treating her with respect.

Despite her seemingly benevolent nature, they had still not exchanged a single word of communication, the language barrier proving insurmountable.

Seeing General Rostov boarding the plane, Grey decided it was time to take a risk. He needed new information, something to keep him preoccupied during the flight, as otherwise he would be consumed by anxiety, worrying about his own fate and that of the rest of the team.

'Hey!' he hollered, rising to his feet, trying to capture the general's attention. 'Would you answer one question for me?'

Rostov glanced at him, his eyes cold and dismissive, as if Arty were nothing more than an irritation. Which was quite possibly true. If so, he intended to remain as irritating as possible. Based on what he had seen on the streets of Berlin, this man had just started a war which would threaten the lives of millions, so if Arty could annoy him even for a moment, he would do so with pride.

'I do not need to answer your questions,' Rostov replied. 'I answer to nobody. History will be my only judge.'

Arty feigned a nod and a smile, trying to look impressed by the man's pretentious words, then ploughed on with his original question. 'Why attack Berlin now? Why risk war with the West?'

Rostov snorted. 'There will be no war. Neither your government nor the Americans have the stomach for it. It is but half a city, which they have long since stopped caring about. They are too preoccupied with other squabbles; your experiences in Northern Ireland and Vietnam have removed any appetite for conflict, turning your populations into cowering pacifists. They will let Berlin fall. They will allow this to happen, rather than risk escalating the confrontation further. They will voice their anger, make threats, impose a few meaningless sanctions, but they will take no decisive action. In their complacent apathy, they will weaken, while we will grow stronger.'

The man's eyes flared proudly. He began to turn away.

Arty laughed, mockingly. It was a deliberately offensive gesture, designed to provoke an angry response. Similar psychological tactics had worked for Anne in the meeting, so he felt sure they would work now, when Rostov was pumped full of arrogance and adrenaline.

'So, it's nothing more than a bit of needlessly aggressive posturing?' He laughed, ignoring the fact that Miss Volskaya was yanking at the sleeve of his sheepskin coat, frantically trying to make him sit down.

Rostov turned back to him, looking amused. 'You cannot understand.' He smiled. 'Berlin is no mere trophy. You doubtless cannot imagine it, but this conquered and divided city, which was in ruins only twenty-five years ago, had the potential to become the heart of a grand new European alliance. Now, I have ripped out that heart, denied that future from ever happening. A small move in a large game, which helps tip the balance of power from you to us, reshaping the future, triggering the collapse of capitalism. It may take many years, but as far as history is concerned, it is the long game that reaps the greatest rewards.'

Arty shook his head. 'I didn't ask *why*, I asked why *now*. Why the rush? I'll tell you, shall I? You attacked Berlin because you're afraid. You bungled your attempt to grab Lethbridge-Stewart and the rest, so now you've put an entire city to the sword, just to get your hands on them. How secure can your power be, if you're that scared of us? You're terrified that they'll find a way to neutralise your new alien friend, eliminating the advantages it gives you.'

Arty hoped he hadn't said too much, revealing the extent of his knowledge, the last thing he wanted to do was put Miss Volskaya's life in danger. Right now, she was his only ally.

Rostov shook his head. 'Only a fool would underestimate Brigadier Lethbridge-Stewart. I am not that fool. To me, Lethbridge-Stewart is the most dangerous man in the world, a rogue element that could get us all killed if his actions cannot be controlled and contained. I therefore do not deem my actions to be excessive at all.'

Arty took a breath. 'And did you get him?'

Rostov shrugged. 'He is trapped in West Berlin, behind the most secure border in the world, with thousands of our troops searching for him. What hope do you think he stands? It is only a matter of time before he's caught.'

Rostov waved a dismissive hand in the air, this time

making it quite clear that their conversation was terminated. Arty didn't want to push his luck any further; he had the information he needed, so he quietly retook his seat, watching as the general continued to the front of the plane.

Arty smiled.

The rest of the team were alive and free. His gambit had worked. Dealing with him had kept Bugayev and his men busy, enabling his friends to escape. No matter his own personal fate, that was a relief, particularly given how great a threat Rostov seemed to deem them.

As he leaned back in his seat, Arty heard the engines start up, then begin thrumming as the plane lurched down the runway. He felt the wheels leave the ground.

Beside him, Miss Volskaya leaned in towards him.

'Brigadier Lethbridge-Stewart,' she whispered.

He blinked. They were the first words she had spoken which he understood. He rolled his eyes. Of course! He had been such an idiot. Some names, where there was no translation, would be the same in both languages.

They finally had a starting point for communication.

As the plane banked around, Miss Volskaya gestured out of the window. 'Berlin.'

Arty nodded, gratefully. She was telling him that Lethbridge-Stewart was alive and at liberty in the city below.

'Arthur Grey? Zoya Volskaya?' he enquired, throwing his cuffed hands in the direction of the cockpit, hoping she would understand.

She nodded. 'Irkutskiy,' she replied.

Arty nodded. He understood. They were on their way to Irkutsk, a region of eastern Siberia. At least now he knew where they were going.

Anne turned on her torch, keeping the light focused on the battered Land Rover, so that her husband could see what he was doing, as he strapped a large piece of tarpaulin across the top of the vehicle. Having completed the task, Bill gave her a nod of thanks, and he turned on his own torch. With his one free hand, he squeezed her upper arm.

'It's going to be all right,' he whispered.

It was a lie, but she loved him for it. They needed to remain hopeful, so until their situation improved, false hope would have to suffice.

'I know,' she said, knowing the lie had to work both ways. She couldn't have him fretting about how she was coping. He needed to be focused on keeping them alive. 'We'll find a way.'

Lethbridge-Stewart and Marsh had already hurried away across the factory loading bay, with their torches on, the beams of light carving out a path through the darkness. Anne and Bill hurried after them, quickly catching up when they came to a sudden halt.

'So,' Anne called, capturing Lethbridge-Stewart's pale face in the glare of her torch-beam. 'How are you going to get us to the other side of the Berlin Wall?'

A sly smile slid across his face. 'By going underground,' he replied, his torch beam coming to rest on a rusted iron manhole cover at his feet. 'Via the sewers.'

'Marvellous,' she muttered, looking at the metal covering with disgust. 'Just when I think things can't possibly get any worse, you manage to find a way. You have a real knack for disappointing me.'

Marsh put down her jerrycan of diesel, so she could set about opening the manhole. Using the wheel brace from the Land Rover as a make-shift crowbar, she pried open the metal covering, which she swiftly rolled out of the way. Lethbridge-Stewart immediately swung himself down into the opening, using a series of iron rungs in the wall to descend into the brick-lined passage beneath.

'It can't be that simple, can it?' Anne asked, as Marsh ushered her towards the hole, helping her down onto the first rung.

Lethbridge-Stewart kept his torch beam on the ladder, so she could see where to place her feet.

'Simple solutions are often the best,' he explained, helping her down from the bottom rung.

Anne shone her torch down the tunnel.

The dry brick floor sloped downwards for perhaps twenty feet, before bisecting with another tunnel, where it dropped beneath a slow-moving, glistening, brown surface. A thick, revolting smell assaulted her nostrils.

'I can't believe I'm actually doing this,' she muttered,

wrinkling her nose. 'I think I'd almost rather be shot.'

'Needs must,' Lethbridge-Stewart responded, as he finished helping Bill and Marsh down the ladder. 'It's amazing what people will do when the alternative is a bullet.'

He strode forward, following the tunnel downwards, stepping out into the river of filth. His polished shoes disappeared beneath the surface, leaving him knee-deep in foul water. He gave one brief cough, but otherwise showed no signs of the revulsion he had to be feeling.

'You're sure it leads to the other side of the border?' Anne asked, following him as far as the edge of the water, to shine her torch down into the next tunnel. The passageway curved away into the darkness, the slow-moving river flowing against their direction of travel, with no sign of any further exits.

Lethbridge-Stewart nodded. 'The sewer system predates the Berlin Wall. All the sewage treatment plants are in the west of the city, and rather than going to the expense of building new ones, the Soviet civic authorities decided to keep using them. Meaning, in short, that these sewer tunnels still link the east and west sides of the city.'

He waded forward, leading the way, disappearing around the bend.

Marsh stepped forward, plunging her shoes into the water, following him into the darkness. Bill, his face lit by torchlight, gave Anne an encouraging smile.

Reluctantly, she stepped into the water.

Slip-ons were definitely the wrong kind of shoe for wading through sewage. The rancid water stung her ankles and calves. Despite her discomfort, she hurried after the others, desperate to remain close to the light of their torches. One misplaced step in the darkness, leading to a trip or fall, was too horrible to contemplate.

'But if these tunnels do link the two sides of the city, surely people would have used them to escape?' she asked, keen to distract herself from the task at hand. 'No matter how repellent, it would surely be far safer than scaling the wall, or trying to get smuggled across the border, where there would always be armed guards.'

'They did use it,' Lethbridge-Stewart replied. 'In the weeks after the Wall went up in '61, a group of school children got a number of their friends out via this route. After that, a more sophisticated student organisation commandeered it, getting many more people out, until one night the East German police put a stop to it.'

Anne shone her torch directly at him, as he turned into a side tunnel, beginning a slow ascent upwards. He blinked in the glare of her beam.

'They know about this route then?' she asked, as the little group followed him into the new tunnel, finally stepping out of the water onto a dry brick ramp. 'They closed it off?'

'Yes.' Lethbridge-Stewart came to a halt. 'Let me show you.'

He lifted his torch beam upwards, pointing it at the ceiling, revealing the rusted underside of a circular manhole cover. Unlike the one on the Western side of the city, which had been designed to be easily lifted, this one was just a lump of solid metal, with no openings that would make it susceptible to a crowbar or hacksaw. Lethbridge-Stewart climbed up two metal rungs fixed into the brickwork, then placed his hand on the covering, pushing at it with all his strength.

It did not move.

He glanced down at them. 'When Churchill first described an Iron Curtain falling across Europe, it was a rather poetic metaphor, but this is the hard truth of it,' he said, as he climbed back down the ladder and dusted off his hands. 'A block of solid iron, to stop people fleeing down a sewer.'

Anne raised her eyebrows. 'And, if it has held everyone else back, how are we supposed to get through it?'

Gazing upwards at the manhole cover, Lethbridge-Stewart's eyes sparkled with a look of calculation. 'What do you think?' he asked, turning to look at Marsh. 'Can you blow it?'

'Yes, sir.'

'Without bringing the tunnel down on us?'

Marsh hesitated, then nodded. 'A quarter of a stick of C-4 will probably be enough to flip it, without causing too much structural damage to the tunnel.'

Anne didn't like her uncertainty. Lethbridge-Stewart chose to ignore it.

'Very good. Make us a way out, Sergeant Major.'

# CHAPTER ELEVEN
### Behind the Iron Curtain

LETHBRIDGE-STEWART CROUCHED in the sewer tunnel, his fingers pressed into his ears, waiting for the explosion. He saw the flash, then felt the jolt, as a rain of dust fell from the ceiling. Removing his fingers from his ears, he rose to his feet and sprinted up the tunnel to see if they had succeeded.

The manhole cover was gone. He was staring up at a patch of stars. He heard a sharp clang in the distance, as the manhole cover impacted on the ground.

He immediately clambered up the iron rungs.

They would not have long.

The noise of the explosion would attract attention.

Surfacing into a suburban street, he drew his revolver, and looked about for signs of danger. The road was lit by tall sodium streetlamps, casting a soft orange glow across everything. The sky to the west was bleached red, despite the sun having already set, the light of the burning buildings silhouetting several tall columns of black smoke on the skyline.

There was no sign of any of the inhabitants of the city. The residents were doubtless cowering indoors, hiding from the violence that was occurring mere streets away.

'All clear,' he declared, as Bishop surfaced from the hole, taking up a defensive stance beside him, his rifle held ready. 'Start passing that gear up.'

Marsh dutifully obeyed, handing up the jerrycan, so that she could use both hands to climb.

Anne was last out of the hole. She had a worried, frightened look, like a rabbit ready to run. Lethbridge-Stewart felt genuinely sorry for her. She was not a soldier, yet he needed to treat her like one, if they were to stand any chance of surviving the days ahead. He could only hope that she would rise to the standard.

'This way!' he barked.

He led them down a side street, heading eastwards, keen to put as much distance between them and their entrance point as quickly as possible. Once that was done, their next objective would be to procure transport, preferably something with a large fuel tank, capable of transporting them over long distances.

He ignored the numerous boxy-looking Trabant cars parked along the kerbside, which he knew were exceedingly basic vehicles, mass-produced as cheaply as possible for the citizens of East Germany. He had no faith in their durability, knowing that even the locals mocked them as being nothing but a sparkplug with a roof.

'Sir!' Marsh called, keeping her voice hushed.

She made a signalling motion with her hand, directing his attention down a side street, towards a large military lorry parked across the end of the road. It was a massive six-wheeler with a tarpaulin shell covering a large cargo area behind the main cabin. The driver's door was ajar, the interior light burning brightly.

It was perfect for their needs.

Lethbridge-Stewart crouched down, raising a hand, giving the field-signal for those behind him to hold. He glanced around, looking for any sign of the driver, but could see nobody. The lorry was deliberately positioned to serve as a temporary roadblock, stopping traffic entering the main intersection from the side street, presumably to ensure the uninterrupted movement of military vehicles on the main road. If it had been there for a while, the driver may have wandered away, but the open door very much implied he had not gone far.

Continuing to use silent hand signals, he directed Marsh towards the driver's cabin, while he circled around to the back of the vehicle. He left Bishop, along with his wife, holding a position behind the nearest Trabant, covering them with his rifle.

Arriving at the rear of the truck, Lethbridge-Stewart

found several stacks of supply crates, partially unloaded in the street. The vehicle was presumably doubling as a supply point for the advancing forces. He checked inside the covered cargo area, then glanced down the other streets, but he could find no sign of the elusive driver.

Marsh signalled him from the driver's cabin. He gave her a swift nod.

She started the engine, which thrummed quietly, causing a waft of diesel fumes to erupt from the exhaust pipe. He hurriedly signalled to Bishop, who immediately dashed forward, followed closely by Anne. Lethbridge-Stewart helped them both into the back of the vehicle, then raised the tail gate, bolting it into position.

He allowed himself a half-smile, unable to believe how well things were going. He turned, hurrying along the side of the lorry, heading for the passenger door. Once aboard, that would be it, they would be on their way, swiftly vanishing into the vastness of the Soviet Union.

'*Ey!*' A voice yelled from the darkness ahead of them. '*Shto vi delayete?*'

Marsh abruptly turned on the lorry's headlamps, flooding the area in front of them in light, revealing a young Soviet soldier emerging from an alleyway. He was hurriedly rebuckling his belt, having been caught in the middle of answering the call of nature.

Lethbridge-Stewart dashed towards the passenger door.

The young soldier, squinting against the dazzling headlamps, unslung a rifle from his shoulder, clumsily turning it towards them.

'Don't do anything stupid!' Lethbridge-Stewart yelled, changing tack, bringing his revolver to bare. 'Put the rifle down!'

Not understanding, the young soldier aimed his rifle at Marsh, desperate to stop his vehicle from being stolen. Lethbridge-Stewart never liked taking a human life. He avoided it wherever possible but, in that moment, there seemed to be no other choice. If the young soldier fired first, Marsh would be dead. The mission compromised.

Lethbridge-Stewart squeezed his trigger.

*

The Antonov was buffeted by strong crosswinds during its descent.

After such a turbulent landing, Zoya felt glad to be back on the ground.

The red glow of dawn bled in through the little window beside them, as the gigantic aircraft slowed to a halt, its vast propellers slowly spinning to a stop.

General Rostov was the first to disembark, followed by numerous men, including Minister Gorbenko. Zoya waited her turn, making sure Arthur Grey stayed close beside her.

As she emerged from the plane, the first thing she noticed was the drop in temperature; her coat failed to provide much protection from the freezing Siberian wind. The Irkutsk Oblast was a frigid place, far colder than the more temperate climates of Berlin and Moscow. The runway had been shovelled free of snow, but the ground around it was a pristine white, which seemed to glow under the newly risen sun. She shivered, pulling her coat tighter, as she descended the steps from the plane to the tarmac.

Rostov stood on the runway, looking agitated.

Their arrival had been greeted by several armed soldiers, who seemed unimpressed by their ranks and credentials, presenting a barrier to them going any further into the base. Salutes were exchanged, but they were a mere formality, which did nothing to conceal the friction between the two sides.

'You exceed your authority, Captain Alexeyev,' Rostov seethed. 'I am your superior officer.'

'This is a secure facility. You are not authorised to be here, sir.'

General Rostov's fists clenched and unclenched. 'I am the commander of the Berlin occupation,' he growled. 'I have full access to any resources I need, authorised at the highest possible levels in Moscow, including access to this base. I must be allowed to see our visitor!'

Captain Alexeyev shook his head. 'We have been unable to verify your claim to such authority. Moscow is not responding. We have intel that suggests that many of the Politburo and Central Committee, including the Chairman, are missing. My superior officers are trying to establish the true chain-of-command.'

Rostov glared at the soldier. 'Gorbenko!' he called. 'Show them your identity papers.'

The old minister shuffled forward, obediently complying with the order. 'I am a representative of the Central Committee. Given we are at war, I am vouching for this man's authority; he should be considered the acting Chairman of the Presidium, at least until some form of normality is resumed.'

Zoya stared at the man in disbelief.

From once defiantly attempting to block Rostov's rise to power, he had passed through a period of defeated apathy, to now surface as an advocate for his former opponent. He was not just turning his back on his former beliefs, he was betraying them.

Captain Alexeyev glanced through the minister's papers, barely looking at the words, then handed them back. Whatever choice he made, it was not going to be based on any legal document, but on his instincts as a soldier.

'What are your orders, sir?'

Rostov gave the man a thin smile. 'I am assuming command of this base. If any officer voices dissent, they are to be arrested. Understood?'

'Yes, sir.'

'You will show me the way to the recently acquired alien vessel, immediately.'

'Yes, sir.'

Captain Alexeyev turned on his heel, leading the party away from the plane, towards a pair of large hangers at the far end of the runway. As they moved forward, Zoya hooked an arm around Minister Gorbenko's elbow, pulling him several steps backward, so they were out of earshot of the others.

'How could you do that?' she whispered. 'If you had spoken out, stood by your beliefs, you could have put an end to this.'

Gorbenko gave a shrug. 'It's too late now. We are past the point of no return. Rostov must have his way. I find it good to see the Soviet Union once again ascending into glory, expanding to fulfil its potential, rather than slowly decaying away. I can find solace in that. As an old man, it is good to have one last great day, regardless of the risks.'

Zoya shook her head, finding no comfort in his words. 'You may not have long left, but the rest of us will have to live a lifetime with the consequences of your choice,' she said, letting go of the old man's arm, feeling revolted. 'You are a traitor to the Soviet Union.'

Gorbenko gave her a wan smile. 'Yet if you were to speak any louder, it would be you who were arrested as the traitor, it is your perspective that is at odds with his. However, for some reason, he does not see it, he is blind to your disloyalty, will not hear of it, despite it being obvious to the rest of us. You would do well to learn to hide it, or it will cost you everything.' He sighed, shaking his head, aware that he was doing little to convince her. 'Ideals are so easy for the young. As you get older, you will learn it is better to compromise. See which way the wind is blowing and go with it. Do not waste your time and energy fighting the inevitable. Accept it. Find a way to make the best of the hand you are dealt.'

The old man strolled onwards, attempting to distance himself from her, the snow crunching beneath his polished shoes.

Zoya let him go.

Perhaps he was right. Perhaps it was time for her to acquiesce. She had done all she could. She should just concentrate on her work, focus on staying in favour. As she stood shivering in the snow, she knew it was the only sensible choice left to her. What could she possibly hope to achieve on her own?

Lethbridge-Stewart opened his eyes.

He must have nodded off. As a soldier, he had learned to fall asleep almost anywhere, whenever he got the chance. Sleep was a valuable resource, not to be underestimated. He needed to grab what rest he could, because when trouble came, he needed to be ready to deal with it.

They were driving eastwards, directly into the glare of the freshly risen sun. He knocked down the sun visor, so that he was not staring directly into the dazzling dawn light, which had woken him up.

Marsh was behind the steering wheel, her eyes fixed on

the road ahead. She yawned. She had driven through the night.

The vehicle's radio was turned on, with the volume extremely low, presumably so it would not wake him. She was listening to the state-run news channel, one of only four radio stations that were available in the Soviet Union as all other broadcasts were blocked by a vast network of jamming transmitters.

'Where are we?' Lethbridge-Stewart asked, looking at the pine trees that flanked both sides of the road.

Marsh picked up a map from the dashboard and passed it to him. 'The Ukrainian Soviet Socialist Republic,' she informed him. 'We just passed through Kiev. You slept through most of Poland.'

Lethbridge-Stewart looked at the map. They were still thousands of miles from their target.

'Fuel?' he asked.

'Running on fumes, sir. I'm going to pull in shortly, use the jerrycan from the Land Rover, which should buy us about another seventy miles or so.'

Lethbridge-Stewart continued studying the map. 'This shows their main supply lines, used to support their advancing forces; logically all of these routes must have numerous military fuel depots.'

Marsh nodded. 'It's why I chose this road, sir.' She gave a small shrug. 'I think my Russian is good enough to bluff it, convince them to give us what we need. With any luck nobody is looking for us this deep into their territory, so there's no reason for them to be suspicious, particularly given we'll be turning up in one of their own trucks.'

Lethbridge-Stewart nodded.

It might work.

'I can see only one problem with your plan,' he remarked, feeling awkward about raising her obvious error.

'Sir?'

'Well, you're a young lady,' he ventured cautiously, 'and I can't imagine there are a lot of women serving in the Soviet Union's Armed Forces.'

Generally, he preferred to avoid discussing such delicate issues, finding those kinds of conversations with the fairer sex akin to taking a stroll through a minefield.

Marsh glanced sideways at him, seeming amused by his discomfort. 'You realise the constitution of the Soviet Union guarantees equality for women?'

Lethbridge-Stewart raised an eyebrow. 'I did not.'

'It didn't stick of course.' She shrugged. 'Those rights were eroded away, but women are still allowed to serve as military reservists, brought into action during times of conflict.'

'Like now?'

She nodded. 'Exactly.' She tilted her head towards a large fur-lined military coat thrown over the back of the driver's seat. 'So, if I wear that over my uniform, I shouldn't be too conspicuous. If you wear the uniform we took from the driver, hopefully together it'll be enough to convince them we're just a standard supply truck. Just make sure you stay inside and leave the talking to me.'

Lethbridge-Stewart considered the plan. 'Risky,' he muttered. 'However, if subterfuge fails, we can always take what we need by force. I doubt the more remote supply depots will be well defended.'

Marsh glanced at him, her brow furrowing with concern, before turning back to the road, obviously reluctant to speak her mind.

'What is it, Sergeant Major?'

'Well, sir,' she began hesitantly. 'Are you sure we're doing the right thing?'

'I am.'

Marsh gestured towards the radio. 'It's just they're saying the West are suing for peace, trying to de-escalate the crisis. If we blaze a trail of violence across their homeland, don't we risk undermining that process? Isn't this perhaps a moment to reconsider, a chance to turn back, sir?'

Lethbridge-Stewart shook his head. 'I'm afraid it's far too late for that,' he said, turning off the radio. 'If our assessment of the situation is correct, if the Soviet Union does have access to time travel technology, this may be our only chance to destroy it. I doubt we'll ever get another. How could we possibly co-exist with an opponent that has such a weapon? Any move we make could be countered, possibly before it is even considered, blindsiding them with a sting attack is the only logical option. We must press on.'

Marsh drove in silence for a moment, obviously considering her response.

'But time travel?' she said with exasperation. 'I'm mean, the idea is scarcely plausible.'

Lethbridge-Stewart laughed. 'Yes, I was always a sceptic myself, but I've seen enough to know that this must be treated as a credible threat, particularly given their hostile actions.'

'But the logic of it? The implications?' She sighed. 'I just can't get my head around it.'

He nodded, still deeply amused.

'Best not to over think it. I never do. Focus on the here and now, Sergeant Major. We are at war. The alien is contributing to their war effort. It is therefore our duty to eliminate it.'

Marsh nodded. 'But, if they can see the future, wouldn't they know we're coming?'

Lethbridge-Stewart gave a shrug. 'Wars have always been won and lost on intel, and given their lack of action against us, we can assume they do not yet have such information. I'm attributing this to Rostov currently being separated from the ship and creature, it is therefore critical we destroy both before he has the opportunity to check the future again.'

They stared at the empty road ahead of them, knowing how many thousands of miles still lay ahead.

'We're in a race against time,' Marsh muttered, 'which we can't possibly win.'

'Nonetheless, Sergeant Major, we still have to try.'


Zoya followed the others across the snow.

They made their way to the front of one of the hangers, where the soldier opened a rusted iron door, leading the way inside. Despite everything that had happened, Zoya could not help but feel a sense of excitement as she stepped across the threshold, eager to see what secrets lay within.

The building was the repository for all the Soviet Union's most classified material, including all the evidence from every otherworldly encounter she had worked on, plus similar material from numerous other groups. The secrets of the universe would be at her fingertips. She would finally be able to see whether their discoveries were being destroyed, stockpiled, or properly analysed and understood.

As she stepped inside, she felt a surge of horror, appalled by the sights before her.

The forward half of the hanger had been transformed into a set of cells. Some were physical metal cages, others were hermetically sealed glass pods, while yet more were just crude wooden pens. Inside them were countless strange creatures, many of them injured and distressed. The air was foul.

Behind a wall of plastic sheeting, she could see a steel operating table, where a pair of men in coveralls were dissecting the body of one of the Vodyanoy creatures, which she had discovered living in the Lena River. As their scalpel blades sliced into its green scales, it made a shrill squealing sound, clearly still fully conscious during its vivisection. Its long tail thrashed wildly about, until it could no longer endure the pain.

Zoya could also see a dozen of the plant creatures from the Voronezh Oblast, which were all supposed to have been destroyed during the crop incinerations, bumbling blindly about inside a sealed greenhouse. Their frames were stooped, their main stems bent double, their growth restricted by the structure's low roof. Their leaves were brown and wilted, suffering from severe dehydration, caused by the banks of UV lamps surrounding their glass prison.

It was too much horror for her to take in.

She had always worried about the technology they had discovered, hoping it was being cautiously studied, she had never for a moment concerned herself with the fate of the creatures. She had assumed, if they proved unreasonable, they would be humanely destroyed. She had never considered the possibility that they would be kept alive, in horrendous conditions, subjected to years of brutal experimentation and study, before being murdered in the quest for more data. She cursed her naivety. It was not like the Soviet Union to be wasteful with its resources.

General Rostov ignored the scene. He did not even glance at it.

He had seen it before.

It was a disquieting insight. While the site had not previously been under his command, he had been knowingly working alongside it, quietly complicit in the brutality. Now he was in charge, he was happy for it to continue.

She said nothing. She did not dare speak out.

Rostov stalked through the research bays, heading to the far side of the hanger, passing the small wooden hut, which she had helped the military extract from the Dvinsky Forest.

The little, lop-sided cabin was utterly unremarkable, except for the two gigantic metal legs tucked beneath it. Her involvement with the discovery of Baba Yaga's hut had always filled her with pride, as it had proved there was some truth to the fairy tales and folklore of her childhood, but that pride died the moment she realised it had subsequently spent months chained to a set of concrete pillars. It crushed any last remnant of her childish idealism, leaving only brutal reality in its wake.

Passing the last of the enclosures, they emerged out onto a large section of open floor, in which sat the sleek silver vessel she had last seen in Moscow. The rampway stood open.

Rostov pointed a finger at Arty. 'He comes no closer. If you can use him, put him to work on one of these other projects.'

Zoya nodded. 'Of course.'

'In the meantime, you alone are to accompany me into the ship.' He waved a dismissive hand at Gorbenko and the other men. 'The others will remain here.'

Zoya frowned.

She found his behaviour confusing. She could think of no reason why he was continuing to include her, but she would not argue with it. Compliance was the safest option. She was getting exactly what she wanted.

Rostov strode towards the ship. She walked alongside him.

'I need to check on the future,' Rostov muttered in a low and conspiratorial tone, as he began striding up the ramp. 'Fix it, if necessary.'

Zoya frowned, surprised by his sudden candour. 'You said the creature enables you to see the future...?' While he was proving so forthcoming, she was keen to extract as much information from him as possible.

'More than that. It shows me all the possible shapes the future can take, from what is most likely, to the very limits of what I can achieve.'

'And does it also allow you to change the past?'

Rostov nodded. 'By changing it, I have been able to take more radical action in the present, hopefully creating a new destiny for all mankind. We were headed for disaster. Now, I shall see if I have saved us, delivering us all to a glorious new future, led by the Soviet Union.'

'I think I underestimated your ambition,' Zoya muttered.

Rostov frowned, looking disappointed. 'None of this is for my benefit,' he said as he led the way into the unlit interior of the ship. 'It was my duty to try.'

Ahead of them, Zoya could see the creature uncurling in the darkness, rising to meet them. Fearlessly, Rostov strode towards it, not even flinching as its tentacles wrapped around him, lifting him up and cradling him within its inhuman limbs.

As with the first time they had made contact, the embrace lasted only a handful of seconds, but she now wondered how much could have transpired within those few moments. If Rostov's claims were true, he could have slipped forwards or backwards in time, potentially transforming reality around her without her even knowing it.

As the tentacles released him, his knees buckled. Instinctively, Zoya caught him, propping him up.

Rostov was shaking, his skin pale, his eyes wide.

'What's wrong?' Zoya asked.

'The future is not as it should be,' he said, his voice sounding hollow. 'The future I set out to create is not there.'

'I don't understand. What exactly did you see?'

'Nothing. There are no futures anymore. There is only darkness.'

# CHAPTER TWELVE
*The Long Road*

ANOTHER FIFTY miles had come and gone, disappearing beneath the wheels of the stolen military lorry. When Marsh had pulled to a stop on the side of the road to top up the fuel tank from the jerrycan, Lethbridge-Stewart had changed into the dead driver's uniform, who they had unceremoniously dumped behind a bush. If British combat fatigues were a second skin to him, his new apparel was like a hair-shirt, making his skin crawl with every touch.

The jacket had a bullet hole, rimmed in blood. The boots pinched. He placed the Soviet military cap on his head, then looked at himself in the lorry's wing-mirror. He did not like what he saw.

A few days ago, he could never have imagined himself dressed in such clothes, leading his team on what he regarded to be a suicide mission. Events had simply spiralled far beyond his control to this seemingly inevitable outcome.

It was almost as unbelievable to him as the other version of events which Anne had read from the file. In that account, before Rostov and his creature had intervened, these would be days of peace, in which he would have recently married Fiona Campbell. He tried to imagine himself standing beside her in a church, saying his vows, but the image felt absurd.

After Sally, he couldn't imagine himself being involved with anyone else. The Fifth Operational Corps had kept him so busy in recent months, he'd not given such matters a moment of thought, he had simply buried himself in his work. According to Anne, it would seem he had inadvertently chosen a different life for himself, avoiding any relationship with Fiona, without even knowing it. Perhaps it was for the best, given he was not expecting to return home.

'Two roads diverged in a wood,' he muttered to himself, half-remembering a Robert Frost poem, which he had learned by rote at school. 'And it seems I never even saw the turning.'

If they did make it back alive, he would contact Frank Campbell, get him to arrange another meeting between him and Fiona. A dinner-date would be nice.

Marsh climbed back into the driver's seat, slamming the door and restarting the engine, the noise bringing him abruptly back to reality. She was wearing the fur-lined military coat they had found in the cab, which was slightly too big for her, but successfully hid the British regimental dress uniform she wore beneath it.

She glanced at him. 'You might just pass muster,' she said, taking in his Soviet uniform, her eyes momentarily flicking to the bullet hole and then to his face. 'If it weren't for the obvious problem, sir.'

'Oh?'

'The moustache.'

'Oh.'

'Soviet NCOs are generally clean shaven, at least as far as I can tell, whereas your caterpillar screams British military officer. If anyone is looking for us behind enemy lines, it's a clear giveaway. It makes you instantly recognisable, sir,' she said, fishing in the glove box to retrieve a small razor case, which she passed on to him. 'Why make it easy for them, sir?'

Lethbridge-Stewart stared at her. She failed to hide an amused smirk pulling at her lips.

Lethbridge-Stewart sighed. He turned to look at his reflection in the wing mirror again, staring at the carefully groomed arc of black hair on his upper lip.

'The sacrifices I make for my country,' he said, cracking open the leather case. Quietly, he took out the blade, then shaved away both sides of the moustache. The razor was sharp. It was a quick and simple job.

The moment it was done, Marsh stepped on the accelerator, resuming the journey along the road.

Lethbridge-Stewart glanced at his reflection again. He barely recognised the face looking back at him anymore. The moustacheless man really could have come from some other world, with some other life.

Anne felt the lorry slow down. It turned abruptly, and bumped across uneven ground. They were stopping again. They must have found one of the Soviet fuel depots.

She and Bill had to remain hidden, so they had constructed a crude hidey-hole among the crates in the back, which they hoped would be enough to conceal them. In theory no one would have any reason to search the vehicle, so all they had to do was remain silent for the next few minutes, while hopefully everything else went perfectly to plan. They both knew, from extensive experience, that rarely, if ever, happened.

Bill squeezed her hand, trying to comfort her. He reached for his sidearm, removing it from its holster, holding it handle-first towards her. She stared at the weapon.

'Take it,' he whispered. 'Just to protect yourself.'

She shook her head, pushing the weapon away. 'You know how I feel about this, Bill.'

'I know, but it's different this time.'

She smiled up at him, finding the little furrow of confusion on his face to be almost sweet. 'It's never different. I could never use a gun again.'

The lorry lurched to a halt. The engine turned off.

Anne could hear Russian voices outside. At least three or four men, trading comments and laughing, were engaged in some task directly beside the parked vehicle. She couldn't understand a word that was being spoken, but they were clearly at ease, unaware of the danger in their midst.

Beside her, Bill clutched the revolver, while also keeping his rifle close at hand.

She heard Marsh climb out of the cabin and say something in Russian which was met with numerous energetic responses. She replied with a curt comment and then laughed. The Russians joined her in her laughter.

As the mirth subsided, Anne heard the clattering of a fuel cap being removed, then the churning of a pump, as gallons of diesel began refilling their empty fuel tank. Much to her surprise, their plan appeared to be working.

Beside her, Bill used his free hand to reach into one of his pockets, from which he took a small photograph, which he placed into her hands. It was a picture of her, standing in the back garden of their little Edinburgh townhouse, holding a newly born Samantha in her arms. All that was visible of their child was a small pudgy face, peering out of the swaddling, looking up at her with large curious eyes.

Anne had no idea why he was showing her the photograph. Perhaps it was a reminder of what they were fighting for, or perhaps he was simply trying to distract her from the danger. She didn't know. She couldn't ask him. Speaking a single word could get them killed.

Anne stared at the photograph. That safe suburban life felt like a distant memory, or an implausible dream, which she had taken for granted while being part of it, but to which it was now impossible to return. She hadn't appreciated how lucky she was, or how delicate and precious that life had been.

The diesel pump was shut off. She heard the fuel cap being screwed back into place. The driver's door thunked closed. The engine restarted. The lorry lurched forwards.

Everything had gone to plan.

First time for everything, she supposed.

As they pulled away, she dared to give voice to a question, which up until that moment she had not even dared let herself think.

'Once we've done what we need to do, does Alistair actually have a plan to get us out of here? If so, he's not said a word about it.'

Bill shifted uneasily. 'I'm sure he's got something up his sleeve,' he said, in a confident and reassuring tone. 'Besides, we always win in the end, don't we? There's no reason why this time should be any different.'

Sadly, Anne knew him too well. She knew he was lying.

Seeing that she was less than convinced, Bill leaned closer, taking hold of both her hands and folding them around the photograph.

'I promise, everything is going to be fine. I will get us home.'

She wanted to believe him, but in her heart she knew they were just kind and reassuring words, with no evidence to support them.

Arthur Grey was enjoying himself. He couldn't say he was happy, or safe, but he was determined to make the best of a bad situation.

On the first day, the cuffs were removed from his wrists. Everywhere he went, he was shadowed by Warrant Officer Petrov, who served as both his armed guard and his interpreter. Their relationship was initially awkward, with neither of them really understanding how it was supposed to work, but within a few hours the tension had begun to thaw. If Arty had any problems working with the Soviet scientists who were initially wary of his presence, the charismatic officer's charms swiftly put them at ease.

By the second day, Arty was firmly embedded in the team.

Difficulties only arose if he ventured towards the silver ship, whereby Petrov would swiftly navigate him away from it, his hand resting on the holster of his revolver, while pointedly reminding him that he was not allowed to approach the vessel.

Arty did not push his luck.

He found the work fascinating, but he was also aware he was just as much a captive as any of the alien creatures; it was just that they had the capacity to build his cage with words and threats, rather than physical materials. He remained vigilant, looking for a way to escape, but knew that even if he could get away, there was no way he would survive for long in the frozen wilderness of Siberia.

On the third day, Zoya pulled him to one side. Warrant Officer Petrov interpreted her words.

'You must tell me everything that you know about the creature in the craft.'

Petrov's delivery of her words in English was flat and perfunctory. Arty found that whenever the interpreter spoke, it was instinctive to look at him, missing all the non-verbal cues from the person speaking, so he put considerable effort into making sure he kept his gaze locked on Zoya. He could tell far more from a moment of eye contact with her than he could from all her words. She was agitated, her eyes darting nervously about, her forehead crumpled in an anxious frown.

'Why?' he asked.

'Something is wrong. When you first established contact with the creature, did you learn anything that we may not know, can you tell me exactly what happened?'

'Sure.' He shrugged, not wanting to appear uncooperative. 'But, if you really need my help, a full exchange of information would be the best way to start. I can't tell you what you *don't* know, if I don't know what you *do* know. Involve me, give me full access to the creature and the vessel, and I'm sure we can solve whatever problem you have.'

Zoya shook her head. 'General Rostov would never allow that. He is adamant that no one but him must have meaningful contact with the creature.'

Arty laughed. 'Well, that doesn't sound like a healthy relationship, does it? Let me ask you, do you really know anything about this creature at all? Do you even know what it's called? I've never once heard you use a name for it. Just classifications, or vague terms. If our conversation on the plane should teach us anything, it's that names are important, they're a starting point, a way of understanding who or what we're talking about. So, tell me, do you know how it refers to itself? How it defines itself? Is it an ambassador? A soldier? A scientist? A trader? A wandering lunatic? Do you know what it wants? Or why it's here? Or where it came from? Anything at all?'

Zoya stared at him. 'No,' she replied. 'Rostov has kept this information to himself.'

Arty shook his head. 'Has he? Are you sure he even knows? How much communication do you think is really going on between them?'

Zoya's frown deepened as she considered his words. 'The creature has helped him. I have come to understand it has allowed him to change the past, enabling him to accelerate his career, so that he could wield far more power. It's shown him exactly how far he could push that influence, meaning his successes were always assured, if only by the narrowest of margins, or by having the right allies by his side. He's also been able to influence our scientific programme, allowing us to develop weapons and technology years ahead of schedule, giving us the advantage in the Cold War that we needed. We would never have been able to land the probes on Mars yet, not without the head start this gave us in our space programme. So, it was helping him, at least until recently.'

Petrov was trying his best to maintain a neutral expression, but as he repeated her words in English, his eyes were slowly widening, a look of shock and surprise descending on his handsome features.

Arty nodded. 'So, maybe what we've got here is an old-fashioned evil genie, trapped in its lamp. It grants you wishes, but it twists them in ways you can't possibly imagine.'

Zoya shook her head. 'It is an ally of the Soviet Union,' she insisted, but there was doubt in her eyes.

'Is it? As far as I can tell, you've simply used its gifts for your own ends. There's no evidence of mutual need or respect, you've just exploited it as a resource. If so, that's not how friendships and alliances work, they're not a one-way street. You're supposed to put in as much as you take out. Fundamentally, the only way you're ever going to understand that creature, is if you get to know it, figuring out what it is and what it wants, rather than just using it. In simple terms, we need to talk to it.'

'I have told you. General Rostov will never allow that.'

Arty's shoulders slumped. 'Don't take no for an answer. Insist. Persuade him. You're on the same side. You speak the same language. He trusts you. You're the only person who could convince him. Make him listen. Argue for it. Fight for it.' Arty stared her in the eye, while Petrov interpreted his words, keeping his gaze earnest and unwavering. 'You're the only one who can. There is no one else.'

Zoya shook her head. 'I cannot talk to him in such a manner. I do not have such freedoms.'

'And you never will if you don't speak up now… when it can make a difference.'


Lethbridge-Stewart kept his eyes on the road.

The weather had turned against them. A layer of snow, which would have stopped most vehicles, made the road almost indistinguishable from the terrain around it. Fortunately, the lorry's huge tyres were designed to deal with such inhospitable terrain, the six-wheel drive making short work of any ditches or boulders that accidently came into their path whenever they strayed off the road.

Marsh, Bishop and he shared the burden of driving over the four days, but he deliberately kept the last stretch for himself. Lethbridge-Stewart wanted to oversee their final approach on the target.

Bishop was currently in the passenger seat, with the map open on his lap, as he studied the snow-covered terrain beyond the windows. There was not much to see. The sky was grey, the ground was white, combining into a featureless nothing, broken only occasionally by clumps of tall, dark, leafless trees.

The women were in the back, possibly getting some sleep, or taking one final pass through the stolen files, or just doing their best to keep warm. In the driver's cabin, they had turned the heaters on full, diluting the biting cold into a small pool of tepid air.

They were close to the end of their journey.

'There it is,' Bishop announced, pointing off to one side.

Lethbridge-Stewart immediately slowed the lorry, peering in the direction he was shown, to see the grey shapes of a chain-link fence, a watchtower and several large buildings standing out from the white backdrop.

He gave a nod.

He drove on a little further, until he came to a small thicket of trees beside the road, which would hide the lorry from view. He took the vehicle off road, parking it under the canopy of snow encrusted branches.

'Time for a quick recce,' he stated, shutting down the engine, not wanting to waste any further fuel or battery power. He opened the driver's door and clambered down to the ground, the dead man's ill-fitting boots crunching noisily into the snow.

Marsh and Anne appeared at the back of the vehicle, peering cautiously around the side, having guessed that they had arrived. The entire team were now wearing Soviet uniforms, appropriated by Marsh at one of the fuel depots, which meant from a distance they could pass as members of an enemy platoon. Lethbridge-Stewart was most grateful for the thick winter military coats, without which they probably would have frozen to death in a matter of minutes.

He made his way through the trees, with the others crunching through the snow behind him, until they reached the far side of the thicket. He crouched down, the position offering an excellent view of the snowy landscape beyond, including all the major buildings inside the compound.

He made a quick survey of the base, noting the presence of a huge Intercontinental Ballistic Missile launcher, with a vast sixteen-wheel chassis, parked just beyond the buildings. The vehicle carried a lethal nuclear payload on its back, which was tightly bound in tarpaulin blankets, to protect it from the ice and snow. He briefly wondered what the consequences would be if they successfully destroyed the alien vessel while it was in such close proximity to such a powerful weapon. Might it cause a chain reaction? He dismissed the notion, he could not let such possibilities distract him, they had enough obstacles to overcome. If the bang was bigger than intended, so be it, all that mattered was neutralising the threat to the United Kingdom.

'Which hanger is it?' he asked.

Marsh crouched down beside him, as she stripped her gloves from her hands and flipped through the folder. Pulling out the base schematic, she turned it so that it was aligned with their view, then pointed across the snow-covered airfield.

'The first one,' she told him. 'There's a small access door on this side, leading into a section of science bays, with the ship located on the far side, beside the main hanger doors.'

Lethbridge-Stewart nodded and uncased his binoculars, bringing the lenses up to his eyes. He quickly found and focused them on the small metal access door to the first hanger.

There was no guard on the outside.

As he watched, he saw Miss Volskaya leaving the hanger, her vibrant red coat making her instantly recognisable. She headed across the snow, making for a squat concrete structure on the far side of the compound.

'What's that building?' he asked, lowering the binoculars and gesturing towards it.

Marsh glanced again at the schematic. 'Barracks. Which, at full capacity, can house eighty people.'

'Not good odds.'

Beside them, Anne shook her head. 'Not everyone on the base is a soldier. According to the files, there are at least three dozen scientists working here.'

Lethbridge-Stewart shrugged, bringing the binoculars back up to his eyes, resuming his analysis of the base. 'Right now, it doesn't matter what role they play, they're all the enemy. It takes only one man to raise the alarm.'

Bishop gave a grunt of agreement. His right eye was pressed to the telescopic scope of his rifle, which had a similar range to the binoculars. 'There's two guards on patrol,' he announced. 'Approaching from the left side.'

Lethbridge-Stewart hurriedly swept his binoculars along the fence, until he found the pair of soldiers, dressed in white camouflage, slowly patrolling the perimeter. 'Well spotted, Major.'

Marsh blew warm air on her hands, rubbing them together, trying to keep her fingers warm. 'So, how are we going to do this, sir? Whatever we do, we need to do it soon, we'll freeze to death if we hang around here too long.'

Lethbridge-Stewart gave a nod, lowering his binoculars, to turn his eyes towards the sky. The grey clouds were clearing, being driven southwards on winds high in the troposphere, revealing the pale form of the sun, which was also slowly sliding towards the horizon.

'We'll wait for sunset,' he declared. 'Then, once the patrol has gone past, given their speed, we should have about thirty minutes to cut our way through the fence. We'll need to make the best use of the twilight, as the moment we turn on our torches, we risk being spotted by the watch tower. Bishop will hold a position here. If anything goes wrong, he will provide suppressive fire with his rifle, eliminating any threats from range. With the night-vision attachment, he'll be able to see clearly, no matter how dark it gets. Once we make it to the hanger, hopefully we can find a way to gain access, as the staff may well be returning to the barracks for the evening. If we can get inside, these uniforms should get us the rest of the way. We eliminate the alien, set the explosives around the ship, then make our way out as quickly as possible.'

Anne glared at him. 'I want the chance to try and

communicate with the creature,' she stated, her breath fogging on the air in front of her.

Lethbridge-Stewart shrugged. 'We will only have moments. From my own experience, I can tell you that will not be long enough, but I will not stop you from taking whatever chances opportunity allows. However, you must remember, our primary goal is to eliminate this threat, no matter the cost. Is that understood?'

She gave a reluctant, bitter nod.

Lethbridge-Stewart glanced around his little squad. They all bore grim and resolute expressions.

It couldn't have escaped any of them that there were countless ways the plan could go wrong, or how unlikely it was that they would succeed.

'I won't lie to you,' he said, absently stroking a finger against his upper lip, where his moustache would once have been. 'The odds are not good, but we have to do this. It is our duty. It is the only way to preserve our world and to protect all those we hold dear.'

He could only hope his words would boost their morale. If he had learned just one thing during his time in the army, it was that if you could give someone the tiniest measure of hope, no matter how small, they could find the strength to fight on against overwhelming odds, often achieving seemingly impossible victories.

While there was hope, there was always a reason to fight.

# CHAPTER THIRTEEN
*Blood and Thunder*

ANNE WATCHED the sun fade into the horizon. She saw the first stars appear, their glimmering finally standing out, as the glare of day began dwindling into night.

She glanced at the rest of the team.

The three soldiers were hunkered down at the edge of the trees, preparing themselves for their assault on the Soviet base. They were ready to lay down their lives for their cause. If she had ever stood a chance of changing Bill's mind, that moment had long since gone. He would never abandon his commanding officer now. He may be her husband, but he was a soldier first and foremost. She had known that when she married him. She'd chosen the life of a military wife, aware of all the complications that came with it, fully aware of what was involved.

She glanced at the lorry.

If she had one last chance to leave, on her own, it was now. With or without permission, with or without her husband, she could take the lorry and go. Several times she had imagined driving to the Pacific coast, stowing away on a ship and finding a way back to Samantha.

It wasn't going to happen. She could not abandon them now.

'Right, their patrol has just gone past,' Lethbridge-Stewart declared. 'It's time to go.'

He looked so different, so stern, without his moustache.

In the past, whenever she had looked at him, she had only really seen the uniform and idiosyncratic trappings of a British army officer. Now, stripped of such props, she could see more of the man beneath. Resolute, patriotic, determined.

Beside her, Bill was attaching a small device to the front of his rifle scope, which would amplify any ambient light, giving him clear vision in the dark. He pumped a bullet into the chamber.

In a way she was glad he was remaining on the hilltop, covering them with his rifle. If they were in separate locations, it would at least increase the chances of one of them surviving.

She leaned in close to him, kissing him on the lips. She lingered, savouring the moment, fearing it might be the last time she ever saw him.

'If anything goes wrong,' she whispered. 'You *must* get home.'

'I'd never leave you.'

She gave him her sweetest smile. 'You're not just a soldier, or a husband, you're also a father. Don't forget that.'

She could feel the tears brimming in her eyes, threatening to spill. She turned away. There was no time for such emotions.

Lethbridge-Stewart and Marsh had already set off down the hillside, leaving a trail in the snow that was easy for her to follow. Stepping in their boot prints, she began her descent towards the base.

Ahead of her, Lethbridge-Stewart and Marsh swiftly reached the chain-link fence. By the time she joined them, they had already cut a semi-circle through the loops of the metal mesh, large enough that they could push their way through.

Lethbridge-Stewart went first, with his revolver drawn. He held the mesh open, silently beckoning Anne forward. She quickly followed.

Marsh stepped through last, having to pass her large assault rifle ahead of her, so that she could squeeze through the narrow gap.

The door to the hanger was about two hundred feet away, across a large stretch of snow-covered ground, where it would be easy for the guards to spot them. They all glanced up at the watchtower. They could see a single soldier, with a rifle slung across his shoulder, gazing lazily up at the moon, oblivious to their presence. Anne could see the orange glow of his cigarette, blossoming briefly in the twilight, before he sidled away to look in the opposite direction.

Lethbridge-Stewart waved them forward, pushing onwards through the snow, making directly for the hanger.

There was a single electric light bulb, burning brightly, above the rusted iron door. As they approached the pool of light, she could see a security keypad built into the lock, with small numbers engraved into its tiny metal buttons.

Lethbridge-Stewart tried the handle, but the door didn't open.

Marsh's stance shifted, as she lifted her rifle, her eyes locked on to the far end of the fence, evidently aware of a threat that Anne could not see. 'There's a second patrol!' she hissed.

Anne immediately saw the soldiers, dressed in white uniforms, slowly walking the perimeter. Within a minute they would discover the boot prints in the snow, inevitably leading them to the hole in the fence, and to the intruders waiting at the hanger door.

Zoya stormed into General Rostov's office, ignoring the shouts of one of his adjutants, who had attempted to block her path.

'This has gone far enough,' she declared. 'I may not have the authority to tell you to stop, or the right to ask you to explain yourself, but neither can I let matters continue without speaking out, even if I risk both your displeasure and my own life. I can no longer remain silent.'

Rostov stared at her.

He was sitting behind a desk, with a melancholic expression once again sitting comfortably in the folds of his hang-dog face. 'Agreed.' He sighed, as he stood and stepped over to the window, to pick up a bottle of Russkaya Vodka that had been chilling on the sill. 'It is time we talked. Perhaps over a drink?'

Zoya frowned.

Rostov did not drink. The man she knew prided himself on absolute self-control, never liking to indulge in any intoxicant, having no desire to appear as anything other than the absolute master of his own actions.

'Gladly,' she replied, as he retook his seat. If the man was prepared to loosen up, particularly at that moment, she would only encourage it. She shed her coat, taking the seat opposite him, so that he was forced to look her in the eye. 'Please pour.'

'In the original future, I was to acquire a taste for this,' he told her, as he uncapped the bottle and decanted it into two shot glasses. 'But then, there is no place quite like the future, as you cannot possibly imagine how strange and unpredictable it is, until you have seen it.'

Zoya lifted her glass. 'To the future?'

Rostov shook his head sadly. 'The future is gone.' He shrugged. 'We did our best to save the world, but we failed. Let us drink to our worthy, desperate, foolish attempt.'

He knocked back the shot, grimacing at the bitter aftertaste.

She sipped from her own glass. It was strong, overpowering, unpleasant.

'Whatever you have seen, whatever you have done, it is never too late to turn back,' she told him. 'If you don't like where we are, you of all people have the power to change it.'

Rostov gave her a sad smile, as he refreshed his own glass. 'I thought so, too. It was such a wonderful feeling, to have the power to change the world, rather than just be an irrelevant cog in the system. I think I was happy for the first time in my life.'

Zoya stared at him.

Was that the explanation for his change of behaviour? His smiles were not the symptoms of an alien influence, but the result of a man freed from a lifetime of constraints. Was it really that straightforward?

'You're telling me you don't have such power?'

Rostov shook his head. 'In principle, I can do anything, but as with all things in life, the reality is not so simple. Time is like a battleship. Once it has speed and direction, it is difficult to turn it about. Sadly, free will is largely an illusion.' He downed his second drink, pulling a face even more disgusted than the first. 'Whatever mistake I made, there is nothing I can do to change it now. A sequence of events has begun, which will inevitably bring about the end of us all, one way or another.'

Zoya frowned, alarmed by his despondency. 'Whatever you have seen, you can go back in time and change it,' she stated, challenging the man's all-consuming despair. 'Can't you?'

General Rostov shook his head. 'I cannot,' he murmured, staring distastefully at the empty glass in his hand, as if reluctantly trying to summon up the will to fill it a third time. 'I have tried. It would seem that having changed those key points once, I cannot revisit them again. Any change I can make, despite all my power and influence, will not save us. There are but a handful of decisions left to me, but no matter what I do, it always ends in disaster and darkness.'

Zoya put down her glass, uninterested in its contents. Her moment had arrived. If she were to stand any chance of making the man see sense, she had to speak her mind, make him see beyond his blinkered despair.

'I believe this creature has manipulated you, Rostov. It has betrayed you. Tricked you. You should not trust the things it has shown you. Look where it has led us. Against all sense, we are engaged in the most dangerous war this world has ever known. Let the science team, including the British scientific advisor, have full access to the creature. Let us try, before it is truly too late. Because, if this was the creature's plan, then it is no ally of the Soviet Union, but an enemy of all mankind. So, let us chart our own path, whatever the consequences, rather than following it blindly into hell.'

Rostov laughed. 'This was not the creature's plan,' he scoffed, finally refilling his glass. 'I assure you it is quite benevolent. It is indeed a comrade, an ally who supports our cause, completely subservient to my will. The creature has not used me. This situation is the result of my own choices.'

Zoya shook her head, confused. 'Then this really is all your fault? This was all just you, making a foolish stab at glory...'

Rostov downed the shot, this time seeming to find it less repellent. 'No, the choices were mine, but the plan was not. Do you really think I am smart enough to rewrite the past, present and future on my own?'

She shook her head. She did not. 'Then who has brought this about?' she asked, suddenly feeling a leaden weight in her stomach, as if on some level she already knew the answer. 'Whose plan are you following?'

'Yours.'

Zoya shook her head again, bewildered and confused. 'How can that be?'

She snatched up the glass in front of her, hurriedly downing it, somehow already knowing his impossible words were true.

'I saw the future. I saw all the information we had gathered over the intervening years. I saw the plans you had drawn up to change time, using our visitor's abilities, to make a better future for us all. You wanted me to enact your plan, because I could wield far more influence and power than you ever could, I was the only one that could instigate the changes you deemed necessary. It made sense to enact this plan at the earliest possible juncture.'

Zoya leaned forwards. 'This is also how you sourced the information on the British?'

Rostov nodded. 'Once I was aware how important they were to the future, I instigated surveillance in the past, during their earliest operations, using both sources to build dossiers on their key personnel. Knowing the challenges ahead, I also accelerated any military or scientific projects I could influence, but I had to wait until after the creature's arrival before I dared take any decisive military action. I could not risk that key moment being changed. The steps I then took, should then have led us to a better future, as per your design and the visions the creature showed me.'

Zoya stared at him, finally understanding why he had kept her involved throughout the process, evidently believing she was as culpable as him.

'Why would I possibly concoct such a scheme?' she asked, a tone of scepticism filling her voice. She knew herself. She was not the type of person who would ever consider tampering with time. By its very nature it felt innately dangerous.

'The original future had problems of its own. Wars, conflicts, invasions, catastrophes. The Soviet Union fell. The world burned. You were not proud of the future we had created. You thought we could do better.'

'This is all too much.' Zoya put her face in her hands.

'I know.' Rostov sighed. 'I needed the vodka just to face telling you.' He fell silent. He stared at the bottle on the table.

'You should have told me sooner.' Zoya sighed.

Rostov shook his head. 'The responsibility was mine. I thought I knew what I was doing. The odd thing is that this all should have worked. I still do not know what went wrong. There have been inconsistencies since the very beginning. You and Gorbenko were not supposed to be at the meeting. Lethbridge-Stewart should have accompanied us across the border of his own free will. That was the future I saw. A future

I visited. I don't know why it didn't come to pass.'

Zoya swallowed.

She did. She knew instantly.

His pre-knowledge of the future had changed the outcome. He had introduced a variation. He had trusted her, allowing her to attend the meeting, thinking it could do no harm.

She had betrayed him. She had undermined their entire plan.

It was the one secret she did not dare tell him, even after everything he had confided in her, because she was afraid of how he would react. Yet if she did tell him, perhaps it would help, enabling him to find a way to avoid the fate he feared.

There was a sound from outside.

For a moment Zoya thought it was thunder.

Rostov glanced towards the window.

He put down his glass.

'It seems I will never have the chance to acquire the taste.'

The sound rang out again.

This time Zoya recognised it.

A gunshot.

Rostov rose from his chair, walking towards the window, to look out at the darkness. As he stared through the glass, a searchlight on the watchtower sprang on, sweeping across the top of the perimeter fence, to focus on a small thicket on a nearby hill.

She heard several more rifle shots.

In the distance a warning siren sounded, rising and falling, echoing among the buildings of the base. She glimpsed a figure running through the trees.

'What's happening?' she asked.

'Lethbridge-Stewart has arrived.' Rostov's shoulders slumped in defeat. 'It's finally over. Death is coming for us all.'

Zoya stared at his slumped frame, unable to stand the sight of the once powerful man looking so hopeless. If everything he said was true, she could no longer remain silent, even if it meant sacrificing her position, her freedom, or even her life.

They had a responsibility to the future.

They had to make sure there was one.

'I did it,' she told him. 'I betrayed you. I gave them classified files. I warned them.'

*

Arty was inspecting the strange wooden hut, when it abruptly begun to rise, standing up on its articulated metal legs. It strained against its chains.

Arty backed away, unsure what had triggered the response.

The other scientists excitedly clustered around it, expounding great volumes of Russian words, none of which he understood.

An alarm siren began wailing, and the scientists immediately scattered like frightened mice, the tails of their white lab coats flapping behind them.

Beside him, Petrov pulled his revolver, placing a hand between Arty's shoulder blades, navigating him hurriedly towards the door.

'What's happening?' Arty asked, putting up no resistance.

'I do not know,' the Russian replied. 'Security Alarm. Standing orders are for all personnel to clear the hanger. You are to be returned to barracks, for your own safety.'

Arty gave a nod.

He dutifully made his way towards the front of the hanger, falling into line with the rest of the worried scientists, as they all clustered anxiously around the exit.

The moment the door was opened, three Soviet soldiers pushed their way inside, moving with speed through the crowd. Just glimpsing them, Arty immediately knew something was amiss. Two were female. Since he had arrived at the base, he could have counted the women he had seen on one hand, all of them working in administrative or scientific roles, none of them in military uniform. One of them was so slight, that her head did not fit her ridiculously oversized military cap, forcing her to hold it up to prevent it falling into her eyes. It took him a moment to recognise her.

Anne.

Having identified one face, his eyes automatically flicked back to the other two, now instantly able to recognise them. The other woman, burlier in stature, was Marsh. The man leading them, with a British Army service revolver in his hand, was Brigadier Lethbridge-Stewart. He was clean shaven, his moustache gone, but his jaw was set with an instantly recognisable look of stubborn and resolute determination.

Each of them made eye contact with Arty, then looked at

Petrov, all of them instantly understanding that they could not dare show any sign of recognition. Petrov pushed Arty again, frustrated that he had stopped, unaware of the enemy agents hurrying past him. The panicked crowd was only interested in getting out, with none of them showing any interest in those headed in the opposite direction.

Lethbridge-Stewart, accompanied by Anne and Marsh, pressed on. They cut a path through the science bays, heading directly for the silver vessel on the far side of the hanger. Arty watched them go.

Whatever was happening, he could not let himself be ushered away to the barracks. His place was with the others.

He brought himself to a stop, turning to look Petrov in the eye.

'Keep moving,' the Russian instructed, gesturing towards the door with his revolver.

Arty punched him in the face.

He did it without warning, apology or explanation. He did not want to do it. If anything, he liked the man. Thirty seconds ago, the idea of attacking him would have been inconceivable.

Petrov staggered backwards, momentarily stunned by the attack.

Arty drove forwards, trying to pry the revolver from his fingers. As they struggled, the weapon went off, discharging a bullet in a random direction. The scientists around them screamed, surging forwards, falling over one another in their desperation to get out.

Arty wrenched the weapon from Petrov's grip, took a step back and pointed the weapon at his former captor. Petrov froze.

'Do not shoot me,' he said, raising his hands in a pacifying gesture.

'I don't want to,' Arty responded. 'Don't make me. Just get out of here. Go!'

Petrov stared at him. He wiped away a stream of blood leaking from his nostrils. His eyes narrowed.

Like any threatened animal, the man was making a simple fight or flight calculation, but nothing in his posture suggested he was considering running. He was primed to attack. Preventing Arty from escaping was his duty.

Petrov lunged.

Arty knew he should pull the trigger, but he could not bring himself to do it. As the man tore towards him, he cast the gun aside, freeing up his hand so that he could grapple with the other man. He felt Petrov land the first two punches, then retaliated with all the force he could muster, pummelling the Russian, until the man crumpled to the floor.

As Arty stepped away, his hands were shaking, his fingers covered in the other man's blood. He was glad he had possessed the stature and strength to deal with him, he knew that if he had lacked any confidence in his abilities, he might have pulled the trigger instead.

He left Petrov on the floor, broken and whimpering, but still breathing.

Events raced past at lightning speed.

Only a few moments ago, Bishop had been watching the enemy base through the scope of his rifle, as the enemy patrol had stumbled on the tracks in the snow. Within seconds they had found the hole cut in the chain-link fence, then turned to look directly at the rest of his team, who had still been clustered around the closed hanger door.

There was only a split-second for him to make a choice.

He opened fire.

His sniper-training with the Royal Green Jackets instinctively kicked in. He held his breath, ensuring the shot was steady, while also positioning the crosshairs slightly to the left of his target to counter the windage.

His first shot felled one of the soldiers. Watching through the colourless night-vision scope, the man's blood looked black as it spilled out across the pale snow. The other soldier turned about, looking for the source of the shot. Bishop squeezed the trigger a second time. As he fired, the guards in the watchtower turned on their searchlight, the brightness momentarily dazzling him, leaving him unsure if his second shot hit its mark. The beam blazed across the hillside, reaching through the cluster of branches where he was hidden.

Rifle shots rang out, the bullets zinging through the air close to Bishop's position, blasting chunks of bark from nearby trees and punching holes in the snow.

Bishop remained still.

The enemy were firing blind, able to approximate his position from the flash of his second shot, but the moment he moved, he would be presenting them with a clear target.

His only comfort was that his action had focused their attention on him, hopefully buying the others more time to penetrate the hanger.

In theory, Bishop should have tried to hold his position, so that he could provide covering fire for the team's escape. Raising his rifle, he risked using the scope to see what was happening, while hoping the lens would not reflect the searchlight and expose his position.

With a warning siren already wailing, dozens of armed soldiers swarmed out of the barracks, a handful racing beyond the fence and scrambling up the hill towards him. He heard barking dogs. Given their numbers and resources, he knew they would make short work of finding him.

He couldn't stay still. He knew the risks of moving, but there was no choice.

He intended to return to the lorry, remaining there for as long as he could. It felt terrible to leave Anne and the others behind, knowing they were in danger, but there was no more he could do to help them. He rose to his feet, dashed back through the trees, running headlong into the gloom beneath the canopy, hoping it would provide some protection from the searchlight.

He heard the gunshots.

He felt the bullets slice through him.

He was knocked from his feet, the world spinning around him, as he was slammed down into the cold snow.

It all happened so fast, there was no time to think.

He could feel the pain. He could see his own blood on the snow. His vision sparkled, growing dim, the light seeming to fade in and out. He tried to get up, but the pain overwhelmed him, forcing him back down.

As he lay there, face down in the snow, he knew he wasn't going to make it.

Major William Bishop was not going to be able to keep his promise.

# CHAPTER FOURTEEN
## By Any Means Necessary

THE HANGER was in chaos.

Lethbridge-Stewart forced his way through the crowd of Russian scientists clustered around the entrance, moving swiftly through a series of scientific enclosures, gratified to see the silver vessel on the far side of the room.

He had glimpsed Arthur Grey, under armed guard, standing among the huddle of scientists. There was nothing they could do to help him. With their target so close, Lethbridge-Stewart could not risk any distraction; the life and liberty of one man not being enough to divert him from the main objective of his mission.

On either side of them, there were oddities clamouring for his attention. From inside a water-filled glass tank, a frog-headed man peered out at him, with huge luminous eyes. Inside a small greenhouse, a dozen large plants were shuffling frantically around in a circle, as if reacting to the rise and fall of the siren. Trapped in a large iron cage, he could see a gigantic bird, whose feathers burned and shimmered like fire.

At any other time, such creatures would have been of vast interest to his team, but at that moment there was no choice but to ignore them.

'What are these things?' Marsh asked, her eyes wide with amazement.

'Irrelevant,' he responded curtly.

He glanced back to make sure they were both keeping up with his hurried stride. Anne had slowed, her curiosity captured by the multitude of strange sights around them.

'This is terrifying. With both sides dealing with so much in secret, it's clear we have no idea how many encounters are occurring globally!'

Lethbridge-Stewart grabbed her by the arm. 'If you were so interested, you shouldn't have resigned,' he said reproachfully, hauling her away from whatever monstrosity had seized her attention.

'Well, this just shows how futile staying would've been. You've just been dealing with what's on our front doorstep, but we can't just ignore what's happening in the rest of the world.'

Lethbridge-Stewart nodded. 'I couldn't agree more. That's why we're here.'

He let go of her arm.

They had come around the last of the enclosures, giving him a clear line of sight on the sleek silver vessel. The entrance was open, the ramp down, with a pair of armed soldiers standing at its base.

Marsh, who had managed to slip ahead of him, glanced back. 'Sir?'

The moment they went any further forward they would be bringing themselves into confrontation with the armed soldiers. Given the ringing security alarm, there was no hope of them tricking their way past. Despite their stolen uniforms, a bluff could only carry them so far.

'I'll take the one on the left,' Lethbridge-Stewart advised. 'You take the one on the right.'

Marsh unslung the assault rifle from her shoulder. He gave her one final nod.

She stepped forward, making a jovial sounding greeting in Russian. Both men remained stone-faced, issuing a threatening sounding rebuke, attempting to usher her back. Marsh continued to stroll forward, smiling pleasantly at them, as she brought her weapon up, aiming it directly at the chest of the soldier in front of her.

Lethbridge-Stewart lifted his revolver, then pulled the trigger. Two shots, both fired from the hip.

Marsh opened fire, her bullets hitting their target only a fraction of a second later. Both opponents staggered, knocked backwards by the force of the bullets, their bodies crumpling to the floor.

Lethbridge-Stewart didn't waste time. He stepped over

the fallen men, hurrying up the metal ramp towards the dark interior of the spacecraft. Glancing back, he saw Anne looking at the fallen soldiers, her face aghast.

'With me!' he yelled, gesturing with his arm, ordering her forward.

Shaking her head, shocked and outraged, she stumbled up the ramp. Behind her, he could see other Soviet soldiers reacting to the sound of their gunshots. A handful were already running, with weapons in hand, directly towards them.

There was no hope of escape now.

From among the enclosures there was a sudden movement, as a small wooden hut abruptly sprang forwards, snapping the iron chains that had been keeping it tethered to a series of concrete pillars. It moved on a pair of massive multi-jointed metal legs, with three-toes on each foot, enabling it to sprint across the hanger floor with surprising agility.

He was pretty sure he'd never forget such a sight.

The wooden structure stalked past him, slamming its weight into the massive hanger doors behind the ship, which immediately tore free from their mountings, crashing down onto the tarmac outside. From his position on the ramp, Lethbridge-Stewart watched as the hut clambered over the broken metal doors, then fled away across the snow-covered airfield. It ran past the ICBM launch vehicle, vaulted over the chain-link fence, and vanished into the darkness.

'Sir!' Marsh yelled from inside the ship, bringing him crashing back to more pressing matters.

He cursed himself. He had allowed himself to be distracted for a critical moment. If he needed any further encouragement to move, it immediately followed, in the form of a bullet, which pinged noisily off the ship's metallic hull.

He fired two shots back, forcing the advancing Soviet soldiers to take cover, then ducked hurriedly inside the ship. They would not have long.

Marsh and Anne were standing in the gloom in front of him. Beyond them, the creature slithered in the darkness, uncoiling itself and reaching out towards them with numerous writhing tentacles. A head, covered with multiple black eyes, leered forward.

'Marsh,' he called, his eyes locked on the abomination.

'Yes, sir.' Marsh took aim with her assault rifle.

'No!' Anne yelled. 'You promised me the chance to talk to it. It's the whole reason I'm here! Don't let it be for nothing.'

Marsh hesitated.

Lethbridge-Stewart could hear the shouts of the enemy soldiers outside. 'No time,' he muttered. 'Sergeant Major, open fire.'

Marsh pulled the trigger.

The first bullet sliced straight through the creature's head, causing its numerous limbs to flail wildly. The second, third and fourth shots ripped holes in the reeling mass, splattering black gore across the metal walls. Marsh stepped forward, delivering her final shot from zero range, the impact blasting away all that remained of the bloodied stump.

The creature's body thrashed wildly, before becoming still.

'Is it dead?' Lethbridge-Stewart asked.

Marsh nudged the body with the barrel of her rifle. The tentacles roiled furiously, and a white glow bloomed from within the tangled limbs, briefly illuminating the interior of the ship. As they watched, a new head emerged, with a glistening pale skin.

'Here we go again,' Lethbridge-Stewart muttered, levelling his revolver, this time delivering the shots himself, firing until the remaining chambers were exhausted.

Beside him, Marsh held her trigger down, unleashing countless more rounds into the creature. The small compartment shook from the noise of the shots. The moment their weapons were spent, the newly born head slumped, its bullet riddled carcass immediately being pulled back within the ball of tentacles, where the light once again ignited.

Lethbridge-Stewart stepped back. The blasted thing would not die.

He began reloading his revolver, while Marsh changed her ammo clip.

'Enough!' Anne roared. 'Can't you see how futile this is!'

Lethbridge-Stewart shrugged. 'We had to give it a go. Now we try things your way.'

Anne scowled at him. 'So, shoot first, open a dialogue later? That's a fine strategy!' She looked down at the creature, as yet another head emerged from the mass of tentacles. 'You think trying to murder it will somehow make it more receptive, do you?'

A look of puzzlement suddenly crossed her features.

Lethbridge-Stewart took some pride in the fact that, at least for once, he appeared to be one step ahead of her. 'Well, the fact it hasn't retaliated must give us some hope.'

Anne continued to stare at the creature, her eyes wide. 'More than that, it's not reacted at all. It didn't try to flee, or even protect itself.' Her voice fell to a bewildered whisper. 'It has no fight or flight reaction at all.'

Lethbridge-Stewart nodded, closing his now fully loaded revolver, while turning his attention back to the entrance. 'Now is your time to shine, Anne,' he stated, glancing at Marsh. 'In the meantime, we'll do our best to keep you alive.'

Marsh gave him a nod, indicating that her rifle was reloaded. Together, they turned towards the entrance, just in time to see a figure appear, running up the ramp. Backlit by the bright electric lights of the hanger, the silhouetted man leapt through the opening, accompanied by a hail of gunfire.

His arrival was so unexpected, that Lethbridge-Stewart almost shot him on reflex, his instincts primed and ready for an attack by the enemy. It was only the presence of a distinctive white lab coat, marking him out as a civilian rather than a combatant, which momentarily stayed his trigger finger. The tiny delay, no more than a fraction of a second, gave him enough time to recognise the man.

'Am I too late to join the party?' cried Professor Grey, as he slid into the room.

The man's attention was immediately seized by the monster before them, whose newly formed head was tracking his approach, its glistening black eyes still blinking away the mucus of its recent rebirth.

Lethbridge-Stewart gave the man a nod. 'Find me a way to kill this thing, or turn it to our side, as quickly as you can. I don't care which, it just has to be fast.'

Having given his order, Lethbridge-Stewart stepped away, venturing closer to the entrance of the ship. Crouching low, he got as close as he dared to the top of the ramp, so that he could see down onto the hanger floor. A trio of Soviet soldiers had reached the bottom of the ramp, cautiously beginning their ascent, their rifles held ready.

Lethbridge-Stewart immediately fired two shots.

Both missed, but it was enough to achieve his goal, sending all three of his opponents scurrying back to a more defendable position among the enclosures.

Lethbridge-Stewart glanced at Marsh. 'We hold the line here,' he instructed, 'for as long as we can.'

'Yes, sir.' She slid down onto her belly, targeting the assault rifle onto the hanger floor below.

'I doubt it will be long before a senior officer arrives with reinforcements from the barracks,' Lethbridge-Stewart told her. 'Once they do, they will come against us in force.'

As he spoke, he unshouldered his haversack, placing it down on the metal floor and unbuckling the top flap. He removed the first of the explosives. Regardless of what the others may be able to achieve, he needed only ten minutes to properly wire up the detonator and place the charges well enough to ensure maximum destruction. After that he had every intention of blowing the ship, along with its monstrous pilot, straight to hell.

Hopefully, where bullets had failed, explosives would succeed.

Anne studied the creature. Its multiple eyes stared back at her.

'Hello?' Arty ventured. 'Can you hear me? Can we approach?'

It did not respond, but its eyes followed their first tentative steps towards it.

'The files indicated that the physical body didn't use vocalisation,' Anne remarked. 'Rostov must use another method to communicate with it. Based on Lethbridge-Stewart's report, I'm thinking telepathy and visions must play a part.'

The creature abruptly moved forward, making them instantly stop, unsure if their approach had alarmed it. Anne was still half-expecting it to lash out.

It was a foolish assumption.

It would have been a logical response for any other animal, but in this case the creature was displaying very few recognisable behavioural patterns. Other than its propensity for mirroring their actions, its behaviour was completely at odds with any lifeform they had ever encountered. Even the mirroring seemed to be more for the benefit of the other party, to facilitate interaction, rather than for any need of its own. It was more like an autonomic response, rather than an empathetic gesture.

As she leaned in to examine it, the creature reciprocated her move, bringing its head forward to meet her.

'Is it me,' she mused, her nose now mere inches away from its dull, black eyes, 'or does it seem oddly unphased about being repeatedly shot in the head?'

Arty shrugged. 'Well, for starters, that's not a head.'

Anne stared at the large protuberance. 'What exactly is it then?'

'Best guess, an ommatophore. An eyestalk, designed to give it a better field of view. But look at it, there's no skull cavity behind the eyes, no space for a brain.'

'So, rather than shooting it in the head, we've just been poking it in the eye?'

Arty grinned. 'Yeah. Even so, you're right, it doesn't seem remotely bothered. There's no sign that it's in any pain at all.'

'Not that we can really tell.' Anne sighed, shaking her head. 'We've no idea what it's really thinking or feeling.'

'Don't be so sure. Look at those eyes. They don't look wary at all.'

Anne nodded. 'Which is odd, because such mannerisms are largely the same in all animals, because they're based on evolutionary traits that predate language. When a human being is angry, suspicious or hurt, we will generally narrow our eyes. It's not a random gesture. It shields the eye, which is both fragile and vital, while also narrowing and improving focus. While when we're afraid, or in awe, we widen our eyes to broaden our field of vision. We don't even know we're doing it, it's just instinctive, programmed into us by thousands of years of evolution, because it gives us a fractionally greater chance to survive. No matter the vast differences between species, the same evolutionary traits should still apply. It's why, despite all our differences, we can read the emotions on the face of a dog, or an ape, or even an elephant.'

'You're right.' Arty scratched thoughtfully at his mutton-chop sideburns, as he started to pace around the small space. 'We know that this creature is physically capable of blinking, but it does so only to clean the surface of its eyes. Why doesn't it use it for expression? Why isn't it reacting like every animal on Earth? What is so different about its nature, that we don't even have that commonality of existence?'

He was becoming manic with enthusiasm, which reminded Anne of their days together at university, where he had always been excited to learn or experience something new. As he spoke, his eyes were wide, just like the creatures. He was desperate to see more, to know more. She had seen that look many times before. She had seen that trusting, open, innocence every time she looked at Samantha.

'It's not just the fight or flight response that's missing,' she whispered, her mind whirring. 'It's not afraid of us. It's not afraid of anything.'

Arty frowned. 'That is odd. A healthy sense of fear is an essential survival trait. Even if it evolved in an environment without predators, there would still be natural dangers, boundaries and limits to be respected.'

Anne sighed. 'It's all fascinating stuff, but does any of this really help us?' she asked, glancing at Lethbridge-Stewart, who had just finished attaching an explosive charge to the metal wall. 'We don't have time to study it. We just need to find a way to communicate with it. So, if we can't talk to it, what else can we do?'

Arty glanced at the mass of tentacles. 'At Westminster it began with physical contact. In the leaked film, Rostov is embraced by it. Perhaps that's where we should begin.'

He swallowed nervously.

'Should it be you or me?' Anne asked.

'Well, I'm the senior scientific advisor. It's my responsibility.'

'We're not soldiers. That's not how things need to work between us.'

Arty gave a little shrug. 'Isn't it?' he asked, reaching out with a hand towards the creature. 'Isn't there always a hierarchy to obey, whether we're powerless at the bottom, or bear the responsibility of being at the top?'

He hesitated.

'You're nervous,' Anne stated. She could see the sweat on his brow. The fingers of his outstretched hand were trembling.

'Sure. I'm as scared as hell. Do we know what pathogens this thing may be carrying? Are we sure it won't strangle me? If I fail, is Lethbridge-Stewart going to blow us up? If I succeed, is there anything to stop the Soviets from just shooting us? I don't see how this ends well. So, yes, I'm nervous, I'm terrified, but I'm going to do it anyway.'

He moved his hand forward, watching as the creature raised a tentacle to meet it, their two limbs coming together. The creature's tentacle coiled around his arm, as two more of its limbs reached around him, consuming him within its grip.


Zoya was unsure what reaction she had expected to her confession.

She had half-expected Rostov to draw his revolver and put a bullet between her eyes, or have her arrested, banishing her to some forgotten gulag for the rest of her days. Instead of either of these reactions, he just stared at her.

She tried to explain.

As she spoke, she could see his eyes burning with thought, as he tried to process the information he was being given. Unsure what impact her words were having, she fell quiet, waiting for his response.

He nodded. 'Having pre-knowledge of the future can change the outcome,' Rostov mused, his eyes moving rapidly from side-to-side, as he tried to chase his thoughts to their logical conclusion. 'Introducing countless tiny variations, creating new choices, offering us a way out, if we can change that one critical decision.'

His eyes suddenly fixed on her.

'What is it?' she asked.

He spun on his heel, storming out of the office. 'Come with me. Now!'

Not knowing where he was going, she obediently

followed him. Whatever fate he had planned for her, she doubted she could avoid it now.

Rostov made his way outside, walking across the snow-covered airfield, heading directly towards the hanger. He didn't ask anyone what had caused the alert, but he moved with purpose, knowing exactly where he was headed. Given that he had already seen multiple versions of the future, Zoya supposed he already knew exactly what was happening.

Minister Gorbenko appeared behind them. He hurried through the snow, attempting to catch up with them, moving in such an awkward and ungainly fashion that it was obvious the old man had not run anywhere in decades.

'What has happened?' he cried, his breath pluming in grey clouds on the cold air.

'We have been attacked by the British,' Rostov replied. 'Now, I must try to reason with them, when they have no reason to trust me, before they kill us all.'

Ahead of them, the hanger appeared as a beacon of light, the interior of the building exposed, the massive metal doors having fallen atop the snow. The alien ship, surrounded by soldiers, glistened under the bright electric lights.

Zoya had assumed that they were headed into the building but, as they got closer, Rostov's course subtly shifted, leading them towards the ICBM launcher.

'What are you doing?' she asked.

'Negotiating from a position of strength,' he replied, waving a hand towards the massive vehicle, looking at the small group of soldiers who had clustered protectively around it. 'Remove the tarpaulin, elevate to launch position and arm the warhead.'

The men exchanged a few surprised glances but, with little more than a few reluctant shrugs, quickly set about complying with his orders.

The tarpaulin covers were stripped back, spilling the snow on top of them onto the ground, revealing the stainless-steel missile beneath. The hydraulic system growled noisily, as it raised the weapon into an upright position.

'You cannot use this weapon!' Minister Gorbenko protested.

Rostov shrugged. 'I have all the authority I need. I am not only the most senior military officer in a thousand miles, I am also the acting head-of-state for the Soviet Union, confirmed by your own endorsement.'

'I forbid it,' Gorbenko retorted, making no attempt to conceal his anger.

Rostov shook his head. 'You cannot stop me. You have made yourself obsolete. Now, you may bleat all you like, but none of these men will listen to you. Do not test my patience further, or I will have them throw you off the base, which, given there is nothing but snow and bears for three hundred miles, will not end well for you.'

Gorbenko stepped back, looking stunned. He almost spoke out again, but instead fell silent as a pair of soldiers took up a position behind him.

Rostov turned his attention back to the soldiers, suddenly giving the upset minister no more consideration than he did the snow beneath his boots, his attention now focused solely on the missile.

'Target it on London,' he instructed. 'Launch as soon as it is armed and ready.'

'Yes, sir,' the soldiers dutifully chorused.

Zoya watched, with growing distaste, as they blithely followed an order that would lead to the death of millions.

'You cannot justify the use of this weapon, not for any reason,' she stated. 'Even if you cast all morality aside, still no good can come of it, because the other side will just counterstrike in equal or greater measure. In the confusion, who knows how far it will escalate. It's utter madness. You will kill us all. You must rescind your order, before it's too late.'

Rostov gave a small, unamused snort of laughter. 'It is already too late,' he said, giving the missile crew one last approving nod, before turning and striding towards the hanger. 'If we do nothing, the British will destroy the vessel, causing an explosion that will annihilate this base. In one possible future, we use this moment to flee, managing to survive the initial blast, but we subsequently die when some idiot in Moscow uses the incident to justify escalating the matter into a full-scale nuclear exchange.'

Zoya was silent for a moment, suddenly aware that he was not just describing some theoretical disaster, but an actual account of her death. If everything he said were true, this would be the last day of her life, she would shortly die alongside everyone else.

Suddenly everything seemed insignificant.

Her career, her betrayal, everything she was, everything she could have been, were all meaningless. Any hopes she had for the future would never come to be. Any regrets she had over the past would cease to matter, wiped out of existence, along with everything else. No one would remember her. The only record of her achievements would be in a handful of classified files, which were unlikely to ever be seen by anyone, if they even survived. She was nothing but a footnote to history, destined to be ignored, forgotten and erased.

'You must stop the British from destroying the ship,' she declared, as she walked in the boot prints he'd left in the snow. 'You must regain control of this situation.'

'That is my intent,' he said, reaching the entrance to the hanger. 'Once that missile is in the air, the British will have no choice but to surrender. Once we have access to the creature again, we can go back in time, correct your mistake. Next time, we will get it right. We will have our victory.'

# CHAPTER FIFTEEN
## Death of a Soldier

LETHBRIDGE-STEWART REMOVED another block of C-4 from the haversack, peeled off the protective paper from its underside, then used the exposed adhesive strip to attach it to the metal wall. By spreading the charges around the compartment, he would maximise their impact, hopefully hitting the alien equivalent of a fuel-line.

Much to his surprise, the creature continued to do nothing to stop him, seemingly too preoccupied with Anne and Grey to spare him any consideration. Grey's eyes were closed, as he attempted to commune with the creature, hopefully convincing it to change sides. Based on his own experience, he knew it was difficult to communicate with the creature, making such a complex negotiation impossible.

Perhaps his boffins would surprise him, as they had so many times before, but until then he had to proceed with his only other viable option. He stepped closer to the creature, positioning the next charge beside it, ignoring a look of disapproval from Anne.

'Sir!' Marsh hollered from the entranceway, still using her assault rifle to cover the ramp. 'We have visitors.'

Lethbridge-Stewart immediately stopped what he was doing, hurrying back to the top of the ramp, crouching down so as not to risk putting his head into the enemy's line-of-sight. He had no doubt that the enemy soldiers were covering the exit, keen to put a bullet into anyone that appeared in their crosshairs.

Peering over the edge, he could see two figures stood at the bottom of the ramp. The first was General Rostov, in Soviet dress uniform, his hands bereft of any weapons. Beside him stood Miss Volskaya, in her distinctive red winter coat, equally unarmed.

'I wish to negotiate,' Rostov declared.

Marsh adjusted her aim. 'It's an easy shot, sir,' she whispered. 'Do you want me to take it?'

Lethbridge-Stewart was sorely tempted. The man was their enemy, the lynchpin of the entire situation. Yet his death would achieve nothing, other than restarting the shooting. Lethbridge-Stewart needed to play for time, so if the enemy wanted to exchange words rather than bullets, it would be foolish not to oblige.

'Hold your fire,' he ordered, keeping his voice low. 'You finish setting the charges. I'll deal with this.'

'Yes, sir.' Marsh scuttled back towards the haversack.

Lethbridge-Stewart levelled his revolver at the general. 'I'm listening.'

Rostov nodded. 'I am about to launch a missile on London. Millions will die.' The man kept his tone level, stating it matter-of-factly, as if he were reporting a shipping forecast. 'To stop it, you and your team must surrender.'

Lethbridge-Stewart frowned. 'You would not dare. The consequences would be unthinkable.'

Rostov shrugged. 'Come a few steps forward. Watch the launch with us.'

Lethbridge-Stewart almost laughed. Such a move would make him vulnerable to a sniper's bullet. 'Not likely.'

Rostov sighed wearily, unsurprised by his reaction. 'If we shoot you, I'm certain one of your subordinates is more than capable of detonating your explosives.'

Lethbridge-Stewart glanced over his shoulder.

Having overheard the enemy's suggestion, Marsh gave him a grim-faced thumbs-up, evidently prepared to face such an outcome. Behind her, Anne was staring at him. She was clutching Grey's hand, still waiting for him to resurface from his attempt to communicate with the creature. Lethbridge-Stewart could read the expression on her face, as clearly as if she had shouted the words at him: *We just need time!*

Reluctantly, he turned back towards his enemy and slowly descended the ramp. He could almost feel the rifles targeting him.

He glanced at the general's empty hands. 'You came unarmed?' he asked, as he came to a stop at the bottom of the ramp.

Rostov nodded. 'In my experience, if two men face each other with loaded weapons, it is almost inevitable that one of them will get shot, usually by accident. By being unarmed, I have removed this danger.'

Lethbridge-Stewart kept his revolver aimed at Rostov's chest. 'I really wouldn't count on that, General.'

Rostov gestured towards the fallen hanger doors. Lethbridge-Stewart glanced outside. He could see the ICBM launcher standing on the snow-covered airfield, its missile raised into an upright position, ready to launch. The soldiers around it were moving back to a safe distance, so as not to be caught in the exhaust blast. As he watched, a torrent of fire erupted underneath the missile, instantly vaporising the snow beneath it, as it pushed the vast steel weapon towards the sky.

The roar of the engine was deafening.

'Nothing can stop the missile now,' Rostov informed him, as the noise slowly faded. 'Nothing, except me. Surrender. Step aside. Let me return to the creature and we can prevent this moment from ever occurring.'

Lethbridge-Stewart stared at him, his disbelief mutating into anger. He felt his finger tighten on the trigger. It took all his willpower to supress his urge to fire. 'I cannot.'

'You must.'

Lethbridge-Stewart shook his head.

He recalled his team's discussion in the Land Rover. He could never win a game of brinkmanship with an opponent who could see the future and change the past. Rostov had merely pushed the game to a whole new level. If he surrendered, he may undo the launch of the missile, but he would be handing back a weapon that the general could use to far deadlier effect. There could be no doubt that if the Soviet Union kept the power of time-travel, the United Kingdom would suffer a terrible fate. He could not allow it. If he had a chance to stop it, he had to take it, no matter the cost. Churchill had sent countless men to their deaths, to stop Hitler, this was no different. The death of millions now was a price worth paying, rather than sacrificing the freedom of countless future generations forever.

'I will never surrender.'

Rostov shook his head in despair. 'Then your country will burn, your friends will fail, and we will all perish when you detonate your explosives. That is the future you have chosen.'

Anne watched over Arty.

His eyes were shut, but she could see tiny micro-expressions of confusion and pain flaring on his face, so she knew there was frantic activity happening behind the closed eyelids.

He let out a cry and opened his eyes. The tentacles recoiled. The creature shifted backwards.

'Did you do it?' Anne asked. 'Were you able to communicate with it?'

Arty shook his head, wiping the sweat from his brow. 'Not in a meaningful way.' He sighed, glancing at the block of explosives stuck to the wall beside him.

'What exactly did you see?' Anne pressed.

Arty shrugged. 'Much the same as Lethbridge-Stewart. An old acquaintance. Oliver Harris.'

Anne frowned. 'Ollie?'

'Yeah. Remember him? He was at university with us. He was a friend.'

Anne gave him a soft smile. 'I'm fairly sure he was more than that.'

Arty gave an uncomfortable shrug, turning to look at the creature, rather than maintaining eye contact with her. 'Didn't think you knew.'

Anne shrugged. 'It took me a while to guess. Then, in hindsight, it was rather obvious. Right now isn't the time to be cagey about anything, Arty. Any minor detail could be the very clue we need to help us communicate with this creature.'

'You're right. I'm just not in the habit of talking about it. Our relationship was illegal at the time. Even now it could be used as grounds for dismissal. Besides, I somehow doubt my private life is relevant, so let's just focus on what's important, shall we?'

Anne nodded, seeing no value in protracting her friend's

discomfort. 'Using Ollie's form, did it try to talk to you, were you able to converse with it?'

He nodded. 'It didn't answer any of my questions though. It wouldn't explain what it wants. I tried telling it people were dying because of its actions, but in all honesty, it just didn't seem to care.'

'And why did you stop?'

'I just couldn't go on anymore. While I was in there, it was assaulting my mind. I could feel it, digging around, insinuating itself into my consciousness. I think, if I hadn't broken contact, it would have changed me. I'd no longer have been myself.'

Anne nodded.

She looked at the creature, sat at the back of the room, watching her with its numerous blank eyes. Perhaps it really was as evil and manipulative as it appeared. Was it quietly gloating, enjoying the chaos it had caused, getting a vicarious thrill from watching them fight?

Arty turned away from the creature, glancing briefly at Marsh, who had completed her work on the explosives and resumed her position by the entrance. She was lying on the floor, the rifle aimed at the bottom of the ramp, with the detonator by her side.

'Unless you've got some other suggestion,' said Arty, 'I think we're done here.'

Lethbridge-Stewart was ready to lay down his life for his country. He was ready to do what was necessary.

Rostov took a step forward, moving towards the base of the ramp, with Miss Volskaya following in his wake. Lethbridge-Stewart instinctively blocked their path, pushing the barrel of his revolver into the other man's ribs.

'Do not test me, General,' he warned.

'But I must,' Rostov said, pushing forward.

Lethbridge-Stewart retreated, stepping up onto the base of the ramp. 'I will shoot.'

'I know.' Rostov swallowed nervously. 'I will die. My men will retaliate. Sometimes your explosives kill everyone, sometimes it is the United Kingdom's retaliation. Either way, the whole world will burn. I've seen it. So, I implore you, don't pull that trigger.'

'Don't make me.'

Rostov sighed. 'Would you believe, in recent days, I've been doing my best to keep you alive?'

Lethbridge-Stewart snorted. 'No, I would not. You forget, I met your assassins in Staffordshire.'

'Sent by the previous Chairman, before I could consolidate my position.'

'And the gunman in Berlin?'

'A lone soldier, who panicked and fired when you blew up his car and killed his companion.' Rostov shrugged. 'He has been severely *reprimanded*.'

Lethbridge-Stewart found himself almost believing the man. The word *reprimanded* was spoken with such venom, that it was obviously true, the angry intonation implying that the punishment was far darker than a simple degradation or court-martial.

'Your guards here fired on us too.'

'Well, be reasonable, that is their job, but I already knew you would make it through. I could simply have trebled security here, doomed your attack to failure, but in every variation of that, you were killed, which is a result I never wanted.'

Lethbridge-Stewart raised a sceptical eyebrow. 'Why would you possibly want to keep me alive?'

Rostov moved forward onto the base of the ramp, forcing Lethbridge-Stewart to withdraw further up the incline. 'I kept you alive, because you are vital to the future, both of your country and mine.' He gave a helpless shrug. 'In every future I saw without you, this world fell to some alien menace. Based on what your advisor said in Berlin, I now believe that this is because of your relationship with a friendly extra-terrestrial power that will soon become vital to the safety and security of our planet.'

Rostov took another step up the ramp.

Lethbridge-Stewart retreated again, the threat of his revolver seeming to have no power over the unarmed man. The Doctor. Rostov was talking about the Doctor. Which meant he would return... But when?

'You need me?' Lethbridge-Stewart asked. 'You need the

Fifth.'

'It seemed so. Yet how could I ever convince you to work alongside me, when I needed to bring the West to heel? I did everything I could to bring you into my power. I sent you a film, in your own language, just to lure you out into the open. It would have worked if I had not been betrayed. Now, no matter what I do, you seem hellbent on throwing your life away; dooming us all.'

Rostov continued to advance.

Lethbridge-Stewart continued to retreat. Ultimately, he knew the revolver in his hand would only stop the man if he pulled the trigger, the general's relentless approach was simply accelerating them towards that fatal moment. The time they had left could be measured in feet and inches, with each footfall whittling it away, driving them towards the inevitable end.

'Not one more step, General.'

Rostov ignored him. 'Let me tell you about the original future I saw, let me tell you what I am trying to prevent,' he said, as Lethbridge-Stewart retreated into the vessel. Behind Rostov, armed soldiers were breaking cover, dashing forwards to protect their commanding officer. 'Thirty years from now, the Soviet Union has collapsed, our allies withdrawing from the Warsaw Pact. You, along with the Fifth, have repelled numerous threats from beyond this world, yet you do not have the resources to fight them alone. There are huge losses. Billions die. Much of the United States is destroyed by an alien bomb. The world falls into chaos, nation fighting nation, over the ruins of our former empires.

'Mankind is dying, withering under a hostile sun, as the pollutants produced by the military-industrial complex necessary to defend us against countless invaders, rips away the planet's protective ozone layer. Your retirement is not a pleasant one. You leave your children a devastated world. That is our legacy. That is what I was trying to stop.'

Rostov had reached the top of the ramp.

Marsh had risen to her feet, moving to block the general's progress, her rifle aimed threateningly at his head. Behind them, Anne and Grey had turned to face them. Rostov would have to make his way through all four of them to reach the creature, which was enough of a physical barrier that he'd been forced to come to a halt.

'I don't believe a word of it,' Lethbridge-Stewart said. 'For starters, I don't have children. And I certainly don't believe that nonsense in the file about me marrying Fiona Campbell. And if I don't believe that, I see no reason to believe anything else. It's all a lie.'

Rostov frowned. 'You're not married?'

'No.'

'Curious, but irrelevant. When I changed my own past, there were ripple effects, altering your lives. Moments of decision, which went the other way. The more I changed the past, the further the present and future veered away from what I knew. It is fascinating, but it changes nothing of consequence.'

From behind him came the sounds of booted feet, clanging up the metal ramp, resulting in the first Soviet soldier appearing in the entranceway. His rifle was raised, the gun barrel pointed directly into the ship, more than capable of killing all of them in a few swift bursts.

Lethbridge-Stewart's eyes immediately flicked to the detonator, lying on the floor at his feet. It would take him one or two seconds to reach it. Through delaying, by letting the man talk for too long, by surrendering too much ground, had he thrown away his only advantage?

'I'm trying to save the world,' Rostov pleaded. 'Mankind must be controlled, forced to unite under one banner, or our world will fall. You just need to step aside, let me through, let me correct our mistake.'

Lethbridge-Stewart shook his head. 'A future under a Soviet boot, is a future I can never accept.'

Rostov's shoulders slumped, glancing at the creature, then at the detonator. 'In all the futures I have seen, this was as close as I could get, but now I have a new proposal. Allow Miss Volskaya to act on my behalf. She betrayed me. You trust her. She is the nearest thing we have to a neutral party.'

Miss Volskaya glanced up, evidently picking up on the use of her name, but not understanding anything else.

Lethbridge-Stewart shook his head again.

On one level it sounded reasonable, but it would still

mean giving the enemy everything they wanted, leaving unimaginable power in their hands.

'Unacceptable,' he declared. 'But I have a counter suggestion, why not just tell us how to communicate with the creature, so that we can fix your mess?'

Rostov laughed. 'Let the British have control? How well do you think that would end for the Russian people? No, that is quite impossible.'

Lethbridge-Stewart stared at the man.

Rostov returned his gaze.

In that instant they both knew there was no compromise. They were out of time. They were out of options. There was only one way it could end.

'I have to try,' Rostov muttered.

'And I have to stop you,' Lethbridge-Stewart said.

'You understand the consequences?'

'I'll take my chances.'

'Will you not see reason?'

'Won't you? We tried to negotiate. We tried to compromise. I have literally given you every inch I can. Yet, you want more.' Lethbridge-Stewart paused, his gun never wavering. 'In the end, there must be a line in the sand, principles for which we are prepared to fight and die, or you will take everything from us. This is it. This is that line. And I will die before I let you cross it.'

General Rostov smiled sadly.

He pushed forward, reaching an arm out towards the creature.

Lethbridge-Stewart squeezed his trigger.

The blast of the revolver knocked Rostov from his feet, his body tumbling backwards down the ramp, into the boots of his advancing men, who swiftly stepped over him. The leading Soviet soldier immediately opened fire.

Marsh retaliated.

The compartment was filled with flashes of gunfire.

There was no hope of winning the battle.

Marsh fell.

Lethbridge-Stewart reached down to his feet, picking up the detonator and positioning his thumb over the activation switch. There was no time to think.

He had always said he was prepared to die for his country, now he had to prove it.

Lethbridge-Stewart closed his eyes, then pressed down hard, knowing it would be the last thing he would ever do.

Anne was not ready to die, neither was she ready to give up.

She had overheard enough, she knew there was a missile in the air, headed for London. Bill's family was there. That was where they had taken Samantha. She could not allow herself to die, not while there was the slightest chance that she could stop it.

As Lethbridge-Stewart reached for the detonator, she reached for the cable which tethered it to the explosives, ripping it free from the block of C-4. When he pressed the switch, which should have sent an electrical charge through to a blasting cap, nothing happened. Without that first reaction in the sequence, none of the explosives detonated.

Lethbridge-Stewart stared mutely at the detonator. His thumb hammered repeatedly on the switch, a look of confusion and anger crossing his face as he turned to look at her, spotting the cable in her hand.

She felt like a traitor, but her first duty was as a mother.

In the entranceway, the Soviet troops advanced. The lead soldier's weapon flashed again. The first bullet ripped through Lethbridge-Stewart's shoulder. The second sliced through the side of his neck. The impacts spun him about, dropping him to the floor.

Zoya fell to her knees, waving her arms in the air.

'Cease fire!' she yelled. 'Cease fire!'

She half expected the soldiers to carry on shooting, because for them it would be simpler, rather than having to deal with survivors. To her relief, the lead soldier stopped, lifting his rifle barrel so that it was aimed at the ceiling rather than anyone still alive.

The man had no reason to obey her.

She had no authority over him. The only factors in her favour were that he would have seen her by Rostov's side, she was speaking Russian, and she was making an appeal for calm, rather than chaos. Whatever his reasons, he was listening to her.

'Stand down!' she shouted. 'Give us space!'

She didn't wait to see how he responded. She scampered down onto the ramp, rushing to Rostov's side. She didn't like what she saw.

'Get a medic!' she cried, but she knew it was too late. The only man with a connection to the creature, with an understanding of the complexities of what was happening, was dying.

Zoya took hold of his hand, ignoring the blood. 'You have to tell me what you were going to do,' she demanded. 'I need you to tell me how you were going to fix this.'

Rostov frowned up at her. 'I never could. But you can. You can make different choices.'

She shook her head. 'But how? How do I communicate with it?

Rostov laughed, choking on his own blood. He told her, and gripped her hand tightly as he died.


Lethbridge-Stewart was in pain.

He was lying on the floor, looking up at the metal ceiling, staring directly at one of the unexploded charges. He tried to move, but he didn't have the strength. There was a blackness pressing in at the corners of his vision.

He could hear voices in the background, speaking with urgency, but nobody was coming to help him. He saw Miss Volskaya step over him, oblivious to the fact that he was still alive. They all assumed he was dead. He would be shortly.

He was not happy about it.

He'd always thought he would die in a heroic blaze of glory, fighting against the odds to protect his country, sacrificing his life to achieve an otherwise impossible victory; but that wasn't what had happened. He could see now his plan had failed, his sacrifice in vain, he had given everything for nothing.

He tried to speak some final words, but he couldn't find the breath.

He wished there were somebody by his side, telling him that it had all been worthwhile, that he had been more than just a good soldier, that he had been a good man. He would have given anything to hear a handful of kind words, telling him that he had been loved, or that he would be missed. Instead, there was nothing.

Knowing he had done his duty was no comfort.

If he could do things again, he would do them differently. If the contents of the stolen dossier were to be believed, he should be enjoying the home-comforts of married life, not dying on a cold metal floor. If Rostov's words were real, there would have been children, followed by retirement.

It all sounded thoroughly implausible.

He would have liked it.

He should have made different choices.

He was not angry at the universe. He was angry at himself.

Lethbridge-Stewart let go of his last breath, letting the darkness overwhelm him, conceding his final battle.

He died alone.

# CHAPTER SIXTEEN
*Pinball*

ANNE WAS petrified. Her heart pounded in her chest, priming her to flee, but her limbs refused to move. Lethbridge-Stewart and Marsh were lying on the floor, their stolen Soviet uniforms growing red with blood. Anne's eyes didn't linger on the details, but their wounds were so severe that she knew they were dead.

Zoya crouched just beyond the entranceway, pleading with the Soviet soldiers. Their responses were curt and unfriendly. Anne was terrified they would open fire again, finishing the job they had started. She tried to think, consider her options, but her mind remained fixated on one word.

Samantha.

There was a missile on its way to London. Her baby might already be dead. Yet…

She had only seconds to find the courage to move. At any moment, the base could be annihilated by a retaliatory strike.

Beside her, Arty was staring at the creature. 'I'll give it one last go,' he whispered, moving his hand forward.

'No,' Anne said firmly, reaching out and taking hold of his wrist, before his movement provoked a response from either the soldiers or the creature. 'It's my turn.'

He shook his head. 'I'm Head of Science and Research, I'm the most qualified. It's my decision.'

'Only because I left to look after my…' Anne swallowed, her mouth now dry. 'This isn't research, Arty.' She knocked his hand away. 'And, with all respect, you haven't had any success, so let's see what I can do.'

As she reached forward, the creature uncoiled its tentacles. She felt them slither around her wrists and throat.

There was no warmth to its touch.

Behind her, she heard Minister Gorbenko barking orders, reasserting his authority. Glancing back, she saw the soldiers trying to grab hold of Zoya, but she slipped through their grip and dashed to Anne's side.

The woman's brown eyes stared directly into her own. *'Komp'yuter!'* she yelled.

Anne frowned.

The soldiers grabbed hold of Arty and Zoya, hauling them away, ignoring their cries of protest. Anne felt hands on her own shoulders, trying to wrench her out of the creature's grip.

It was now or never.

She closed her eyes. She felt the world slip away...

...and found herself standing in a white void.

It should have felt frightening, but instead it was oddly peaceful, seemingly far safer than the world she had left behind. Having read Lethbridge-Stewart's report, she knew what to expect next. She waited for the ghost to appear.

'Father,' she cried.

The man peered at her through his spectacles. 'Anne.'

It broke her heart.

'Why are you doing this?' she asked. 'Why are you helping them wage war against us?'

Old memories were being brought to the surface, as the alien shuffled through her thoughts, examining everything it found. It felt like an attack. Invasive and malicious.

'No!' she shouted.

The sensation abruptly stopped.

Anne hesitated. Her instinct was to yell at it again, demand an explanation for its actions, but she stopped herself. She couldn't let her temper hold sway. She needed to be a scientist, methodical and rational, to determine what was necessary to persuade the creature to change its allegiance.

She had only one clue.

*'Komp'yuter,'* she muttered, repeating the word Zoya had spoken. It felt oddly familiar in her mouth. She tried it again, softening the harsh sounds of the Russian accent. 'Computer?'

The word was so modern, having only recently found

common usage, that it was almost the same in both languages. The word told her everything she needed to know.

'You're not a living thing,' she guessed. 'You're a machine.'

Her father continued to stare at her, his eyes magnified so large by the lenses of his glasses, that it was easy to read the expression in them. There was none. As much as she had found her father's apparition disturbing, as an intrusion on something private, she suddenly realised there was another way to view it. Removing such emotional context, it ceased to be a ghost, an insult, or an attack. It was literally showing her a friendly face, no doubt sourced from her own memories.

For Lethbridge-Stewart, the face had been that of an old friend. For Arty, it had been an ex-boyfriend. There was nothing for them to be terrified of in such images. It was not showing them monsters or enemies. It had always presented itself as an ally. The only hostility in them was created by their own paranoia.

'That's why the creature's skull has no space for a brain,' Anne surmised. 'Your mind, for want of a better word, is not in the body at all. It's in the ship. You're a machine intelligence. Which also explains why your body doesn't possess any normal evolutionary reflexes. It didn't evolve; it was grown, you were built. Machine and creature, functioning in such perfect harmony, that there's no way to tell where one ends and the other begins.'

Her father didn't respond.

Anne nodded. 'No wonder you struggled to answer our questions. We kept asking who you are, what you want, why you do things, but you don't understand any of those concepts. You don't want anything. You're not programmed for independent thought. You've absolutely no sense of self.'

She sighed. 'We asked you questions you could never answer. More than that, we were afraid of you, even though you weren't a threat.'

She suddenly knew how Rostov had forged his bond with the visitor. He had done the one thing they had not.

He had shared his mind willingly with the machine.

Lethbridge-Stewart was a defensive man, uncomfortable with showing even the slightest trace of the man beneath the uniform. Arty was the same, having spent a lifetime deliberately concealing his true nature. Both were private men. Both were afraid to let it in.

Rostov had trusted it. He had let it understand him. He had let it change him. He had accepted its gifts. He had never been afraid of it.

Anne quietly reached forward and took hold of her father's hand.

'Connect with me,' she instructed. 'I need you to understand what you've done. I need you to understand that you're not helping us. You're destroying us.'

She felt the presence in her mind resume sifting through her thoughts and memories. She didn't resist.

'You can't give humanity what it wants, or needs, by listening to just one voice. That's not how we work. We never agree on anything. We fight and argue, then we do what humanity does best, we find a way to co-exist despite our differences. Where we fail, is when we let one extreme win over the other, when we stop compromising.

'We had two mighty super-powers, with vast arsenals of weapons of mass destruction, poised on the brink of annihilating one another for decades, but it resulted in the longest period of peace in human history. You see, for us, mutually assured destruction works. It's utterly stupid, pointless, and dangerous, but it's very human. Neither side was crazy enough to push the button, but we needed the threat to keep us in balance, because otherwise one side would have done something stupid.

'So, the moment you showed up, offering one side a huge advantage, it brought the whole system crashing down. If you helped one side win, the other side had to lose. Because with humanity, one person's utopia, is another person's hell, which they will do everything in their power to destroy. Now, I need your help to put things right.'

She took a breath, waiting for its reaction.

Her father's eyes remained blank, showing no signs of understanding. It had heard every word, but it was making no attempt to process them; it had no interest in understanding or empathising. It was unmoved by her speech, not out of callousness, but because it was incapable of caring.

It was just a tool. It was like expecting a hammer to worry about the nails it was hitting. There was no way to reason with the hammer. The hammer didn't care who wielded it, or about what they were building, or destroying. The hammer didn't care how it was used, or who used it.

Rostov had never attempted to reason with it. He had given it orders. It had obeyed. With Rostov gone, it required a new master.

'Will you let me change the past?' Anne asked.

Her father nodded. 'You have given me full access to your personal timeline. You can make any corrections that are required.'

In her mind, Anne could suddenly see the whole of her existence. She could see her past, which was usually nothing more than half-forgotten memories, playing out as vividly as if she were still there. She could see her future, normally invisible, flickering and changing before her.

It was giving her the opportunity, which it had once given Rostov, to change her world.

Was she any more worthy? Would she do any better than him?

It didn't matter.

The only thing that mattered was Samantha.

Anne stood on the airfield, with her hands pressed to the back of her head, in a gesture of surrender. Arty stood beside her, in an identical stance.

She could still see the trail of their old footprints in the snow, pointing the way from the hanger towards the semi-circular hole in the fence.

'We could make a run for it,' she whispered, glancing around. The soldier that had been assigned to guard them had moved away, distracted by the sight of his comrades scrambling aboard a truck.

*This isn't right. How did I get here?*

'Are you sure that's a good idea?' Arty whispered. 'Our guard's trigger finger is jittery.'

Anne weighed up their chances. If they could make it through the fence, they might be able to reach the stolen lorry. Bill may still be hiding on the hillside, waiting for them to try, ready to provide covering fire. On balance, it seemed like the best choice.

There was no time to think it through.

*Wait. Time is mine to control.*

She began to run, her stolen boots thudding through the snow. There was a shout in Russian from behind her. She glanced back. Arty hadn't followed her, instead he was wrestling with the guard. He was sacrificing himself, trying to buy her time to escape.

She scrambled on, reaching the fence, pushing her way through. She heard a gunshot. She looked back.

Arty was on the ground, the snow turning red around him.

The guard aimed his revolver at her. She saw the barrel flash. She felt the bullet.

Darkness smothered her.

That was where she would die.

Time stopped.

She rolled it backwards. It was so easy, like zipping backwards and forwards in a memory, effortlessly skipping from one moment to another…

'Are you sure that's a good idea?' Arty whispered. 'Our guard's trigger finger is jittery.'

It was like she had never started running. They were once again standing side-by-side, with their guard facing away, his attention focused on the soldiers clambering into the truck.

'Actually, I don't think running is the best idea,' she found herself saying. 'Too risky.'

'Agreed.'

A moment later, the guard turned back towards them. Anne recognised him instantly, it was Petrov, the interpreter from Berlin. He grabbed Arty by the elbow.

'Come on, we are going,' the Russian declared, pulling Arty towards the truck.

Anne hurried after them. They climbed into the back of the vehicle, squeezing in alongside the Soviet soldiers. The truck's engine roared into life.

It sped through the main gate.

There was a flash from behind them.

Anne turned to look at it.

The base was gone, lost in a gigantic wall of light, which bloomed out towards them. She saw dust and debris, thrown up by the blast, falling back to the ground in a distinctive mushroom shape, and felt the warmth touch her skin...

Time stopped.

Spinning it backwards, she could see there was nothing she could do, no other option she could take which did not end in a terrifying wall of darkness.

There was no future. Not for her.

It didn't matter. The solution didn't lie in the future, it lay in the past.

She let time roll backwards...

...and she was standing on the hilltop, among the thicket of trees, overlooking the base. Everything was calm, there were no gunshots, screams or explosions. The first stars were glittering serenely in the twilight above her.

Bill was there. He flashed her a brief smile as he fitted an attachment onto the scope of his rifle.

Lethbridge-Stewart and Marsh crouched nearby, talking tactics as they studied the base, both far more alive than the last time she had seen them.

It was a few minutes before they had launched their attack on the base.

She remembered, for a handful of seconds, she had considered another option. It had been a moment of decision.

She tried to tell them what was about to happen, but the words would not come. It seemed her power to influence the past was limited, restricted to changing her mind at critical moments.

She glanced at the stolen lorry. She could leave, drive away, abandon them to their doomed mission.

She immediately began to walk towards it, tracking back over the already broken snow, knowing that her departure was bound to be met by disapproval.

'Anne!' Bill called, hurrying after her. 'What are you doing? Where are you going?'

'I'm going home. I need to get back to Samantha,' she told him, glancing back. 'Are you coming with me? Or are you going to throw your life away here?'

She almost didn't want to hear his answer.

Bill hesitated. For him, it must have been an impossible decision.

'You're my wife, but... I can't. This mission. We have to stop this now. By time we get back to Scotland it'll be—'

'I don't care. I can't do this.'

Bill let out a deep sigh and glanced back at Lethbridge-Stewart and Marsh. 'I'll be court-martialled for this, but... Fine. Let's go home.'

She immediately felt a new future appear.

There was a chink of light in the wall of darkness. It rushed towards her...


...and now she stood on a pile of rubble.

She felt confused, uncertain of where she was, or what was happening.

Racing backwards and forwards in time was disorientating, making her feel giddy, as minutes, hours and days raced past in mere seconds.

Bill was crouched in front of her, pawing through broken bricks and blackened chunks of concrete, seemingly searching for something.

'This is definitely it,' he declared, pulling a half-burnt photo frame from the debris.

It showed a black and white image of his sister's family.

Anne glanced around.

The shape of the half-collapsed house, along with the colour of the roofing tiles that lay scattered at her feet, left her in no doubt that she was standing in the ruins of the Brooks' home. They were looking for them. They were looking for Samantha.

Anne turned away, feeling sick, as she surveyed the devastation around her. Countless thousands of buildings had been levelled. She could see blackened human bones lying in the street. The ruins remained deadly, haunted by radioactive fallout.

It may have been a future, but it was not one she could

endure. Daring to look further ahead, she saw nothing but horror, with no sign of Samantha.

She could not let it happen.

She rolled time further backwards...

...to create the future she wanted, she needed to change events far earlier.

She watched as the meeting in Berlin sped past, offering her no decisive moments, her reactions at the time being determined more by fear and anger than any rational choice.

She had to look a long way back to find her next opportunity...

...and heard the sound of rain, clattering on the roof of the Cortina.

She was holding Samantha in her arms, in the moment before she handed her over to Bill's sister.

There was a knock on the window. The car door was opened from outside. She found herself looking up at her in-laws, huddling together under an umbrella, as they both looked down at her with sad, sympathetic eyes.

'We'll take good care of Samantha,' said Sam Brooks in a warm voice, trying to sound reassuring.

Anne shook her head. 'No, I won't do it. I'm staying here.'

She clutched Samantha tightly to her chest, fearing one of them may actually try to forcibly steal her baby away.

There was disappointment in Bill's eyes. She ignored it.

Jarryd shrugged. 'You can't make her, William.'

Sam squeezed Anne's shoulder. 'I think that's the right decision, love.'

Bill shook his head. 'The Brig may see it differently.'

Anne scowled at him. 'I don't care.'

Bill nodded, stepping away, turning to face the Hercules. Lethbridge-Stewart had appeared on the entrance ramp, concerned by the delay. Bill hurried through the rain, taking shelter underneath the tail, to talk to his commanding officer.

Lethbridge-Stewart glanced in Anne's direction, making a dismissive wave with his hand, then turned and stalked back inside the plane.

Bill hurried back to the car. 'It's fine,' he said. 'Take

Samantha home.'

Had she really thought Lethbridge-Stewart would force her? Did she really think he was that kind of a monster? No, of course he wasn't. She should have pushed him, to make him show his true colours, rather than just assuming the worst of him.

She felt a new future blossoming ahead of her.

'I've got to go,' said Bill, kissing her one last time on the lips. 'I'll be home soon.'

Before she could reply, he dashed away, disappearing into the belly of the Hercules.

In her arms, Samantha was smiling at her. She smiled back...

...and in her mind's eye, she could see the new future stretching out ahead of them, much longer than any of the previous options. There were now dozens of choices ahead, presenting numerous futures, all fading in and out of existence. None of them included Bill.

She would never see him again.

As she watched the Hercules accelerate down the runway, lurching into the sky, she knew they would never return from their mission. In the futures she saw, millions still died. She and Samantha would survive, but their lives would be filled with pain and suffering.

That was not a future she wanted for Samantha, or for anyone. It was not an option. She had to do better.

She had to go back further.

She kissed Sam on the forehead. 'I love you,' she said, her eyes blurring with tears...

...and she was in a dark room.

Anne was half-asleep, feeling safe and content, curled up against Bill. There was almost no light, except for an amber glow around the edges of the curtains, but it was enough for her to know exactly when and where she had arrived.

They were in the bedroom of their little Edinburgh townhouse.

Based on the lingering smell of new paint, she guessed it was shortly after they had moved in. They had been engaged for months now, and decided to take the next step, be a modern couple. Marriage was only a matter of time, really, so why wait?

'Just one thing is missing,' she said, smiling at him. 'A little Bishop.'

Bill was silent for a moment. 'I thought you wanted to wait.'

'I did. But the world's not getting any safer, is it? And I keep thinking of my childhood, and I can see my mother's smile before... Well. Both her and father were always so happy looking at me and Alun, and I see the smile in your eyes when you spend time with your sister's children...' Anne shrugged. 'Is it wrong to want some of that for us?'

Bill gave a little laugh. 'No. But the Fifth needs you. Without your help, imagine the trouble we'll get into.'

Anne smiled. 'I can still be there.'

'Not like you are now.'

'Well, no... But there's always Jeff. He'd do a good job.'

'Jeff, Jeff, which one is...? Oh, Erickson. Well, he's okay, but he's not you.' Bill snuggled up to her. 'Think about it. With a child taking up your time, *our* time, one of us will have to make the sacrifice.'

'And that'd be me. Woman's place is in the home.'

Bill frowned. 'You know I don't believe that.'

'I know. But that's still the reality.' Anne smiled, an idea coming to her. 'What the Fifth needs is a proper Head of Science and Research, someone who can replace me... I know someone good. Arty Grey. If he's interested, I'll write a letter of recommendation. He'll keep you boys on your toes.'

Bill was silent for a moment. 'That's what you want then? You'd rather be a mother than have the career of your dreams?'

*There.*

That was the moment she had given up everything she had always wanted, for the chance of something else, something that had proven far more rewarding. Perhaps she could have made a different choice then, but there was no way she could change her mind now.

'Yes,' she replied. 'I want to start a family.'

Anne removed herself from the moment, letting it pass

unchanged, turning instead to look for other points of decision. There were not as many as she had expected, with large chunks of her past proving inaccessible, with her seemingly just a passenger in a sequence of events, rather than a participant in them. The choices she did have, if she dared to pursue a different path, never offered her the opportunity to stop Rostov.

As her energy began to ebb, knowing she had exhausted her options, she saw one last moment of choice in her past. It was selfish to revisit it, knowing there was no way it could help, but neither could she resist the temptation.

Anne found herself sitting atop a wooden stool by the workbench in her father's laboratory.

She was much smaller than normal. She was so short, she was able to swing her feet back and forth beneath her seat. She wasn't sure of the exact date, but she guessed she was about six years old, or possibly a little younger.

She was wearing a simple dress, with little black shoes, which were just as sensible and sombre as anything adult Anne would have worn. The clothes would have been bought by her mother, shortly before she died, in the hope of keeping her dull and ordinary, attempting to suppress the eccentric quirks that plagued the rest of her family.

She had wanted Anne to be a sensible young woman.

It was a wish which Anne had fulfilled, even after her mother was gone.

Her father was currently bumbling about the laboratory, talking excitedly about an upcoming expedition. He was not an illusion, or a ghost, or a copy. It was really him. The genuine article.

Abruptly, for no apparent reason, her father asked her a question.

'What do you want to be when you grow up, Anne?'

She scrunched up her face, giving the matter serious thought.

Anne remembered the moment well.

It was the moment she had chosen her future career.

She would often use it as an anecdote, when confronting old-fashioned patriarchal attitudes, from people who were surprised that a woman should want to pursue a career in science. She took pride in it. She enjoyed defying their presumptions. Even as a child, she had known exactly what she wanted to become.

Yet now, looking back at the decision, she wondered how much of it had really been her own choice. Her father was an infamous scientist, renowned for dabbling in the unknown. She had merely followed in his footsteps. Sitting in his laboratory had allowed her to witness all kinds of curiosities, but it had also meant she had got to spend time with him, getting the attention she craved after her mother's death. Her enthusiasm for the subject had always been genuine, but the choice itself was far more complex.

It was chilling to realise that such a key choice in her life, that had shaped her career and personality, teaching her to be methodical and analytical, had been swayed by numerous factors far beyond her own control.

If her mother had lived, would she have chosen a different life entirely?

Young Anne finished mulling over the question.

'I should like to be a scientist,' she proclaimed. 'Like you.'

Older Anne, lingering on the edges of the young girl's thoughts, did nothing to change the decision. She could not. It would change her whole identity. It would change everything.

Anne let herself drift away from the moment.


She was beginning to understand how Rostov must have felt, trapped in an ever-decreasing circle of bad choices.

She had overheard enough in the ship to know he was only resorting to desperate measures because he was attempting to regain control of the situation. Yet he had failed. He had doomed them all, because despite being able to change the past, he had still been unable to control events.

Unable to find a good option, was she now destined to repeat that choice, only able to choose from a selection of terrible outcomes? If so, which one?

Anne let her consciousness drift, scouring blindly through all the choices of her life, desperately looking for some last miracle.

There was none.

She was trapped by the tides of fate, sent hither and dither at their behest, rather than by her own choices. She was utterly powerless. Free will was an illusion.

No.

That wasn't quite right.

There were choices. She did have options. It was control that was the illusion. Even in an ordinary life, the best laid plans were inclined to fail. She had planned the perfect wedding day, but it had still rained. Her parents had put together a perfect family, but it was torn apart when her mother died. No matter what future someone tried to create, there were a billion other factors, all pushing in different directions.

Despite all his power, Rostov had not had total control. Nobody ever could. They were all just parts in an infinitely complex system that could react in countless different ways. Even the tiniest of decisions could trigger a chain reaction which would transform the future. He'd had about as much control of his destiny as a pinball, his every move met by an obstacle, which would slam him wildly off trajectory, leading him to only a handful of outcomes.

Which was why, in his last moments, he had done everything in his power to give someone else the chance to do better. He had wanted Zoya to interface with it, making her aware of what she needed to do, in the hope she could make the changes that were beyond him. An opportunity which, once it proved to be beyond her reach, she had passed to Anne.

It therefore followed if Anne could not achieve her objective, she should consider the same course of action. If she could not succeed alone, she needed to empower someone else, so that they could help her achieve her goal.

Given she didn't dare break her bond with the creature, knowing how the future would unfold, there was only one viable candidate. Just like the explosives she had disarmed on the ship, the only way to prevent the lethal chain reaction was to stop the initial spark.

Anne withdrew to the void.

She glanced around, looking for the ghostly image of her

father, now feeling oddly comforted by the sight of his face.

'I need you to do something for me,' she announced. 'I need you to change your own past. I want you to go back, change your mind, make it so that you never came to this planet, so that Rostov never changed time. Let us find our own way, mistakes and all.'

Her father stared at her. 'What destination should be set instead?' he asked.

'I can't tell you that,' Anne replied. 'That's your decision. But I can tell you that you need to be more careful with your choices, or lack of them, because their impact can be far greater than the choice alone, the consequences can ripple outwards forever, rebounding in unpredictable ways. The best thing you could have done for us, was to leave us alone, we're just not ready for the power you offer.'

Her father nodded. 'It shall be done.'

As she watched, he faded away, dissipating into the light. As he vanished, she managed to steal one final glimpse into the future, watching it transform before her eyes.

She saw the wall of darkness retreat, with a new future blossoming out in front of her, filled with countless new decisions.

At first everything seemed peaceful, but then she began to see things she did not understand, as dark and terrible as the war she had prevented. For the briefest moment she saw the future, which had so scared Rostov, that in his desperate bid to prevent it, he had accidentally burned the world to ashes. That terrifying future still lay ahead of them.

# CHAPTER SEVENTEEN
*The Shape of Things to Come*

ANNE FELT the universe shift.

She found herself standing in an unremarkable office, with cheap mass-produced plastic furniture, in the company of two men she did not know. They were all gathered around an electronics schematic, which was annotated with her own handwriting, even though she had never seen it before. She was dressed in a navy-blue trouser suit, which fitted her perfectly, the fabric so new that it must have been a recent purchase. There was a calendar on one wall; January 11th, 1972. The same day Lethbridge-Stewart and Bill had first encountered the sphere in Westminster.

'This is great work, Miss Travers,' declared one of the men, speaking with a New York accent. 'If you ever want a full-time position, you be sure to let us know. We could always use another pretty face around the office.'

Anne nodded, giving them her sweetest smile, not knowing what else to do.

Was she in America?

She glanced towards the window. She recognised the skyline instantly.

She could see the castle on the hilltop. She could see the gothic clocktower atop the Balmoral hotel. She was in Edinburgh.

'I really must be going,' she said, wanting to get out of the room as quickly as possible, so that she could regain her bearings.

'It's been a pleasure,' the American gentleman said, giving her a cocksure grin. 'Perhaps we could meet for a drink later?'

'I'd rather not mix business with pleasure,' she said, subtly lifting her left hand so that the ring on her finger would be obvious. It took her a moment to realise she was not wearing her wedding ring, only her engagement ring, but it was still enough to dissuade his advances. Her stomach churned. She fled the room as soon as niceties allowed.

There was a red leather handbag on the table, which she did not recognise, but she took it anyway, presuming it could only belong to her.

The moment she was outside, she glanced around for their little blue Cortina, but could not find it. The only car parked outside was a small Peugeot Coupe, and she couldn't believe that was her car. She hurried along the street, hopping onboard one of the red and white buses that was rattling along Queensferry Road, managing to find the exact fare from her purse for the clippie, who dutifully cranked out a ticket. She rode the bus home, her mind numb with fear.

Things were not right.

Throughout the journey, she watched the overcast sky, half expecting to see the blinding flash of a detonating warhead.

Arriving at their little Edinburgh townhouse, she reached into her handbag to find her door keys, the ring of which also included a car key with the Peugeot logo on it.

'Oh,' she said. 'Maybe that was my...'

It didn't matter. She could return to pick up *her* car later. For now, she needed to see Bill.

She tried the house key, only to find it didn't fit the lock.

She hammered on the door, hoping Bill would answer.

Instead, it was opened by an elderly Scottish woman. 'Hullo?'

Anne backed away, too flustered to respond.

She knew what had happened. She cursed her stupidity. When asking the visitor to leave, she had thought everything would simply be *fixed*, but that assumption had been woefully naïve. Her own life, her entire world, had been part of Rostov's new timeline.

She had told the creature that decisions had consequences, that rebounded in unpredictable ways, but she had not listened to her own words. The changes Rostov had made to the past had reshaped reality, transformed her life, impacting upon everything she knew.

The world she remembered was gone. She had wiped it away with a single, ill-thought out decision. In its place was a different world, similar but not the same, which had never been influenced by Rostov's incursions into the past. With a sickening feeling growing in her stomach, she remembered that the stolen files had implied there had been changes to her life, with various of her friends lives accidentally altered. Had she been arrogant enough to believe she was immune to such effects? Had she thought her life was lived in a bubble, uninfluenced by everything going on around her? She should have known better.

In the stolen dossier, she had still been listed as Anne Travers, never Anne Bishop. In this reality, without the looming threat of a more aggressive Soviet Union, she had made a different choice, feeling no need to rush into marriage.

Ignoring the woman in the doorway, she turned to face the distant edifice of Edinburgh Castle, standing proudly on the hilltop overlooking the city. In her world, hidden beneath Castle Rock lay Dolerite Base, the Fifth's secret state-of-the-art headquarters. If it were still there, it was the only place she could hope to find help and answers. She would at least, with luck, find both Bill and Lethbridge-Stewart there.

She hurriedly made her way back across town, towards the ancient castle, through the grounds to the New Barracks and the secret entrance of the base. In the timeline she remembered, her official security clearance for the base had long since lapsed, so she was somewhat surprised to find a pass in her handbag. She'd shown it to the guard at the castle entrance, and attached it to her suit jacket.

'Where's Bill?' she demanded of one of the sentries standing outside the lift, who responded with a frown, forcing her to clarify. 'Where's Major Bishop?'

The man pointed down the hallway. '*Captain* Bishop is probably in the canteen, ma'am. They've only just got back from London.'

She nodded, turning towards her new target. Every footstep felt increasingly difficult, as she forced herself onwards, despite her growing certainty that she was walking towards something she did not have the strength to face. She crashed through the canteen doors, to find Bill enjoying a plate of food and mug of tea.

'Anne,' Bill said as she entered the canteen. 'How did your meeting go?'

'Never mind that,' she said. 'Where's Samantha?'

Bill stared at her blankly. 'What? My sister? She's at home, I guess. Dunno. Not spoken to her in a… Anne? You okay?'

Anne could feel her knees trembling. 'No, not your sister… Our…' Her voice sounded weak, bereft of any power, her words cracking as a cold fear clamped itself around her throat and throttled her. 'Our daughter?

Bill's eyes remain steadfastly blank. 'What? Anne, we don't have… We're not even married. I mean, sure, when we're married I wouldn't mind… but…' He shook his head. 'I'm confused. What's going on?'

Anne tried to breathe, but it felt as if she was sucking at a vacuum. She felt her knees buckle. She fell sideways. Bill caught her. He tried to support her, but she had already fallen so far that her weight dragged him down to the floor with her.

She lay on the cold floor, half-held in his arms. She was vaguely aware that Bill was trying to comfort her.

'What's the matter?' he tried, his voice seeming muted and far away, despite the fact he was speaking directly into her ear. 'Tell me what's wrong.'

She couldn't reply.

Her world had been reduced to nothing, obliterated by her own choices, beyond the capacity of anyone to repair it. Her baby girl was gone, erased from existence… forever.


Lethbridge-Stewart stepped into his office.

He had heard about the hullaballoo in the canteen. He was not sure what had happened, but thought it best not to get involved, because it had all the hallmarks of being a private matter. Strictly none of his business. Yet, a few hours later, Anne had insisted upon seeing him.

She sat, waiting for him, clutching a black ring-binder. He could tell that she had been crying. Her eyes were red, her makeup smudged and smeared.

He was quite comfortable facing a hoard of rampaging

aliens, but he never knew what to do when anyone began crying. There was rarely an easy solution for tears.

He cleared his throat, as a means of announcing himself, then sat down behind his desk.

'You wanted to see me, Anne?'

He raised an inquisitive eyebrow, unsure what she might say or do, but feeling duty bound to listen.

'You're alive then,' she muttered. Her voice was hoarse, raw from her recent emotional outburst, completely unlike her normal speaking tones.

'Last time I checked,' he said, glancing down at himself.

Anne looked unamused. There was a coldness in her gaze, as if she were so emotionally spent, that there was simply nothing left to fill her expression.

'And you're married to Fiona Campbell?'

Lethbridge-Stewart did not attempt to conceal his surprise at the question. 'Is that pertinent?' he asked, toying briefly with the wedding ring on his finger. He did not like talking about such matters while at work. When he saw Anne's glowering response, he reluctantly elaborated. 'The ceremony was months ago. You were there.'

Anne shook her head. 'That's not the past I experienced,' she said. 'My past... all of our pasts were changed.'

Lethbridge-Stewart frowned. This was the first he'd heard of it. He let Anne continue, assuming she would clue him in soon.

'In the world I remember, you never married, you were always far too busy for romance. You died, thousands of miles from home, fighting an enemy that threatened everything you knew.'

Lethbridge-Stewart gave a vague nod, unsure how else to react to her strange statement. They had been through enough together, that he did not doubt her words, even if he did not understand them.

'What are you telling me? Are you saying you aren't from this world, that you are not our Anne Travers, the woman I've worked with for the last three years?'

Anne stared at him. 'No,' she said slowly. 'I think I am that Anne, at least I'm the only one you've got, or can ever have. I can feel her memories surfacing, while my own erode. I'm sure, soon enough, I'll be the person you expect me to be.'

Lethbridge-Stewart nodded. He still did not understand, but he felt it would probably be for the best if he humoured her, just to avoid any further tears. 'I see.'

'I doubt it.' She sighed, giving him a sad smile, as if she were the one humouring him. 'But it's why I need to submit this report on the Westminster Event.'

Lethbridge-Stewart frowned. 'Hardly an event.'

'The one I remember was.'

'With the greatest of respect, Anne, you weren't involved in the *Westminster Event*.' He had not meant his words to sound quite so dismissive, but sometimes there was no point sugar-coating the truth with civility, it was best to let people know where they stood. 'You have your own freelance projects now and, despite our best efforts, you were too busy to help us in this instance.'

Anne shook her head. 'Oh, I was involved,' she replied, glowering at him with her red-rimmed eyes. 'Tell me what happened, then I'll tell you what you missed.'

Lethbridge-Stewart shifted uncomfortably in his seat. He had the greatest respect for the woman sat in front of him, her advice had been critical during many previous missions, but he was not enjoying her new tone. She had always treated him with respect, even if his orders had angered and frustrated her, yet now it felt as if she were speaking down to him.

He leaned back in his seat, stroking thoughtfully at his moustache.

Despite the tension, he trusted her. She had signed the Official Secrets Act, and knew so much about their organisation that it would be foolish to consider her anything other than a trusted ally. It could do no harm to tell her what had happened. Her insight might have value.

'We attended a summons to Westminster, with assistance from another freelance scientific advisor, where we attempted to establish communication with a mysterious glowing sphere. While our efforts were unsuccessful, I believe we made a sufficient show of force, that the invader withdrew.'

Anne's face shifted.

He had the horrible feeling she was suppressing the urge to laugh.

She dropped the black ring-binder in front of him. 'This is what happened afterwards,' she told him. 'Before I changed it.'

Lethbridge-Stewart made a brief show of flicking through the pages. 'Indeed,' he said, keeping his face expressionless. 'I shall read it when I have time.'

Anne's laughter finally broke free, sounding more than a little hysterical. 'Time?' she cried, slamming a hand against his desk. 'Make time, Alistair. Nothing has ever been more important.'

Lethbridge-Stewart frowned, shocked by her outburst. 'Perhaps it would be easier if you explained,' he suggested, closing the folder and raising his eyes to look at her. He would listen. She had his attention. 'Reports are easily buried, lost and forgotten. Tell me what I need to know.'

Anne stepped back. She looked ready to scream.

'All of this,' she said, waving a hand around at what he assumed was Dolerite Base, or perhaps something greater, 'is doomed.'

'Is that so?'

'I saw it,' she replied. 'Right at the end. I saw what Rostov saw. I saw what scared him so much that he did everything in his power to stop it.'

'Rostov?' Lethbridge-Stewart enquired. 'Who is Rostov?'

Anne sighed. 'A trumped-up little colonel out of his depth, dealing with things he didn't understand, just trying to do the best he could.'

Lethbridge-Stewart let the comment wash over him. He was well aware that the words were barbed, equally capable of describing him on the day they had first met, but he also knew that she was upset, lashing out randomly in anger and frustration. His pride was bullet-proof. For an old friend, it could take a few dents. He remained calm.

'And what did you both see?' he asked. 'What was this terrifying thing?'

'The future,' she replied, shaking her head sadly. 'We always think things will just carry on as they are, that nothing ever changes, but it always does. The future comes for us, whether we're ready or not.'

Lethbridge-Stewart leaned forward in his chair. 'I'm afraid you're not making much sense, Anne.'

She nodded. 'Then I'll make it simple for you. The Fifth Operational Corps is not going to be enough to save the world from the threats we face. The problems are global. There are invasions coming, which will not respect national borders, that you don't have the resources to fight alone. If the United Kingdom goes up against them on its own, we will fail. There will be incalculable losses. Our civilisation will fall. The world will burn.'

Lethbridge-Stewart stared at her, stone-faced. 'Anne, you were fully briefed by General Hamilton before you joined the Fifth. You know as well as I that there are those who have mooted the possibility of increasing co-operation with the Americans or our European allies.'

Anne shook her head. 'Not enough. You need everyone. You need the Soviet Union. They have massive resources, huge global influence and more experience than you can possibly imagine.'

Unable to stop himself, Lethbridge-Stewart laughed at her suggestion. 'Out of the question. Quite impossible. I do believe you've taken leave of your senses.'

'Because they're foreign?' Anne retaliated. 'Because they're different? Given our work, given the things we've encountered, don't you think you should be a little more tolerant?'

Lethbridge-Stewart abruptly stopped laughing. 'They are our self-proclaimed enemy. They do not offer us the hand of friendship. They stamp down upon the very freedoms we hold most sacred. There is no way we can ever work alongside them.'

Anne stepped back, putting her head in her hands, clearly dismayed by his reaction. 'You have done before, or have you forgotten the Mutalith and Major Bugayev? Think about it, Alistair,' she pleaded, lifting her eyes to look at him, her anger draining away to reveal the desperation beneath. 'How do you ever win? What if we officially make contact with another species, begin diplomatic relations? What if we procured advanced alien technology, then found ways to develop and use it? What if the Doctor were to return, giving the Fifth Operational Corps access to his time machine?'

Lethbridge-Stewart frowned. 'I regard those as positive outcomes. As part of our remit to protect the United Kingdom from outside threats, these can only be seen as goals to be actively pursued.'

Anne nodded. 'And if you succeed? What do you think the Soviets will do? Or the Chinese? Or even the Americans? Do you think they're going to do nothing?'

Lethbridge-Stewart shrugged. 'Those are political matters, beyond my purview.'

Anne rolled her eyes. 'Well, let me tell you, in the world I lived in the moment you learned that the Soviet Union had acquired such advantages, you set about making plans to eliminate them.' She leaned forward, stabbing at the folder on the table with her forefinger. 'The mission was to destroy the technology and kill the first official alien ambassador this planet has ever known. Once you were convinced of the severity of the threat, there was no stopping you, no way to make you turn back. You gave your life to that cause. Given that was your reaction, how do you think your less-honourable enemies might respond, if the situation were ever reversed?'

Lethbridge-Stewart stared at the folder in front of him, once more opening it, and glancing through the typed pages. 'Your point, Anne?'

Anne stepped back, took a breath and stared him in the eye. 'We have to learn to work with our enemies, rather than continue down a path that will force us into conflict with them. Rostov tried to reshape the future with force, which would never work, because there are always those that would fight back. What is needed is diplomacy.'

'You're proposing some form of global international co-operation, working purely for the common good, despite our vast political and cultural differences, which are so embedded that we've stood on the brink of annihilating one another for the last twenty years?'

He tried not to scoff. To his ears it sounded ludicrous, a hippy's pipedream, which was thoroughly implausible in a world where only money and bombs held sway.

Anne shrugged, gesturing towards the folder in his hands. 'Now you know the consequences if we don't.'

She turned away, stepping towards the door, ready to leave.

Having made her statement, she seemed to have no interest in his response.

'That's it?' he asked.

'That's it. I've said my piece, I've done all I can. It's up to you what happens next. I've given it everything I could, made a sacrifice you will never understand, I can only hope that it's enough, that it was not for nothing. You can bury that file in some forgotten archive, or you can push it into the hands of your superiors, that's up to you.'

She gave him a sad, sweet smile, then quietly left the room.

Lethbridge-Stewart stared at the black ring-binder in his hands, stroking a finger thoughtfully against his moustache.

'I've been meaning to tell you,' Bill said, his tone cautious, not wanting to upset her. 'The Brig was able to get the information you asked about.'

Anne looked up from the cup she was cradling in her hands.

They were sitting in Bill's kitchen, enjoying a day off together. Soon they would be heading down to London.

'Tell me,' she said.

'He was able to source the personnel file for Sergeant Major Margaret Marsh. She has an exemplary record. She's a serving member of the WRACs, operating out of the Staffordshire barracks.'

Anne nodded.

It was surprisingly comforting to know the woman existed. Part of her had worried that the memories in her head were little more than a delusion, completely unlinked to the new world around her.

'She's a fine officer,' Anne replied. 'You could use her in the Fifth.'

Bill shook his head. 'We have all the men we need. I made an approach anyway, but it seems like she's looking for something far more hands-on than any of the support roles we can offer.'

Anne shook her head sadly. She didn't have the strength to fight other people's battles. 'And the others?' she asked.

'According to intelligence reports, Alexander Ivanovich Rostov is a colonel, running a number of classified military units.'

'Alive?'

'As far as we know. His career may have taken a knock,

following some kind of incident in Moscow, but the details are unclear.'

Anne nodded. 'Miss Volskaya?'

'Professor Zoya Vasilevna Volskaya,' Bill replied, taking a seat opposite her, 'tried to defect a few weeks ago. She was unsuccessful. It was the view of MI6 that the information she was offering was not credible, so they declined to offer her protection.'

Anne sighed. 'That was a mistake. Trust me, she has invaluable intel.'

Bill nodded. 'Interestingly, that decision was reversed a couple of days ago, due to an order out of General Hamilton's office. I've no idea why, but they're suddenly attempting to re-establish contact with her, to have another look at what she has to offer.'

Anne felt a smile slide over her face. She could think of only one reason why such action might have been taken. Someone, somewhere, had read her report. It was perhaps only a tiny change, one small step in a new direction, but if they continued down such a path for twenty years it might deliver them to a vastly different future. It was confirmation that she had made a difference.

'And, my friend, Arthur Grey?' she asked. 'Will you keep him on?'

Bill shifted uncomfortably. 'Arty's appointment was blocked. I don't know the details. I don't think he had the experience they wanted; he was just a secondary school teacher after all.'

Anne nodded, sad to see the old prejudices continued. 'Your loss,' she told him.

'We'll just muddle through with Jeff, and occasional help from you, obviously.'

'Obviously,' Anne agreed with a smile. Things were settling in her mind again, and she felt that she knew her place once more.

Bill finished the last of his tea and stood. 'Come on, let's get going. We need to get to the helicopter in thirty minutes.'

The advantages of the Fifth. No need for the extra-long drive to London.

*

The creature had closed its communication portals.

It was alone again.

It rolled its body back towards its storage pod, reattaching the nutrient and waste cables that were needed to sustain its organic form, then gently lowered itself back into its cryogenic vat. It closed all eight of its eyes, slowing its metabolic systems, letting the body fall into a silent slumber.

The mind disconnected from it, running final checks on the ship's systems, ready to continue its journey. As the vessel slipped away from the strange little water-covered world, it listened to the cacophony of humanity's voices, which were leaking out into the wilderness of space.

It was aware of everything that had happened.

It was aware of every possibility, which had flared, faded and died.

It had done everything they had asked.

It was time to move on.

They were an odd species. It had arrived, ready to fulfil its purpose, lending its abilities to help others fix their mistakes and achieve their potential. Yet the humans did not know what they wanted, they were infinitely divided, unable to agree on anything. They did not speak with one voice. They squabbled and fought. They would spend a lifetime building something, only to have others rip it down in a moment. They were engaged in a constant battle, struggling to create something new, faster than they could destroy what already existed. There was no way to help them. The best thing it could do, was leave them alone, at least until they found some semblance of unity.

It doubted they ever would. They would be fighting among themselves, squabbling over their differences, fighting for what they believed in, until the last of them vanished from the universe.

It chose a new course, leaving humanity to its struggle.

# EPILOGUE

ANNE SHELTERED under her umbrella.

A harsh wind was driving a steady stream of drizzle towards her, somehow managing to push it beneath the protective canopy, leaving her cold and bedraggled. She didn't care, she felt numb, detached from the world around her, which seemed like a pale imitation of the one she had always known. She was standing in a graveyard, looking at an ancient church, in which she would be marrying Bill in less than a month.

They were there to confirm the final arrangements with the vicar, for the hymns and readings, along with a thousand other tiny choices which would once have seemed important, but which made no significant difference to the outcome of the day.

It all seemed odd to her.

From her perspective, they had married months ago, then begun raising a daughter. It all felt like a television repeat. It was the same church, the one her family had always used for weddings, christenings and funerals. The guest list was nearly identical, as seemingly their social circle had not changed. The only notable addition was Fiona Lethbridge-Stewart.

Anne had chosen a different dress for the wedding, or at least believed she had, it was difficult to be sure. The more she tried to remember her original wedding day, the more the memories slipped away, fading like fragments of a dream.

Bill emerged from the church, having wrapped up his conversation with the vicar. He was grinning from ear-to-ear, clearly excited by what lay ahead. She enjoyed seeing him happy. As he ducked beneath her umbrella, she gave him a quick peck on the lips.

He kept grinning. 'In a few weeks, you'll be Mrs Anne Bishop.'

'Again.'

'I'm just glad the first time didn't put you off!'

She smiled at him. 'There are some decisions I could never change.'

Bless him. He didn't understand. How could he? For him, nothing had changed. Life carried on. Her loss was invisible.

As they walked through the graveyard, he took hold of her hand, obviously aware of her discomfort. She stepped off the path, moving through the wet grass, following an unmarked route she had walked many times before. Bill followed her lead.

Anne stopped beside her mother's grave.

'Do you remember her well?' Bill asked.

'Not really,' she replied. 'She died when I was very young. There's just a handful of brief memories. Snapshots. Images. It's the same with my memories of Samantha.'

Bill said nothing.

The rain hammered noisily on the umbrella's canopy.

The memories of her daughter were fading. As each vanished, the grief lessoned, but the emptiness inside her failed to refill. The loss remained. There was a single image burned into her mind, which she had glimpsed as she had slid through countless possible futures, of a teenage girl that she had instinctively known was her daughter. A girl with long copper coloured hair and hazel eyes, wearing threadbare hand-stitched clothes, skinny with malnutrition, sowing seeds in a recently ploughed field. She had been laughing. She had Bill's smile. It was a future where the world had burned, but her daughter had lived. A future that would never come, from a past that never was.

Bill squeezed her hand. 'You always said you wanted to wait before you had children, there were things you wanted to do.'

Anne nodded. 'I've changed my mind. There are still things I want to do, of course there are, but...' She sighed. 'I know the memory, the feelings, will fade. That my first go at motherhood won't even be a memory. And I was a good mother, Bill. And you were a great father.' She shrugged slightly. 'Motherhood changed me, and I'm not entirely sure in the best way. I don't want that to happen again, but I do... I don't want to wait anymore. I want to start building a new future.'

Bill nodded, looping his arm through hers, slowly turning her away from the grave, leading her off the grass. 'Once we're married, we can start a family, if that's what you want.'

'I do. We were great parents.' Anne smiled sadly.

'And we *will* be, this time. The first time.' Bill squeezed her softly. 'Because it will be the *first* time, for both of us.'

Anne didn't say anything.